MURDER, ITALIAN STYLE

Murder, Italian Style

Published by The Conrad Press Ltd. in the United Kingdom 2023

Tel: +44(0)1227 472 874

www.theconradpress.com

info@theconradpress.com

ISBN 978-1-915494-33-7

Copyright © Tony Davies, 2023

All rights reserved.

This is a work of fiction. Names, characters, business, and events are the products of the author's imagination. Certain places within the work exist, but the incidents described are from the author's imagination. Any resemblance to actual persons, living or dead, or actual events is purely coincidental.

Typesetting and Cover Design by: Charlotte Mouncey, www.bookstyle.co.uk

The Conrad Press logo was designed by Maria Priestley.

Printed and bound in Great Britain by Clays Ltd, Elcograf S.p.A.

MURDER, ITALIAN STYLE

DETECTIVE BRYN LAWTON PLAYS CATCH-UP WITH A SERIAL KILLER

TONY DAVIES

INTRODUCTION

Sunday 10 February 1952 21.32 hrs

Slowly a very tired man stepped down from the old, rickety, paint-splattered wooden step ladder; the one he had borrowed from his father-in-law months ago and now thankfully had never got around to returning. He felt a whole lot older than his thirty-six years. He stretched his aching back, then wiped his hands on a piece of old rag, before folding the ladder and placing it against the adjoining wall. He turned back to view his handiwork. The thick, bright red flock wallpaper he had used certainly matched the rest of the room. He was pleased that he was able to find a couple of rolls in the loft – thankful that his poor DIY skills had made him buy too many a few years back.

Yes, he was very impressed with the work because decorating certainly wasn't one of his fortes – then he thought, what was? He seemed to be a failure at everything he tried to do in the bloody awful country.

However, in the rush to complete the work, he had managed to push the reason for doing it right out of his mind, but now he had almost finished, like a clap of thunder, it came back to him. He suddenly felt physically sick. He needed to sit down. He walked over to his wife's dressing table and sat on the pink velour chair and caught his reflection in the mirror. He struggled to recognise the face staring back at him; it looked pale and haggard. There were large, black bags under his eyes. He realised just how tired he was, but he knew he couldn't rest yet for he still had a lot of work to complete before the light of morning came.

It had taken him all weekend to board up the shallow alcove in the master bedroom of his old Victorian house. He was rapidly using up money he really couldn't afford to lose but he had no choice if he wanted to avoid the hangman.

'*Papa. Non posso domire, dove e'mamma?*'

The tiny voice shocked him. He turned quickly. He hadn't noticed that his four-year-old son was now sitting on the bed behind him. He was rubbing his eyes with tiredness. As he stared at the boy, dressed so smartly in his Andy Pandy pyjamas, tears began to well up in his tired eyes, then slowly began to roll down his cheeks. The terrible realisation of what he had done began ripping at his very insides. As he got up from the chair, he felt every muscle in his body complain. Slowly he walked over and sat next to his son on the bed. He put his arm around his boy and held him tightly. He felt like he could never let him go.

He quietly answered the child's question.

'Mamma has gone away, hasn't she Leonardo? I have been telling you this all weekend. If anyone should ask, you must tell them that she has gone away with little Lucia – okay – my beautiful bambino?'

'*Sì Papa. Dove e'mamma?*'

'I don't know where they have gone.' The lie was making his voice begin to quiver with emotion.

'*Quando tornera?*'

'Yes. I am sure they will be back soon.'

He continued to hold the boy, stroking his long, blond hair, and gently rocking him until he fell asleep. He was pleased now that, despite his wife's nagging, he had continued to talk to him in Italian as it would help him fit in right away when they moved back to Italy. He gently picked up the sleepy little boy and carried him back to his small bedroom, put him to bed and closed the door. He still had to finish off the painting before he went back to work tomorrow. He knew he needed to sell the house as soon as possible and return to his homeland, back to the place where things made sense to him, if they'd have him back, that is. He knew that now his overbearing father had died the chances were good.

He had no other choice anyway – he had to go back. There was nothing left in Britain now, only the shame of what he had done and execution if it became known.

CHAPTER ONE

Friday 8 February 1952 08.27 hrs

Softly singing her current favourite song from the radio, 'Auf Wiederseh'n Sweetheart', Jenny Salvino carefully manoeuvred the pram out through the doorway, slowly closing the back door of her rambling old home behind her. It was the type of house she and her gorgeous new baby belonged in, even though, in her more lucid moments, she knew they couldn't afford it, not on her husband's measly wage. She turned the large, iron key in the lock and put it in her shopping bag. She returned to her song. She had always loved the songs of Vera Lynn – the person whom she credited with winning the war single-handed and singing them usually cheered her up, but not today. The sadness she felt about her life, which had recently intensified with the death of the King a couple of days ago still remained. She had cried bitterly when she heard of her monarch's death. It had still come as a bit of a shock, even though he had been ill for some time. She felt so sorry for the young princess who hadn't been able to be at her father's side, but was on a royal tour, somewhere in Africa. Her thoughts came back to that wastrel of a husband of hers who had tried to console her – but what would he know of affection for a monarch when he had followed that bloody horrible, strutting, arrogant, little man he always referred to as *Il Duce*, the man she referred to as 'that bastard Mussolini'.

She took her small son roughly by the hand and headed for the gate. She wondered why the child was always so moody. She had tried to like him, but something had always stopped her. She had recently discovered what that 'something' was now it was even harder for her to tolerate him. He was too much like his bloody father!

It was a bright winter's day, and once out in the open air she could try and forget about her domestic troubles, if only for a couple of hours. The path at the side of the house was just wide enough to push the pram along. She was more than a little embarrassed, for it was only a second-hand pram; and this for her gorgeous new baby girl. He said that it was all they could afford. He was so pathetic.

'The shit! He is such a failure – with all his promises before we were married, none of which he ever lived up to.' This she muttered as she looked at her new baby, Lucia, now three months old. How beautiful she was. A true gift from God and at least now she had a child she could love, not like this sullen boy, who was getting more and more like an Italian every day, and all this speaking bloody Iti was getting on her nerves too. She would have to put a stop to that.

In her shopping bag was a letter her husband had received that morning from his rich relatives in Bologna. His older sister Gabriella had sent it to him, two hundred pounds cash for the new baby. He would see none of it, that was for sure. She would put it in her secret account; the account she had been storing up for a couple of years now, ready for when she and now Lucia left him for good; and that time was fast approaching.

Jenny walked the mile into town, annoyed at being unable to deposit her four-year-old son in school as it had been closed as a sign of respect for the passing of the King. She carried on into the High Street to do the weekly shopping. She made an effort to try and avoid speaking to anyone, for all they could talk about was the King's death, and she was depressed enough about that already.

Her temper began to build up inside her again as she thought of the paltry amount she had in her purse to spend on the weekly groceries – all the fault of her underachieving pathetic excuse for a husband – but again the weak sunshine got the better of her and slowly she calmed down. She entered the grocery shop. How the boy loved to watch the tins containing the money fly across the shop on wires, catapulted to the till on the opposite side of the shop. The shop always had tins of broken biscuits that her son loved to dip into – but only when he was a good boy, which was rarely these days, but she bought him some just to keep him quiet for a while.

She stood there seemingly admiring the produce, but in reality, she was working out what she could afford to spend. She would not spend the cash sent from Italy – that was solely for her and Lucia's use later. How she hated being in this position. If he was so bloody wealthy in Italy, why was he such a failure here?

Wednesday 11 June 1986 19.02 hrs

Today was Bryn's first day back at work following his week's annual leave. He had taken the time off to attend Fiona's funeral which had taken place down south in Surrey. He knew he would need the break following her burial to get his head straight and also to use the occasion to appreciate that he was, at last, in the clear about the disturbing things that had happened in Dynas Dre all those years before. He had, however, spent almost the week in a haze of anti-depressants and Jack Daniels, so come that Wednesday morning, sitting there in the CID office, he didn't really feel too much better.

Luckily for him, so far it had been a very quiet day, but he just couldn't get motivated to do anything. It wasn't that he didn't have enough to do – his in-tray was overflowing with crime files he had to complete, but as he sat there, he knew that the clinical depression, which he had been diagnosed with as a kid, was getting worse, and the hangover he was experiencing didn't help either. He realised too that he seemed to spend all his off-duty time drinking and popping pills. What a fucking life, he thought, as he tried to talk himself out of being sick, for he could tell, by the looks he was getting, that his sergeant was getting a bit pissed off with him.

The one and only highlight of the day came when one of the uniformed lads had asked Bryn to meet him on the High Street and when he got there, emblazoned on a newly painted white wall, he saw – 'DETECTIV BRIN LAWTON IS A FUCKING BASTED' in bright red letters a foot high.

'At least they could have had the courtesy to get the fucking spelling right. Can you get the scene of crime lads to get a pic?'

'What – for evidence?' asked the very inexperienced lad in uniform, mistakenly thinking Bryn wanted to start an enquiry about this piece of vandalism.

'No. I want to frame it and put it on the wall.' The young uniformed officer laughed, then realised that Bryn was serious, so he radioed the station to get it arranged while Bryn returned to the CID office for some more pills and a coffee.

He left the office at a little after 5 p.m. and went home to a small flat. It was situated above a very poor-quality Italian restaurant on the outskirts of the town. The owner let him have it for a very low rent, not that Bryn actually paid him anything, nor did the landlord dare to ask. He was a detective after all and had the power to make his life hell.

The flat was cold and unwelcoming and always smelled of garlic. Everything in there screamed that he was a failure. He had moved in over two years ago, ever since his marriage to Laura had disintegrated in a blaze of acrimony and violence, yet in every room there were still cardboard boxes he hadn't even bothered to unpack. He seemed to disappoint everyone who ever mattered to him, especially his Fiona, and that was something he knew he would never forgive himself for. That knowledge was slowly tearing him apart; how he badly needed a drink. He went to the cupboard and unscrewed the top off the half-full bottle of 'Jack', then, surprisingly for him, decided against it. He was going back to work in a bit and he didn't want to reek of booze; well, any more than he already did anyway, so he rescrewed the top back on the bottle and settled for a cup of tea, a plate of beans on toast with lashings of tomato sauce, a couple of anti-depressants and a quick snooze on the couch.

When he woke, he splashed his face with cold water, sprayed himself with some deodorant, dabbed on some aftershave, picked up his crumpled jacket from the chair and left the flat. He did feel a bit better; the sleep had refreshed him. He had intended to walk back but the weather put paid to that idea. It had started to pour down.

He returned to the CID office of Quayside police station at a little after 7 p.m. on what was now a very stormy Wednesday evening. He had some urgent paperwork to complete; work he couldn't have been bothered to do during the day. He thought that the office would be quiet at that time in mid-week, hence no distractions. He entered through the control room, which appeared unusually tranquil for what was a very busy police station. Penny, the telephonist, was sitting with her feet up on her desk, doing the crossword and answering the odd telephone call that came in. She always wore her skirts just that inch too short – Bryn had always thought that she had nice legs for a lady of her age.

'Anything doing?' he asked as he picked up the telephone message pad. Then he thought he had only been away for two hours.

'Haven't you got a bloody home to go to?' she said, snatching back the pad, then immediately regretted saying it, for she knew as did most of the station, Bryn's shitty domestic situation. Bryn tugged at Penny's maternal instincts. She really liked him, which was unusual for her as she usually didn't have much time for detectives. She found them arrogant, but not Bryn, he was different, a really friendly guy with a wicked sense of humour, which unfortunately he rarely used.

'No. Nothing, I sent the lads to a RTA on the bypass – that's all. It's been really quiet all day,' she replied hastily, without looking up. Penny had a really husky, sexy voice that always held a fascination for him, even though it was borne out of sixty cigarettes a day. Bryn quietly smiled to himself – he found her very sensual and quite a bit of a girl when she had a couple of drinks. He found this out a couple of Christmases ago when he gave her a lift home following the office party. Neither had spoken of it again, or repeated it, but it was the best blow job Bryn had ever had.

He gave the pad back, smiled wearily, turned and walked slowly up the stairs. She watched him leave. Yes, he really was a nice guy, she thought as she returned to her crossword.

He walked into the CID squad room but didn't put on the light. He went and sat at his desk and looked out of the window. The rain that hit the glass sure seemed to be getting heavier. 'Those poor bastards,' he muttered to himself as he thought again of those uniformed lads out in this weather, dealing with a RTA – police parlance for a road traffic accident. He had always hated dealing with anything to do with vehicles, especially RTAs. He was glad that that type of duty was now a thing of the past for him, at least while he stayed a detective. He leaned across his desk, switched on the small lamp he had brought from home and slowly pulled his work basket over to him. He lifted the first buff-coloured crime file towards him. It was a case where he had had to go to Scotland to bring this lad back to Quayside. He smiled to himself as he remembered the conversation he had had with the young burglar on the way back to Quayside.

Bryn: 'So you were in Scotland for Burns Night, were you?'

Lad: 'That was fuck all to do with me, Mr Lawton – I burned nothing – you're not going to fucking pin that on me; I didn't burn anything.'

God, how Bryn loved these idiots – they made this job worthwhile and, in some cases, a whole lot easier.

He was halfway through writing his statement of evidence when the phone rang. He picked it up and heard Penny say, 'Bryn? Tea's up. If you're interested.'

He was grateful for the distraction and quickly closed the file and went back downstairs for a brew. The uniformed lads had just got back from the accident scene and their coats were on the radiators, steam rising from them, misting the windows.

'Christ it's like a fucking Chinese laundry in here,' he said as he poured himself some stewed tea, using the only cracked, handle-less mug that remained on the shelf. He tried to make it more palatable with four spoons full of sugar.

'Forgotten what it's like to be a bobby now, have you; now you have entered the ESSO department, Oh Exalted One,' said Stefan with a broad smile.

'He never knew what that was like before he went upstairs,' shouted one of the lads from the other room.

'I am far too busy to listen to this carefully rehearsed repartee from a bunch of sodden plods,' he said as he picked up his mug, took a chip from Stefan's plate and returned to the relative quiet of his office. He thought, as he climbed the stairs, how sometimes he missed the camaraderie of the uniformed branch, for being a detective had a tendency to be quite a lonely existence. Then again, that was Bryn Lawton all over – lonely.

He sat at his desk and looked at the half-completed statement, written as always with a fountain pen, the only reminder of his father's influence on him.

The ESSO department – every Saturday and Sunday off – how he wished that was bloody true. He couldn't remember the last weekend he had had off – when was it? It had been ages, well over six weeks. That was the last time he had seen his nine-year-old daughter, Sian. Of course, Laura, who had become the ex from hell, was bitching about it all the time. He had three unreturned messages on his desk now and that was just from today. She was really laying a 'guilt trip' on him – as if he could help having to work. She would be the first to shout if he stopped working and the maintenance payments, which were crippling him financially, suddenly ended. Yes – she was the bitch from hell – then again perhaps he had been the ex-husband from hell, so, all in all, things balanced out. He started to smile.

He had just got himself comfortable back at his desk, and put pen to paper, when the phone rang. It was Penny once again, 'Sorry to bother you again, Bryn, but I've got a man on the phone who is really upset and I can't fully understand what he is saying. It is something about being at home and his mum being dead in the bedroom; can I put him through to you? He is a bit hysterical.'

'Sure,' he said, and then he thought, I don't appear to have anything special to do – I'm just here for the good of my health. He heard the call click through: 'Quayside CID, Detective Constable Lawton, how can I help you?' He still loved saying those words even after three years – Detective Constable Lawton – at long last.

He too had difficulty understanding what the man was blabbering on about. He thought back, as he so often did, to his tutor constable all those years ago, saying, 'This would be a great job if it wasn't for the bastarding public.' To date he had never found anything that had made him contradict that statement. Bryn tried to get him to calm down but it was no use.

He did sound very upset. After a couple of minutes, he thought he got the gist of the story; the man seemed to be saying that he was at home and had found that his mummy was dead in his bedroom. He looked at his watch and noted the time of the call on the back of his hand, the policeman's notepad.

'I'll come straight over, sir,' he said, having taken down the address, once again on the back of his hand. 'That's all I fucking need – a bloody sudden death,' he muttered to himself as he stood up and put his jacket on. He now very much regretted coming back to the office, but brightened up when he realised that a simple sudden death was a uniform problem and not really a matter for a detective. But as he couldn't get into his paperwork, and thinking a little fresh air would do him some good, he decided to go on this enquiry.

He went into his jacket pocket, opened the bottle, and swallowed a couple of anti-depressants – just in case. He shook the bottle – he needed to get some more, and soon.

He slowly walked downstairs, just as Stefan was about to go out on a routine mobile patrol. Bryn asked if he would come with him to the address. He had worked with Stefan for years, and they were firm friends. It always amused Bryn that Stefan believed he was descended from Native Indian stock and in Bryn's words, 'He was not particularly bright, but could lift heavy things' but more importantly, within police circles, he was 'a good lad' – meaning of course that he could be trusted, which was one of the finest accolades any police officer could have.

Twenty minutes later both officers were hurrying up the gravel path of a large Victorian house that was situated not far from the bungalow that Bryn's father, the grammar school-teacher – the one most pupils hoped they wouldn't get – had built twenty-five years before. That house now belonged to a wealthy jeweller. As the police car was driven past the bungalow, Bryn stared at it through the rain-soaked windscreen and his thoughts went to his parents. He had always been a disappointment to them, his school reports always saying, 'has potential but doesn't use it'. He left school without a single qualification to his name. This fact was repeated over and over to anyone who would take the time to listen, by his not-so-proud father.

'Perhaps he won't need qualifications. He will be alright,' said his mum, in an effort to placate his dad, 'he's a bright lad.'

'If he was that bright, he would have got some bloody qualifications,' his dad always retorted.

Bryn knew this particular house well, for as a child he had passed it almost every day on his way to primary school. He and his friends always believed it to be haunted – it looked like something straight out of a *Hammer Horror* movie. The door was opened before they reached it and a middle-aged man in paint-splattered overalls beckoned them inside. The officers identified themselves but the man wasn't listening. Ignorant sod, thought Bryn. They were directed into the dining room where Bryn saw a young woman sitting at the table; her head was in her hands. She was sobbing uncontrollably. He also noticed that the man's face was ghostly white, which made the red paint speckles on his face more pronounced. Bryn realised that the sight of death hit some people like that – but not him, not now, not ever – he had been in the proximity of death too many times to be moved by it in any way whatsoever.

Without any preamble the man said, 'It's upstairs,' and he pointed towards the stairway but made no effort to accompany the officers. Bryn looked at Stefan who simply shrugged his shoulders and together they left the room and climbed the stairs.

On the next floor Bryn looked down the corridor and seeing only one of the doors open he walked to that room and reverently entered, Stefan following, without much interest, their footsteps echoing eerily on the bare wooden floorboards. The room was well lit, and without any furniture. Even their whispered voices seemed to echo around the large room. It was clear that the whole house was undergoing a major renovation. The plasterboard, which was covered with patterned flock wallpaper, had been removed from one entire wall and this had revealed a set of ornately carved wooden doors, one of which was ajar. Seeing no visible signs of a body anywhere in the room, Bryn walked over and opened the door a little wider, peered in, and let out an involuntary shriek. For there, staring back at him, was the dried-up face of a woman. Stefan quickly came over to his friend and he also looked in. 'Fucking hell – it's like that end scene in fucking Psycho,' he whispered as he pulled the doors fully open and entered the tiny room.

Bryn felt slightly ashamed of the noise he had made on seeing the body and he was glad he was with Stefan, who he knew wouldn't mention it to anyone for after all he had a reputation to uphold.

'It's a fucking *mummy*,' Stefan said; his smile always had an innocent quality that Bryn found so amusing.

'Now that's something you don't come across every day,' Bryn said trying to cover the embarrassment he felt following his initial outburst, 'now I know how Howard Carter must have felt.'

'Howard who?'

'Howard Carter; the man who discovered Tutankhamun's tomb in Egypt.'

Stefan stared blankly at Bryn who just shook his head in despair. 'God Stef, you are a fucking Philistine.' What Bryn didn't know was that most of the lads at his station admired his intellect. His dad would have been so proud.

The two officers tried to examine the body by the light of Stefan's torch, the batteries of which were fading fast. So, without actually touching anything, Bryn took out his notebook, made a sketch, and quickly wrote some notes.

The lady was sitting in a rocking chair, and was dressed in what appeared to be 1940s style clothing or so he thought, for being a fan of 40's movies they seemed to fit. It was very clear she had been dead quite some time. There were no obvious wounds on the body. Bryn noticed that she showed actual signs of woodworm in the lower part of her legs.

The detective went back downstairs and asked if he could use the telephone. No one answered him. The man was still desperately trying to console the woman, who now appeared catatonic.

She should receive some medical attention, he thought as he picked up the receiver and dialled the station. Bloody civilians, they always make a mountain out of a bloody molehill, he thought as he waited for the phone to be answered at the police station. He spoke quietly to Penny, summoning the necessary experts.

While he waited for the large number of troops to arrive, he walked over to the couple and tried to speak to them about the find upstairs. He tried to elicit any information whatsoever about the corpse, but they were too upset to talk to him.

Christ, it's only a bloody dead body for fuck's sake. There's no need to make such a song and dance about it. After all, as his mother used to say, 'It's the living you have to worry about, not the bloody dead'. He thought this as he went back upstairs to re-join Stef and the stiff. He chuckled at that. Yes, he thought again, the public do get in the way of us having a good time. How fucking true.

It was two hours later, when all the experts had done their thing, that the lady's body was finally removed to the mortuary. Bryn had ensured that numerous photographs were taken, ensuring he would get his own copies, for he knew that this was a case he could dine out on for months. He returned to the police station, leaving Stefan to take the necessary written statements from the traumatised householders.

'Good luck with that,' he whispered as he made for the door. He knew from the look on his face what his friend was thinking about him leaving and it wasn't pleasant.

When Bryn got back to the nick he approached Penny, 'Something about his dead mummy – he'd found a mummy in his bedroom. You just can't get the staff anymore.' They both laughed. She really did like Bryn, he has such a lovely smile, she thought, it's a pity he so rarely uses it. She thought again, as she did every so often, of that night a couple of Christmases ago, and she smiled to herself about how rude she had been with him and then, with some difficulty, she returned to her crossword.

Bryn went back to his office, putting the dead lady completely out of his mind and tried again with his paperwork but his heart just wasn't in it. He found himself constantly looking out of the rain-covered windows, his thoughts returning to that one subject – Fiona. His love for her. His desertion of her. The guilt that was always chewing at his insides. He took the bottle of pills out of his desk, the ones he called his 'emergency supply'. He swallowed two, then poured himself a large Scotch and downed that in one. He knew the depression, which he had nicknamed 'the black hole', was closing in fast and there was nothing he could do about it.

Fifty minutes later, having given up trying to write anything and was about to go home, the phone rang. Christ, I'd have got more peace in the middle of bloody Piccadilly Circus, he thought as he picked up the receiver. He smiled as he recalled that she had said the same thing to him years ago, back in that shithole of a village. He was soon brought back to reality. It was Stefan speaking from the mortuary, 'You're not going to believe this my old mate – it's a fucking murder. This place is teaming with bosses and they told me to tell you that you are to get over here straightaway.' He heard Stefan chuckle.

'That's all I fucking need to round my night off, a fifty-year-old murder – thank you, God,' he muttered to himself as he put his jacket on, picked up the car keys and headed out into the rain.

CHAPTER TWO

Friday 8 February 1952 09.20 hrs

Jenny called into several shops, trying to avoid anything to do with sweets, despite her son's wishes, as they were still rationed – even seven years after the war had ended – but she did need sugar, so she queued up, presented her ration book to the clerk, and obtained her small paper bag, half-filled with the white granules.

'When will this rationing end?' she asked the spotty-faced young man behind the counter.

'Soon,' was his reply – it was clear to everyone that he really had no idea so he thought that was the best answer. The queue at the butcher's led out of the door so she avoided that, keeping her ration for next week as she had some bacon and ham that her in-laws had sent from Italy, along with the cash.

She went into the Midland Bank. Unfortunately, her sister was behind the counter. She had hoped she could have carried out this transaction without her knowledge. They had never been particularly close, but they exchanged some pleasantries as she deposited the money in her account then her sister watched as she hid the paying-in book in her handbag. She asked for a balance and Jenny saw her sister look in surprise at the amount. Jenny looked at the slip of paper that her sister handed to her, smiled, but said nothing. She tried to hide her excitement when she saw that she had more money in her account than she thought — six hundred and twenty-two pounds and six shillings and eleven pence, more than enough to leave that pathetic excuse for a man.

She went across the road to a milk bar to celebrate. She bought a coffee and a milkshake for the boy and went and sat in the back and considered where she would go — it would be somewhere abroad, somewhere warm, just her and Lucia. As she left, a group of Teddy boys wolf-whistled her — yes, she thought, she still had it and she liked that fact very much.

She walked slowly back home, and pondered how on earth she had got into this mess. The man she married had been a rich, well spoken, successful man — or at least that was what he had told her when they first met — who now, within such a short space of time, had just given up on life. He told her that he had been a solicitor and an army captain back in his native Italy. Now even his rich family back there had all but disowned him when he failed to return after the war. When he did decide to return two years ago, when things had got so bad here and he was unable to pass the solicitor's examination and get a decent job, his family wanted nothing to do with him.

She hated herself for how she felt. Why had she allowed him to give up? Why had she not done something to help him? He didn't even try to defend himself when she physically attacked him, like last night for instance; he just stood there and let her hit him. How she wished it was different but now it was too late. Once, she just wanted him to change, be a man and provide for his family, but now all she wanted was to be rid of him — and seeing the amount of money she had in the bank, today had suddenly become 'that day' to do it. Yes, she would leave today.

Wednesday 11 June 1986 22.28 hrs

It took Bryn well over half an hour to reach the mortuary, a journey that should have only taken ten minutes. 'Why does the rain bring out the idiots who have no idea how to drive?' he muttered to himself as he slammed on his brakes to avoid a rear end collision with another very nervous driver. 'What else did you get for Christmas besides fucking brakes, you idiot?' he screamed at the slow-moving car ahead. He thought to himself, I bet it's a bloody woman. It wasn't, but as he drove past, he gave the driver an evil stare anyway.

He was relieved when he eventually turned in through the hospital gates for the slightest thing these days put him in one of two moods – a deep depression or a violent rage – and he could never tell which one it would be. He drove around to the rear and parked the car under the covered area reserved for hearses. He saw the mass of cars belonging to his bosses and swore under his breath. He had hoped they would have gone by now for, to his way of thinking, bosses always got in the way.

He walked into the morgue; it was as cold as ever. It was a place that always gave him a feeling of foreboding, probably because he realised that in due course everyone ends up here, in one of those fridges. He shuddered. He was thankful when he heard familiar voices coming from the dissection room. He entered quickly.

'Ah Lawton, about bloody time – your job now, I think?' With that the detective chief superintendent and all the other senior officers left without another word. He sniffed under his arms and pulled a face. He turned to Stefan who was grinning which of course made Bryn smile too. He quickly examined the body before him, trying to look for the injury that made this a job for him and not uniform.

'Ah, Detective Constable Bryn Lawton – how lovely to see you again! Long time, no see. I thought you had left the country.'

He turned slowly. He knew that voice only too well. He greeted the Home Office pathologist, Heather Thomas, with a wry smile. 'Miss Thomas – great to see you too – it's been a while.' He said this with more than a little embarrassment. She approached the body on the slab and without taking her eyes from Bryn she nonchalantly handed the two officers a mask and a pair of gloves each, because she knew that the slightest movement of the body caused a choking dust to fly everywhere.

'So, H, what's the story? Got any ideas?' Bryn asked, trying to put the situation back on a semi-professional footing. Stefan was initially surprised at the informality between such an eminent person as a Home Office pathologist and a lowly police officer but then he remembered that there had been a rumour going around the station about six months ago that these two had a history. What that history was Bryn had never shared with him but as Stefan knew, if it involved Bryn Lawton these days, it had to have involved 'shagging', for since his marriage to Laura had come to an end, he knew Bryn had 'a history' with many, many women of the town.

'As usual, Detective Lawton, you never bring me anything simple – do you?' she said with a smile. Bryn had to smile too, for the last couple of deaths they had anything to do with were far from straightforward – there was a headless woman, murdered by her son a few months ago; a child who fell in the river and was found in a horrible state a week later; a young man who had fallen from a great height and had fully impaled himself on a brush stale; one of his prisoners who had hung himself in his cell whilst performing what the press labelled 'a bizarre sex act', and now this one.

'Well, Miss Thomas – I just like to keep you on your toes,' he said, his words slightly muffled by his mask he had just put on.

'Not just on my toes, if my memory serves me correctly, detective – my back and my knees too, if I recall. Have you still got your handcuffs, officer?' she whispered to him as she leaned across to pick up the dissection knife. That was true; they had hardly been vertical throughout their torrid three-month relationship and the kinkiness he had displayed with her he never knew he possessed. She had certainly brought out something in him that should possibly have remained dormant. He was pleased that Stefan was too far away to hear these whisperings and that the mask hid his blushes.

He stood back and let the pathologist get to work and it was clear to him almost immediately that she had forgotten that they were there as she became so engrossed with the body.

After her initial examination that took about quarter of an hour Bryn broke the heavy silence, 'So, Miss Thomas, do you have any idea how long this lady has been dead?'

'Well, detective, from the condition of the body and by the look of her clothes I would say... since about nineteen fifty – give or take.'

'Ten to eight, eh?' Bryn said with a smile that was fortunately hidden by his mask. It was only met with a stony stare from the lady who stood close by. His police humour had always fallen on her deaf ears, but he heard Stefan giggle. Bryn had already surmised that as her garb was from a period just after the war.

There was no sign of a mortuary assistant which pissed Bryn off because he knew what was to come. At the pathologist's request the two officers put on the rubber gloves and started to undress the corpse. Sure enough, the pathologist was right – dust from her was flying everywhere. Heather told them to be careful because in the body's dry state it would be so very easy for them to break bits off her – particularly her fingers and toes. They took their time and managed the task, leaving the body intact. Each item of clothing was bagged as evidence, Bryn signing the evidence slip that he attached to each item.

As they removed her underwear Bryn heard Heather whisper, 'Well Bryn? You always did get turned on by stockings and a suspender belt.' He started to blush again and this time he was sure Stefan heard.

In an effort to distance himself from her he began to examine the holes that were in her blouse. 'Very clean cuts indeed,' he muttered to no one in particular.

When the body was naked, the Home Office pathologist pointed to the two holes in the chest. 'Knife wounds,' she said as she made the first incision into the chest. Bryn excused himself and went to find a cup of tea, leaving Stefan to assist further if necessary. It wasn't that he was squeamish, far from it; he just needed a bit of space from Heather, for that was the cause of their split. She had a tendency to crowd him. He started to feel smothered by her again. He went and sat outside in the corridor and waited. Sometimes this job could be boring as hell, he thought as he looked at the brick walls of the hospital corridor now smooth with countless layers of cream and green paint, colours that you saw nowhere else in the world. He closed his eyes against the harsh florescent light. That and the smell of disinfectant were starting to give him a headache. He got up and stood by the open door – the rain was still pouring. He wanted to go home. He needed sleep. He needed his anti-depressants but most of all he needed a large glass of Jack.

To take his mind off how he was feeling he thought back to his probationary days and the 'mortuary game'.

About twenty years before he joined the job, a dead body had been stolen from the mortuary that was situated in a remote corner of the grounds of the hospital in Crymachno, where Bryn was first stationed. The body was never discovered – not that it mattered to the story. So every night shift thereafter the mortuary had to be checked. It had become something of a tradition.

Bryn thought back to his first time of checking the building. He was told that he had to check that all the bodies were still there. He was given the keys.

So, early that morning he unlocked the large green door and entered the very cold building. As he passed one of the bodies that were laid out on the slab, covered by a white sheet, it suddenly rose and screamed. Bryn remembered that he almost shat himself with fear. Constable Martin Bradley thought this was fantastic fun, and did it to every new probationer. Bradley never knew just how close he came to being struck with Bryn's truncheon that night, but as he hardly ever carried it, he was lucky.

Bryn's new replacement, as he was being posted to Dynas Dre the following week, was a brand-new probationer, Constable Colin Appleton, a tall, lanky ex-public schoolboy, who looked like a strong wind would blow him over.

'Christ, I thought you were bad when I first saw you, young Lawton,' said Sergeant Jack, 'but this new lad takes the bloody biscuit. Not long to retirement, thank Christ.' Bryn saw him look towards the heavens as he said this.

'Is he on mortuary patrol tonight?' Bryn asked Martin over a brew in the canteen.

'Too right he is,' he replied with that sadistic look of glee in his very dark eyes.

'Can I suggest something to make it even better?' asked Bryn as they ate their breakfasts together at around 1 a.m.

Martin listened to his suggestion. He said that to make it scarier Bailey should get inside the fridge and when he opened the door to do the count, 'Bingo. You leap out.'

'I love it,' said Martin, eager to put the plan into motion.

All was arranged for 3 am.

At the appointed time, Martin Bradley, who was lying on a stretcher inside the large fridge, heard someone let himself into the mortuary. He remained quiet in the fridge waiting for the door to open, when all of a sudden, a hand of the body next to him, grabbed his shoulder and said, in a ghostly voice,

'Cold in here, isn't it?'

Bradley's screams could be heard throughout the mortuary and perhaps the whole hospital as he tried to kick the door open.

He eventually emerged to see the whole rota standing in the room, pissing themselves laughing. Bryn came out of the next compartment, laughing fit to burst.

'It took a long time but vengeance is so sweet,' he told his friend Dave Knight back at the station.

Constable Martin Bradley had shat himself.

So ended the mortuary game.

Bryn was still chuckling to himself when, after about an hour, Stefan came out of the dissection room, his uniform jacket covered with particles of the deceased. Bryn handed him a lukewarm cup of coffee he had managed to scrounge from a passing nurse, who, Bryn noticed, gave him 'the eye'. He had made a mental note of the nurse's name for future reference.

'Well, it's a murder alright – she said that both the wounds inflicted on her could have been fatal on their own; one hit the heart and one severed the main artery – but how the hell she could say that I have no idea. It was nothing but fucking dust in there.'

'It's because I am so damn good at what I do, constable,' said the pathologist, who was leaning against the doorframe, removing her thin rubber gloves. Bryn knew Heather well enough to know that she was enjoying the embarrassment.

'You could have told me she was there,' mouthed Stefan, as he took a seat next to Bryn, who just smiled at his reddening cheeks. Bryn then turned to look at Heather. He'd forgotten just how beautiful she was.

'This is definitely murder. I'll have the preliminary report for you in the morning; say around eleven, if you can pick it up?'

'Got any idea of an age for the vic?' he asked as he stood up to leave.

'That's difficult but I would say no more than forty.' She

handed him a gold ring. 'I managed to get this off her wedding ring finger – there is an inscription on the inside but I can't make it out.' Bryn put the ring in a plastic bag. 'One other thing – I think there was another ring on that finger, but it had been forced off post mortem. It tore some flesh off the finger.'

'Thanks, H, I'll get the report picked up tomorrow cos I have a feeling I am going to be a bit busy for the next couple of days,' he said.

'Fancy a drink, or a bite to eat later?' she said as he took his raincoat from the coat hook by the door.

Bryn looked at his watch to give himself a moment to think.

'Sorry, I can't – I have to get Stefan back to the station and get the initial report in to my bosses. I am going to be there quite a while yet but thanks for the offer. Some other time soon, if that's okay?' They both knew what he was really saying – but she let it pass.

'Sure – no problem,' she said and turned back into the dissection room. Bryn could tell he had pissed her off, again. He had become an expert at that.

'You're a jammy bastard Lawton – you were shagging that, weren't you?' Stefan said as the unmarked police car pulled out of the hospital grounds. Bryn was pleased to see that the rain had almost stopped and the traffic was now non-existent – all the law-abiding citizens were in bed – the lucky bastards.

'I have no idea what the hell you are talking about,' said Bryn with a dry smile. Both officers began to laugh.

At a little after 2 a.m. having called in at the police station, deposited Stefan, and dashed off a telex about the murder for the information of his bosses who were also now fast asleep,

Bryn knocked on the door of a large, detached house on the outskirts of the town. He had not been surprised to see the downstairs lights still on when he had stopped his car outside. He had thought for a while about whether he was doing the right thing but... he popped some anti-depressants and walked up to the door.

'Not bothering you, am I?' he said as she answered the door.

'Not at all – in fact there is a JD and ice already poured and waiting for you.'

He entered and Heather closed the door – she watched him take off his jacket – he looked tired. She so wanted to look after him, if only he would let her, which in her heart of hearts she knew he would never do.

She followed him into the lounge and handed him his drink – she was so glad he was here, with her.

CHAPTER THREE

Friday 8 February 1952 10.45 hrs

Giuseppe Salvino had been in work in that small solicitor's office for well over two hours now. He just couldn't get started, his mind always straying back to that terrible argument he and his wife had had last night. It was the worst one yet, resulting in him receiving a black eye and a cut lip from the blows she had landed on him. It wasn't the injuries that concerned him, he was used to those, it was the look in her eyes – pure unadulterated hatred. He had spent the night sitting on the sofa, trying to figure out how to make things right. He loved his wife so much, but he felt such a failure.

The excuse that he had given to his office colleagues that morning for the injuries was that he had tripped over the dog and hit the door frame but he knew no one believed him if for no other reason than they all knew he didn't have a dog – they also knew who the real culprit was. Most of them had witnessed his wife's temper on several occasions over the last year, most recently at the Christmas party, when she embarrassed everyone when she threw a cup of punch over him, slapped him across the face, and stormed out.

So he sat there, in his small rear office, staring out of the window at the brick wall of the butcher's shop next door, a lowly solicitor's clerk, a man who had been a prominent solicitor back home in Italy before the war; a man who had commanded men in battle, a brave commando working behind enemy lines, a decorated war hero who had come to this country as a prisoner of war, become engaged to Jenny and was then able to stay and not be repatriated. A man who now was struggling simply to pay his household bills. It was thought that he would become a solicitor here but he just couldn't pass the initial examination – and this was a constant cause of conflict between him and his wife, who wanted a better life that he just couldn't obtain for her – hence the escalating violence towards him. He truly loved her very much and he felt her frustration and now, with another mouth to feed, his feeble wage was stretched so thin he didn't know what to do. Even his wealthy family back in Bologna had refused to assist him. He didn't know where to turn for help. He felt he was on the verge of tears.

His mind went back to last night's attack on him. He hadn't even tried to defend himself from the blows she rained down on him – he never did – for he knew she was right. He was a total failure and what's more the whole world knew it. He felt he truly deserved her beating.

As he stared into space he muttered, 'What am I to do, Lord?' But he knew, after all the terrible things that he had done during the war, his God had truly forsaken him.

He felt the tears roll down his cheeks, which he quickly wiped away – how he loathed himself.

Thursday 12 June 1986 09.20 hrs

Bryn had been in the office since just after eight. He regretted visiting Heather last night. He had slipped quietly out of her house this morning, before she woke. But last night, for some unexplainable reason that he couldn't quite understand, he hadn't wanted to be alone. He knew that her door was always open to him, despite what a bastard he had been to her during and after their short relationship. The one thing he could never complain about was the sex and last night's, once again, had been fantastic – if somewhat unorthodox.

He sat at his desk and tried to push Heather out of his mind as he sipped his third coffee of the morning. He opened the envelope that contained the photographs of the mummy that he had christened Nefertiti. It surprised him how quickly he had got them; it usually took days. He studied the dried-up face of the woman, her blonde, shoulder-length hair still tied back with a faded purple ribbon. He had thought that hair and nails continued to grow after death, but last night Heather had told him that that was a myth – it just appears like it because the skin shrinks. She generally gave him more information about being dead, than he really needed.

He stared at the photograph and tried to picture Nefertiti in life – but he couldn't. He suddenly remembered the ring, which he took out of his pocket and examined through the plastic – it was a thick gold band. On the inside he could make out some writing but it was not clear enough to decipher what it said and besides he needed to get it fingerprinted before he handled it, just in case the killer had tried to remove it before boarding her up. He rang the switchboard to put in a call to the scene of crime officer, and ask him to call in when he had time.

'Karl's here, having a brew,' said the telephonist, a new girl with absolutely no personality whatsoever and with 'a face like a bulldog chewing a wasp' – well that was the general consensus of the lads downstairs.

Bryn took the ring to the canteen and presented it to Karl, asking for an examination as soon as possible. 'I'll do it now,' was the reply. It was definitely paying off. A couple of months ago he had got Karl's mother off a shoplifting charge – Bryn just never put in the paperwork, more out of laziness than any desire to help out a colleague, but Karl was now firmly in his pocket – hence the speed of the photographs too.

A partial fingerprint was found on the outside of the ring, 'It's not the deceased's print, I'm sure of that,' said the SOC officer. 'It had been a bugger to do, but I got prints from her last night and I can say that it is not hers.' He handed back the ring to Bryn, together with the lifted fingerprint on a clear plastic card.

'If we find the killer, is there enough her to get a match?' he asked as the SOC man was about to leave.

'Sure – there's more than enough to get an ID,' he said with a smile as he left. Karl was pleased he was able to help Bryn – he had been so kind to his mum just a couple of months ago. He often wondered how he had managed to pull it off.

Bryn sat at his desk, pulled out his notepad and began to write down what he knew about the dead woman to date:

NEFERTITI

Female

approx. 40 years old

Brown eyes

Well built

Well nourished

Long blonde hair

murdered

two stab wounds to chest – (heart and aorta) both potentially fatal.

Died 1950 approx. (+/ – 5 years)

Found in a cupboard behind a well-constructed false wall

Fully clothed – all intact except for wound holes

Found sitting in a rocking chair – no signs of a struggle

Reason for good condition of body – very dry with little air

Married? (Wedding ring). With unknown inscription.

Poss. ring missing (engagement ring)??

Bryn sat back and studied the list – not much to go on – perhaps Heather's full report would shed more light on it. He had already put in a call to the local council rates office to try and ascertain a history of the residents of the house and he was awaiting a call back. Then he asked the uniformed inspector if he had a couple of lads to help him with some house-to-house enquiries later. He was given two uniformed officers, both with very little police experience – Bryn realised that this forty-year-old murder certainly didn't rate too highly in the scheme of things today.

Bryn briefed the two lads and sent them off to do the house-to-house enquiries in the street – he gave them a list of questions to ask the residents, the first of course being how long had they lived there. He told them to note which houses were unoccupied so they could be revisited later. He knew he had to spell it out to the not-too-experienced officers.

He took out the ring and studied the inside, but he couldn't make out what was written, the whole ring had been dusty before but now it was covered with silvery fingerprint powder. He went to the bathroom and brought back some moistened toilet paper. He sat back down and started to clean the ring and slowly the inscription became clearer. He wrote down the tiny engraved words carefully:

'Io Sono Il Tuo Prigioiero Adesso!'

He read out what he had written to the two other detectives in the room.

'Sounds Spanish or Portuguese,' said Michael Noonan, the oldest and the most useless detective Bryn had ever encountered. 'It isn't French – that's for sure,' he said, returning to his newspaper, showing total disinterest in the investigation.

'I think it's Italian,' said Lenny Sinclair, a thirty-seven-year-old recent transferee to the Quayside CID office. Bryn agreed and asked the switchboard to find where the nearest Italian embassy was and put a call in to them. He had considered calling the Italian restaurant where his flat was, but then thought better of it – he didn't want to be beholden to them in any way for they might take it into their head to charge him rent.

Twenty minutes later he put the telephone handset onto the cradle and said, 'It means, "I am your prisoner now", in Italian; the shite things people say to each other when they are in love.' He had mentioned that the '*SONO*' was in capital letters – and was told that it meant 'YOUR'.

'So, whoever gave her the ring emphasised the *YOUR*. Why?' he muttered as he studied the engraving.

On his list, Bryn crossed out 'with unknown inscription' and wrote the translation underneath. He added:

Translation –I am YOUR prisoner now

It was almost one by the time Bryn arrived at Heather's office on the third floor of the hospital – he thought that he should collect the report himself, especially after last night and the numerous times they had 'made love' – her words not his. Her secretary sent him straight in – it was clear that she too knew of their previous relationship, and her attitude displayed the fact that she also knew how much of a bastard he had been and how much he had hurt her. He found Heather sitting behind her desk, her many diplomas displayed on the wall behind her, along with photographs of Heather sharing the frame with some very famous people. She looked up and smiled as he entered the room. She looked even sexier when she wore her glasses. She pushed the file towards him; then she stood up, came around the desk and kissed him. He did enjoy her kisses. He now felt embarrassed about the way he had left this morning and he was lost for words but she didn't seem to mind. She returned to her seat and even though she had vowed to herself she wouldn't, she asked, 'Will I see you later?'

'If I can – sure. But I'll call, if I can't.'

She settled for that; after all what could she do? She picked up her pen when he had left the office and tried to concentrate on work. She couldn't, not now that he was back in her life. She went to the window and waited for him to emerge from the hospital building. She watched as he walked to the car. She sensed he was smiling. She watched him get in and drive off. She had never felt like this about any other man and she liked the feeling. She only wished he felt the same.

As he crossed the car park to his car, he somehow knew she was watching him – it made him feel good. He walked a little straighter. He was smiling.

When he got back to his desk, the office was empty – he much preferred it that way. The others, with the exception of Lenny, seemed to be very jaded and cynical. They were just going through the motions until they got their pension. Bryn hated that attitude – he had waited a long time, and had gone through a lot of shit to become a detective and he was not going to take that for granted. He knew also that he had been lucky and his past in that shitty village called Dynas Dre was now covered up for good – he hoped – for he had attended her funeral only last week. He tried desperately to get his mind off Fiona and back into this case.

He sat there and opened Heather's report. He could smell her perfume as he turned the pages. His mind kept straying back to last night. She would let him do anything to her, some of which he knew to be illegal – and he had taken full advantage of that fact. As he sat there, he started to get an erection – there in the office. He continually lost his place so he turned to the beginning again and using all his concentration he put last night's debauchery out of his mind and started adding some more details to his list:

Deceased 35 – 40 years closer to 35??

Deceased had at least one child – shortly before death.

Weapon – thick-bladed knife – blade 8" long

No signs of violent internal trauma (sexually)

No defence wounds on hands

Signs of liver damage

Right upper canine tooth found in throat – poss. injury at time of death.

No distinguishing marks except old/well-healed appendix scar.

Not a great deal of blood on clothes.

Not true blonde – original hair colour light brown.

This last fact had already been brought to Bryn's attention by Stefan as they undressed the corpse at the mortuary when he said, 'The curtains don't match the carpet,' nodding towards the naked body. This comment received a steely glare from the Home Office pathologist who stood across the table, for as Bryn knew only too well – neither did hers.

So, possibly the deceased had been hit in the mouth prior to death, swallowed the tooth, and then was stabbed, twice.

He looked at the picture of the deceased again – yes, now he saw the injury to her lip – not clearly visible unless you looked closely and knew what you were looking for – he looked back at the report – yes, sure enough Heather had spotted it too then obviously went looking for the tooth.

Bryn loved making lists – so the next one had supplementary questions he needed to ask Heather next time he saw her, which probably wouldn't be long off:

Rough idea of timing of baby prior to death.

Was liver damage alcohol-related?

This made him think of his sister – the raging alcoholic. Then he thought about himself – he too had that gene – he too was on the verge of becoming an alcoholic. Verge? His ex-wife often told him that he had a 'self-destruct button' that his finger constantly hovered over. He shrugged the thoughts away by continuing to write:

Any idea of weapon used to knock out tooth?

Any idea of age of the appendix scar?

Why not too much blood on clothes?

When he had exhausted his list, he got up from his desk and went into the small room adjacent to the squad room; the room that his boss laughingly called 'The Conference Room'. It was more like the Black Hole of Calcutta when more than eight people were in it. He took out the clothing and laid each item out on the table. He had to open the window as the dust was quite bad. He thought about how pissed off the cleaner, old Mrs Kennedy, would be tomorrow – he quickly realised that it would be best not to tell her what she would be wiping up though. He slowly examined the contents – not that he really knew what he was looking for, but he was trying to get an impression of the dead woman. The clothes appeared to be of poor quality but he wasn't sure so he called down to see if there was a policewoman available to take a look and get her opinion. He was joined ten minutes later by Barbara Piper, a policewoman with about the same length of service as Bryn. He didn't rate many policewomen but Bryn had a lot of respect for Barbara and she could drink him under the table, and had done so – on many an occasion.

'They look cheap,' she said as she examined each article, 'except the underwear – that seems expensive, but I have never heard of the make, I think it is Italian from the label.'

There it was again, the Italian connection. Was my dead lady an Iti? he thought as he put the clothes back in their plastic evidence bags, having thanked Barbara for her time, and promising her a drink in the very near future. He went back to his desk and added to the list of unknowns:

Deceased Italian??

Clothing – British brands – poor quality except underwear.

Underwear – expensive and Italian

He sat back in his chair and contemplated these Italian references. Then something struck him and he added it to his list in large letters:

WAS SHE MISSED BACK THEN?

He wondered where the missing person reports would be kept these days, particularly since his police force had amalgamated with other forces twice since the '50s so Lord knows where the paperwork would be – if in fact it *was* kept.

CHAPTER FOUR

Friday 8 February 1952 11.47 hrs

Jenny returned home and put on the wireless. *The Light Programme* was her favourite – but it was all too solemn; everything was still about the King's passing and the anticipated arrival of the young Princess Elizabeth, but she left the radio on just for the background noise; it calmed her nerves as she went to prepare for her husband's return. He always finished work early on a Friday. She was going to tell him she was leaving – today. He could keep the boy, whom she had never been able to connect with, but her beautiful Lucia was coming with her.

She put the boy down for his nap; Lucia was still asleep in her pram. What a wonderful child she is, she thought as she picked her up and carried her lovingly to her cot. She stood for a while looking at the sleeping child – 'I love you so much,' she said, bending down and kissing the child's forehead. She went downstairs and poured herself a large glass of gin, putting in just a dash of tonic, and went into the lounge to await his return.

She felt an excitement deep in the pit of her stomach. She had no idea where she would go, but anywhere was better than here and besides, I have enough money to go where I like, she thought as she poured more gin into the glass, forsaking any tonic this time.

Thursday 12 June 1986 16.55 hrs

Bryn put down the telephone to his boss – he had told him what he knew about the deceased, which wasn't much more than he knew early this morning. He had also made several more unsuccessful calls to the council rates department. He remembered what one of his bosses had said one day when he looked out of a window in the court building, which was next door to the council offices. A fire alarm had gone off and the council staff were assembled in the car park:

'Hell, how many people work there?' he muttered.

'About half of them,' came his boss's sardonic reply. Now he found that comment to be very true.

He was also awaiting the arrival of the two uniforms to tell him the result of the house-to-house enquiries. Thankfully his boss seemed surprisingly satisfied with the progress and he told Bryn that he would brief the press later that evening. Anything to get your name in the paper, thought Bryn as he sat and looked at his pad. He was just about to call Heather and clarify those couple of points when the two probationers walked in.

'Nothing – no one knew anything cos most of the houses around there were only built in the late sixties.'

Bryn remembered as a kid playing in the fields where some of those houses now stood.

'How many houses up there were built earlier than that?' he asked and he tried to picture the site as he knew it as a boy.

'Six – we spoke to four residents – all of who moved in during the seventies. There was no reply at two of the houses.'

Bryn asked them to type up a report straightaway.

'We were supposed to have finished at two,' one of them said.

'And your point is…?' asked Bryn, looking at them with venom. 'If you don't like the job – you shouldn't have joined – now do me that fucking report with less lip.'

They said no more, which was a wise decision considering Bryn's mood. They just turned and left. He heard them muttering as they went down the corridor. Fucking plods, he thought as he picked up the phone and dialled the hospital.

'Hi, H – what time you finishing work?' he asked.

'What time can you get there?' she replied then suddenly hoped she hadn't misread his call – as he had a way to make her giddy as a schoolgirl.

'See you at your place in about an hour.'

He heard her agree as he put the phone down and looked back at the lists he had made. He had just meant to ask her the questions over the phone, but he needed some company right now and he knew H would readily supply that. He popped an anti-depressant and washed it down with some Scotch he always kept at the back of his desk drawer, just for emergencies – then he studied the file again.

His thoughts were interrupted by one of the probationers coming into the office. Bryn looked up, 'Where's your mouthy mate?'

'Gone home,' he replied reluctantly. Bryn immediately 'marked his card'. He would heap a ton of shit on that young man. He took the report without a word, glanced over it, and turned to the young officer and said, 'This is a load of crap – you need to get better than this.' The young officer left the office very deflated. Bryn added the report, which to be fair wasn't really that bad, to the growing file.

On his way to H's house, he had to drive past the street where Nefertiti was found, so he took the list, went into the control room, and gave the number where he could be reached to the telephonist, picked up a police radio and went out to the CID car.

He stopped outside the rambling Victorian house. He knew the owners had gone away – he also knew they would not be back – not if that guy's catatonic wife had anything to do with it – he smiled at the thought – nice house going cheap, I might put a bid in. Then he realised that he could never afford it – not with the amount of bloody maintenance he was paying the bitch from hell. He thought about a line in a film he had seen recently that typified his situation perfectly – 'I couldn't get out of sight if it took a pound to go around the world.' He smiled to himself at least.

He knocked on the front door of the first unvisited house. The occupant said he had only moved in last year and he had somewhere a list of the previous owners – he promised to find them and bring them to the police station. Bryn wrote down his name on a piece of paper and made a note to follow this up just in case the helpful citizen forgot his promise.

He then turned to try and find the other house that had been unoccupied. According to the list the uniformed lads had given him, it had the strangest name – 'Priate'. He searched all the gates and located the names of all the houses, which now matched the list he had. He went to the backs of the houses and walked up the alleyway, stopping at the third house, where he found 'Priate' or as it should have been 'Pri ate'. The mark where the 'v' should have been was still visible in the centre of the word.

'Fucking 'Private' – you morons,' he muttered to himself. Those two idiots would experience a living hell – he would see to that – especially that loudmouth wanker. He would be lucky to see out his probation if Bryn had anything to do with it.

When he got to her house, he saw that her brand new, bright red Audi Quattro was already parked on the driveway. That car cost six months' wages, he thought as he looked at the sort of car he would never be able to afford. He turned around; she was standing in the open doorway. 'Just admiring your motor – again,' he said, slightly embarrassed, for he felt she could read his thoughts.

'Just say the word and I'll get you one for your birthday.'

He couldn't reply to that for he knew that she would, if he asked. She knew he would never ask. He walked in and as the front door shut, he grabbed her and they kissed, which lasted for some considerable time.

Once they had finishing making love, this time in the front room, and he had removed the restraints from her wrists, she went and made a meal. Bryn had had a lot of women but only very few meant anything to him – Enya, a black nurse with the rich, racist parents and Fiona, who could have sent him to jail for a long time. He, of course, did not add his ex-wife, Laura, to the list. She had, after all, tricked him into marrying her – the fucking bitch. These days just thinking of her put him into a rage. He was pleased when he awakened from those thoughts by Heather calling that dinner was ready.

Over the delicious meal and the even more delicious and expensive bottle of red wine, Bryn produced his notebook and turned to the page of questions for the Home Office pathologist. 'I wondered how long it would take you to get back to work,' she smiled. And she picked up her glass of wine and settled back to answer the questions that were to come her way. She was in love with him – if only he knew it, or even if she felt confident enough just to tell him – she tried to banish those thoughts and concentrate on helping him, if she could.

He asked his questions and wrote down her replies – putting a question mark next to anything that was just her opinion and not actual fact.

When he had asked all his questions, and had written down her answers, Heather collected the plates and began to wash up. She sent him into the lounge with his wine. He sat on the couch and looked at his notes. What new things had he learned about the deceased he now called 'Sophia'?

She had had a baby not more than 6 months before her death?

Her liver was diseased – possibly alcohol-related.??

Not known if weapon used to knock out tooth.

Appendix scar old – poss. done as a child.

Little blood – heart stopped quickly. Deceased prob. left on her back??

He put his pad away as she entered the room and came and sat next to him – the hiss of the gas fire, the heavy meal, the wine, and the strenuous fuck he had just completed was lulling him to sleep. She watched him, as his head nodded in sleep. Yes, she thought, I really love him. She had from the first moment she met him over the body of that lifeless little boy who had drowned – and that was nearly twelve months ago now. She saw then that he wasn't as tough and heartless as he made out. She had watched him dealing with the parents of that little boy – she saw another side to Bryn Lawton that day and she liked what she saw; the calmness, compassion and humanity of the man was so different to what he usually displayed. She realised then that he, like so many other policemen she had met, wear this impenetrable mask. She had tried to break through but so far, no luck. But she vowed to keep trying – for this was a man who was worth the effort.

She let him sleep, happy to watch him, observing his chest gently rise and fall. She sipped her wine – very content indeed – she knew what went wrong with the relationship last time so she would try and hold back this time and perhaps he would grow to love her and they could be together.

The tranquil scene was interrupted just over an hour later by the telephone ringing. Bryn jumped awake and Heather ran out into the hall to answer it. She returned and said, 'It's the station for you.'

Bryn stood up very unsteadily for he had been in a deep, contented sleep – he looked at his watch. It was now 9.15 p.m. He picked up the receiver – this couldn't be good. It was Penny: 'Sorry Bryn, can you come in – there's a job and I can't reach anyone else.'

'No probs – I'll be there in about ten minutes.' He put the phone down and turned to face her, 'Sorry – duty calls.' She handed him his coat and opened the door. He left without a word, and didn't turn around even when he heard the front door slam. She stood, leaning on the closed door, wondering if there was any point in loving that man. As she didn't know the answer she went back into the lounge and switched on the television, and poured herself another glass of wine – anything to take her mind off that infuriating enigma that was bloody Bryn Lawton.

Bryn had hoped that something might have broken in the mummy case, but he was handed a telephone message. It was from a petrol station manager who had a member of staff stealing money. Bryn had installed a secret camera and from reading the message it was clear it had spawned a result. He went up to the office to get his spare set of handcuffs from his desk drawer – just in case, as he had left his best pair at Heather's. He was surprised to see Lenny sitting at his desk.

'What you doing here?' he asked, somewhat annoyed that he had been called out when a detective was just sitting there – doing fuck all.

'My landlady took the call – I had been out for a run – so I thought I'd come in but they said you were already on your way so I waited. What's the job? Anything to do with the dead woman?'

'No. It involves a female petrol station attendant. She had been suspected of nicking money by her boss for some time so I put a covert camera in and today is the day that she goes and gets herself caught.'

Lenny looked at his colleague – he appeared to be a bit angry so he tried to change the subject. 'By the way – seen the local paper? Your mummy case made page two.'

Bryn took the local rag from Lenny and quickly scanned the article – the words on the page clearly having come from his chief superintendent – utter bullshit, but he gave them what they wanted. Bryn just wondered where the 'team of dedicated detectives' were that were working the case. 'I'll read this crap later – you coming on this job?' Lenny nodded and followed Bryn out of the office.

Bryn, Lenny, and Barbara Piper entered the garage shop just prior to closing. The till was checked and money was found to be missing – £140 in ten-pound notes.

The attendant, who was the only one with access to the till at that time, was arrested and taken to the police station where she was interviewed by Bryn and Barbara. She, of course, denied taking the money. She had the arrogance of someone who was guilty but sure that they would never be able to prove it. She was almost laughing at the two officers – not a good thing to do when dealing with Bryn or Barbara. She was searched, and not surprisingly, no money was found. Bryn told Barbara to stay with her and not let her out of her sight. He returned to the shop where Lenny and two uniformed policemen were also searching for the money. It was nowhere to be found there either.

It was a very pissed off detective who returned to the police station and said to Barbara, 'I want that fucking bitch searched properly if you get my drift; I mean everywhere.' He pointed to his nether regions. 'Call a doctor, if necessary. She must have the money on her somewhere, and I think we know where.'

Barbara understood.

'But rather you, than me,' he shouted as Barbara left the office to return to the cells.

Twenty minutes later, a smiling Barbara handed Bryn £140 in ten-pound notes. It was in a sealed evidence bag.

'No prizes for guessing where she had that hidden,' said Barbara as she removed her surgical gloves.

'£140 – must be a big girl,' said Bryn.

'I reckon that slag could have taken that much if it was in ten-pence pieces. Fucking that would be like throwing a sausage down an entry.'

She had such a way with words.

Bryn took the money to the uniformed sergeant for placing in the locked evidence room.

'Have you counted it?' asked the sergeant, holding up the transparent evidence bag and peering into it suspiciously.

'No, I haven't, but Barbara has. She found it; I'm more than happy with that.'

'Never can be too careful when it comes to cash. There are two things that can get a policeman in trouble – cash and women,' said the sergeant, who had never even bent a rule throughout his twenty-nine years of service, never mind broken one. Before Bryn could tell him where it had been found, he had taken the money from the bag, and begun counting it. He kept licking his finger, bank cashier style, after every twenty pounds, or so.

At the conclusion of his counting Bryn told him where it had been found. He thought the sergeant was going to throw up as he ran to the toilet to wash out his mouth.

When Bryn told Barbara what had happened over a glass of Scotch in the CID office she replied, 'Serves him right, the old git should 'ave trusted me.' They touched glasses and both took a long, hard swig.

He had always liked working with Barbara, she was so

down-to-earth and nothing ever seemed to make her angry. Only Bryn knew that she was a lesbian – he had been pissed at her flat with her and her girlfriend Monica on several occasions.

'How are you getting on with the mummy case?' Lenny asked, after Barbara had left to go back to work and as he downed the last of the Scotch.

'Still no ID – I think she might be Italian though. I am going to the council office in the morning to try to get the records of the house – want to come?'

'Sure – but you seem to have enough on your plate – why don't I go? I don't have anything on at the moment.'

'Thanks – that would take a bit of pressure off. I have made an appointment for nine.'

'Okay – I'll go straight there after my run – see you in the morning.' With that he stood up, picked up his coat, and left the office.

'Out for a run – what the fuck next?' Bryn picked up the telephone and dialled Heather's number. He told her he had to work on so he wouldn't be coming back tonight. She sounded upset but simply said 'Okay.' He replaced the receiver and opened the store cupboard and took out the spare bottle of Scotch kept there for emergencies, grabbed his coat, and went home to his dingy flat – time for a little oblivion, he thought as he walked to his car.

CHAPTER FIVE

Friday 8 February 1952 12.20 hrs

'Right on time,' she muttered as she heard the front gate close – twenty past twelve. Heaven forbid he could break his bloody routine, she thought as she stood in the kitchen, ready to speak her piece, a speech she had been rehearsing since she got home.

He sensed the atmosphere as soon as he opened the back door. It was worse than usual. She glared at him seeing the bruises on his face and not feeling one iota of pity for this pathetic excuse of a man. She watched him as he hung up his keys on the hook behind the door, took off his shoes and placed them neatly on the shoe rack. He put his briefcase on the table while he removed his hat and coat – every movement of his daily routine grated on her already taut nerves. She knew every move he was going to make before he actually made it and it was making her feel physically sick. She sipped on her fourth glass of gin, her eyes never straying from him. He felt them boring into him but ensured he avoided that gaze.

He knew something was coming and it was something big. He expected more violence – it was inevitable.

Friday 13 June 1986 05.10 hrs

The whole bottle of booze he had consumed had only succeeded in giving Bryn a corker of a headache, which he was more than used to by now, but he had been experiencing that other old feeling for a couple of days now – he knew that it was coming; it was just a matter of time. The clinical depression – or as he had come to call it the black hole – was certainly on its way. Usually, booze helped but of late it wasn't having much effect. He had got much worse immediately after the Fiona incident ten years before. He had hoped that it might have improved now that they had found her body and she had been laid to rest and he was in the clear – but that wasn't the case at all – he felt worse. He knew he would enter that black hole and be there for a while – he just didn't know when, for how long, and how bad he would be. He lay there as the light slowly dawned. He looked around his dirty, untidy flat. A train rumbled past – this house used to be the old level crossing guard's cottage. He got up and staggered into the bathroom and threw up. The water from the tap was cold but he used it to wash, the cold water did help a little.

He went into the kitchen and switched on the kettle, put a tea bag in a cup, then went and sat in the lounge. He looked around the messy room; Sian's toys were in a large cardboard box in the corner. It had been nearly two months since he had been able to see her; he just knew that Laura would be starting to poison her mind against him, especially as she now had a new man in her life – a right wanker, a real steady Eddie, just the type of man she would go for, one she could control completely. The poor bastard. He smiled at the thought.

He picked up the newspaper Lenny had given him last night and read about his case. 'Christ, that man could bullshit for Britain,' he muttered to himself again as he read his boss's words. He seemed to be talking about a totally different case.

He thought about giving his old school friend Tommy Bowman a call. He was a reporter on this rag; perhaps he would like the truth. Bryn had done this a couple of times, just to rattle his bosses and earn a couple of quid by passing on the odd snippet of information, but he couldn't really see too much in doing that at the moment – maybe when the case is over, he'd get Tommy to pay for a meal and he could dish some dirt.

He dozed on the couch until eight, then changed his shirt, in the vain hope that this clean item would have some restorative properties – it didn't. He walked the mile and a half to the police station. He wore his cheap sunglasses against the early morning sun that he was walking into. His first port of call was, of course, the canteen – the beating heart of any police station, but it was empty. He made himself a strong coffee and wearily climbed the stairs to his office, avoiding the control room – he had no wish for any of the uniformed bosses to see him in this state – they would never understand his condition for they had never been detectives.

Following yet another annoying telephone call from his boss asking what progress he had made in the enquiry, Bryn was trying to concoct a report on the enquiries that had been made so far into the mummified woman's case – the information he had still didn't amount to much even when written down and flowered up as best he could, but what little he knew went into the report. He looked at his watch and saw it was 10.30 a.m. – tea time – so he put down his pen and was just leaving to go to the canteen, when Lenny came strolling in. Bryn could tell by looking at him that no good news was on its way. Lenny took out his notepad:

'Nothing – the records only go back to 1965, when a family called Jackson bought the place. There is no mention of who they bought it from. They sold it last year to the couple who found the body. Sorry.'

'Fuck,' said Bryn and he walked out of the office. He now badly needed another coffee – his head was pounding. He borrowed some aspirins from Penny and popped them together with his anti-depressants. He hoped they would stay down this time.

He felt a bit better when he had put some more caffeine into his body and was able to try again with the report. Paperwork never was his strongpoint and he was unable to give his written work the added flair that got some of the less able detectives noticed.

He answered the phone.

'Detective Lawton – it is your favourite informant – can I take you for lunch?'

'You sure can – I need to get out of this bloody dump. Usual place?'

'See you there in twenty minutes.'

He put the phone down. Lenny was trying to pretend that he was busy writing. 'I am taking my refs. If you want me, I am with the frustrated virgin.' He took his coat and left.

He saw Heather's car in the car park of the out-of-the-way pub they had used often during their brief affair. She was sitting at a corner booth, a glass of white wine and a JD already on the table. He liked her a lot but wasn't sure if it would lead anywhere. They sat together for a while without speaking – he loved the smell of her perfume. It was Heather who brought up the subject of the mummy.

'Any developments with Nefertiti?' she asked as she sipped her Chardonnay.

'No. Nothing. I am no further forward than I was the other day. Even the council can't help. I have given her a new name though; I think she is Italian so I've rechristened her Sophia after the beautiful Miss Loren.'

'You men are so predictable – put Italian and a woman together and you will always come up with Sophia Loren.'

'That is how I want to die – shot by a very jealous Carlo Ponti.'

She shook her head.

'Miss Loren's husband.'

Heather smiled then said, 'Unfortunately – I think you need to rechristen her again. I took another look at her this morning – I examined the tooth – the one that was knocked out. I saw she had some old dental work done. I called in a dentist friend of mine to take a look and he agreed with me. She had work done when she was very young and both the work and the materials used were British, not Italian.' She was pleased to see him smile as he got up to get another round of drinks.

Bryn returned to the station ninety minutes later. He felt so relaxed, the way only good sex can make you feel. He and Heather had stopped off at his flat on the way back and had what Heather described as a 'lovely quickie'. It was something they both needed, but for very different reasons. He did, however, refuse to allow Heather to send her cleaner over to 'spruce the place up a bit'. It did go on his to-do list though.

Lenny met him in the control room and relieved Bryn of the car keys as a job had come in. Bryn went upstairs to try and complete the bloody report.

'The frustrated virgin?' Lenny asked Penny as he passed through the control room on his way out.

'He was at the Halfway Inn,' she replied with a smile. Lenny just smiled and shook his head.

Bryn sat at his desk and added this latest piece of information about the dental work to his list. So, if she is British – it seems reasonable to assume that her husband is the Italian connection. As he mused, a thought came into his mind. He picked up the phone and dialled.

'Hi, H, can I ask you a question?' he asked without any preamble.

'Sure,' she said. She was quite used to him by now but she did wish he was just a little bit more compassionate for not an hour before they were making love… but that's not going to happen, she thought to herself as she listened to his voice. 'Let me take a look and I'll call you back,' she said. She put the phone down.

Within an hour she called him.

'I'd estimate the ring had been on her finger about ten years – that's a rough estimate but given the way the skin on the finger…'

Bryn stopped her mid-sentence, 'Sorry – but like Joe Friday used to say in *Dragnet*, "just the facts, ma'am".' They both laughed. 'See you later,' he said as he put the phone down. She hoped he would.

He turned to a fresh page in his notepad and wrote:

<u>*Italians in Britain in the 1940s*</u>

Italian descendants

Restaurant owners/waiters

Prisoners of war??

He pondered about that for a while – then he thought that as the war had been over for five years by 1950, any prisoners must surely have been repatriated by then, but it was worth following up. He put a call into the Imperial War Museum in London – he knew they would hold information on this sort of thing.

'Yes detective, a lot of Italian prisoners were in camps here in the UK,' said the rather posh-voiced researcher at the museum, 'then of course their status changed in 1944 when the Italians capitulated and supposedly came over to our side – so the prisoners were asked if they wished to help the Allies and those that did had their restrictions relaxed. They were called co-operators and of course those who didn't want to help were called non-co-operators.'

'Were there a lot of prisoners in the UK by the end of the war?' asked Bryn, making copious notes of what he was being told.

'Well, we caught 130,000 in North Africa alone and most of them came here; some to America, some to Canada,' replied the researcher, who sounded quite bored with the whole thing.

'How many camps did we have?'

'A little over a thousand here in the United Kingdom; but not all for Italians of course – for the entire Axis lot.'

'When were they repatriated?'

'They were gone by the end of 1946; most of them shortly after the war ended – we needed to get rid of them as soon as possible – we couldn't feed them all you see.' He seemed almost apologetic as he said this.

'How could a POW get to stay in the UK and avoid repatriation?'

'If he had a job useful to us, or he got married to a British girl. Both were very common in the post war days. If my memory serves me correctly, about 25,000 POW's stayed after the war but I don't know how many of those were Italian.'

'Was it a difficult procedure for a POW to get married?'

'It was while they were still a prisoner – a lot were refused at the time but after, when the war was over, the restrictions were relaxed and really it was similar to a UK citizen getting married.'

'What happened to Italian civilians who were living here when the war broke out?'

'They were interned for the duration I am afraid –the Isle of Man, I think. I hope I have been of help. Please do not hesitate to call if I can be of any further assistance. Goodbye.' With that he put the phone down.

Bryn still didn't feel any further forward but he had had enough for the day. He went downstairs and signed out; making sure that his name was not on the 'on call' roster. He walked quickly to his flat, opened a new bottle of his anti-depressants – he noticed it was the last. He would need to pay another visit to the chemist who gave him the pills – in return for not doing him for several offences relating to prescriptions that Bryn had discovered several months ago. The arrangement was working out fine for both parties. He got his pills and the pharmacist kept his licence – perfect. He collected his car and was waiting as Heather drove onto her driveway. She was delighted to see him.

It wasn't long before they were in bed.

CHAPTER SIX

Friday 8 February 1952 12.27 hrs

Jenny had seen enough of his bloody annoying routine, so she went back into the lounge and to the drink's cabinet, pouring herself another large gin and emptying the bottle into her glass. Giuseppe went into the bedroom to change out of his suit. She plucked up the nerve, rushed up the stairs and suddenly burst in.

'I am leaving you,' she blurted out, her words slightly slurred. He looked so comical, sitting on the bed in his long johns with one leg in and one leg out of his trousers.

'Leaving – why? Where will you go?' he said, his eyes full of love – which only made her madder, for if he had loved her why hadn't he done more to improve their lives?

'I am going far away from you – and I am taking Lucia. The boy can stay here with you – both you bloody Iti's belong together.'

'Tu non puoi lascaiarmi adesso, ti prego io ti amo tanto.' (You can't leave me. Please I beg you. I love you so much). She knew that strong emotion always forced him back into speaking Italian, and she now knew enough of the language to glean the gist of his words but today it would have no effect on her.

'You pathetic excuse for a man. How could I ever have seen anything in you?' She walked past him. 'I hate you,' she screamed. He could tell she was drunk again. She started emptying the contents of her wardrobe into a large suitcase. He sat there watching her – his pants still around his ankles. He did not know what to do or say to her to make all this right.

When she had closed the suitcase, she went into Lucia's room; the baby was still sleeping contentedly in her cot, and so Jenny quietly placed a small suitcase on the bed and started to pack Lucia's things. She heard him leave the bedroom and go downstairs.

She called a taxi from the bedroom extension, asking them to collect her in twenty minutes. In just twenty minutes she would be out of here and rid of him – and it would just be her and Lucia – as it should be.

Saturday 14 June 1986 08.40 hrs

Bryn sat at the breakfast bar in the kitchen, reading the paper while Heather prepared some breakfast. This was a relaxing fantasy as they 'played house' together. The headlines were all about the Labour Party expelling radicals. Bryn, to the horror of his grandfather, a militant trade unionist, was a staunch Conservative, a true child of Maggie Thatcher, so the machinations of the commi left had no interest for him. He put the paper down as a plate of eggs and bacon was placed in front of him. He tucked in greedily. He realised that he hadn't eaten anything substantial in thirty-six hours – something that was not unusual for him. The guilt he had felt after he called Laura and lied that he had to work today so wouldn't be able to see Sian was slowly fading. He had been given a rare day off for there was very little he could do on the case on a weekend. I will leave it to the 'team of detectives' to carry on today, he thought. He was going to spend it with Heather. She made him feel so good and that was something Bryn hadn't felt for a long time.

'Let's go out,' he said. Heather jumped at the chance and was ready within the hour.

He drove Heather's car and as they left the town, Bryn noticed a police car parked on the large, blue, metal bridge that spanned the river. The blue light on the top of the car was flashing and the driver's door was open. Heather said nothing – she knew he would not just ignore this and drive on. Sure enough, Bryn stopped the Audi behind the police car. He ignored a heavy sigh coming from the passenger's seat. He got out of the car and saw Stefan looking up. He did the same and spied a man standing high up on the bridge's metalwork. He could hear Stefan calling to the man to come down.

'At last,' he thought, a chance to put his hostage negotiator's training to some use – it was all fresh in his memory, as the course only ended two months ago.

He turned to Heather. 'Sorry,' he said, 'this won't take a minute.' He walked over to the uniformed officer, just as he heard him say, 'Oh fuck.' Bryn looked up and the man was nowhere to be seen. They both ran to the rail and saw him floating face down in the river. The strong, incoming tide was carrying the body swiftly upstream.

'There's a boat over there,' Bryn shouted to Stefan. They both ran to it and pushed it out and the officers jumped in. Bryn looked back and could see Heather standing at the rail with a group of concerned citizens. She waved and disappeared.

She was swiftly forgotten. Bryn loved being in the thick of any action.

Stefan was doing the rowing and Bryn sat in the stern of the small rowing boat. He could see that Stefan's strong rowing was allowing them to catch up the body.

'Do you think he's dead?' asked Stefan.

'He is – unless he can breathe through his ears – his face has been in the water for ten minutes.' They both laughed.

'Fucking slow down, or we will catch up with it – let it keep floating.' Bryn looked at him, hoping he would catch his drift. It suddenly dawned on Stefan what Bryn was saying – for two miles further up the river was another force area and if it went there, they would have to deal with it. Stefan slowed his rowing accordingly, and Bryn sat there, enjoying the sun on his face.

A couple of minutes later Bryn was just about to regale Stefan with an amusing story about a lifeboat he had launched during his training to join the merchant navy, which he had joined on leaving school to get away from his parents, when he saw something that he hadn't accounted for. 'Oh shit,' he said when he saw that the body had snagged on a small sand bar. There was now no way to avoid having to collect it, for they were still over a mile away from the other force area and there were people on the bank watching, so refloating it wasn't an option either. They pulled alongside and heaved the saturated body into the boat, Bryn trying not to get too much water on himself. Both officers were surprised at just how old the man was – surely well into his seventies. It was clear from the way his head wobbled about that the neck was broken, but Bryn checked anyway – yes — he was dead.

They were just about to turn the small boat around and head back when Bryn heard shouting from the bank and saw two uniformed officers calling to them. They had crossed over into a different section of their force and officers from that station were on the bank. Stefan rowed the boat over to the bank and Bryn asked the officers, one of whom he was in training school with years before, to help get the body out and to a place where the ambulance could get to it. The two officers pulled the dead man up the steep bank. Bryn quickly whispered something to Stefan – it was a couple of minutes before the other officers realised that they had been left with the corpse and saw that the rowing boat was now heading back to the Quayside patch. The language the men in the boat could hear coming from the bank was awful – but the crew of that small boat roared with laughter all the way back to the jetty.

Heather was sitting in her car in the car park of the pub opposite. Bryn got in and without a word, started the car and drove off. She could smell the river on him, so their first port of call was to get him some aftershave to mask the smell. Bryn couldn't keep it in for long and burst out laughing, and in between giggling he explained what had just happened – Heather wondered if she would ever get used to police humour but she did see the funny side of it – eventually.

Over a lovely lunch Bryn told Heather the story he had tried to tell Stefan:

During the second week of his training for the Merchant Navy Bryn was put in charge of launching a lifeboat from the davits that were situated on the banks of the River Thames. He knew all the theory. All was going well until the boat actually touched the water and the lowering ropes were disconnected. A cry was heard from his mate, Tosh, who was the only occupant of the boat at the time.

He was very quickly up to his ankles in cold water. The instructor took over and the ropes were hurriedly re-attached to the sinking craft. Bryn had forgotten to have the drainage plug in the bottom of the boat 'shipped'.

'Twat,' was all Tosh could say as he squelched past Bryn and into the dormitory, following his profound apologies.

This total lack of practical ability came to the fore on the fourth week of the course. The lifeboat had been successfully launched, and Bryn, surprise, surprise, had been given no part in the proceedings. The boat was being rowed across the Thames towards Tilbury, with each student being given the opportunity to be cox of the little boat. The wind started to blow stronger and the instructor, a very polite, quietly spoken man – a rarity in this institution, who looked strangely like Captain Birdseye – decided that it was time to return to the shore and store the boat back on the davits. It was unfortunate that that decision was made at the time when Bryn was having his turn as cox, and it was even more unfortunate for the crew of twenty-four students and one instructor that no change was made to the cox of the soon-to-be-stricken little boat. Bryn had given the instruction to 'Ship oars' which meant that the oars were lying inside the boat. He then gave the order 'Oars' resulting in all the oars being put in place ready to start off, but by this time the wind was blowing very hard and the tide was coming in. Bryn could see the bore, (the first large wave of the incoming tide) coming closer.

He knew that he needed to get the boat moving and shouted, but not loudly enough, as a slight panic had gripped his voice, 'Give way together.'

The port side oarsmen heard him but the starboard oarsmen

didn't, resulting in one side rowing and the other side not. The boat turned side on the approaching wave, which, driven against the strong wind, had built up several feet high. The real lifeboat had to be launched from Tilbury to come and rescue the floundering student and instructor who were left swimming in the murky, condom-ridden waters of the Thames after the 'Titanic' in which they were rowing capsized.

'Twat,' said Tosh which was echoed two dozen times as the saturated survivors made their way to their dormitories.

'Are you sure you are cut out for this life, son?' said the ever-so-tactful Captain Birdseye.

So that was my very short-lived career in the navy,' he said as they sipped their coffee. She was laughing at his story, and loving the fact that he had opened a little part of his life to her. That was really all she needed to feel close to him.

CHAPTER SEVEN

Friday 8 February 1952 13.10 hrs

Giuseppe now quickly changed his clothes and walked back downstairs and into the kitchen – he had no idea what to do. He was in a blind panic. He started to make himself and Jenny a sandwich – something he always did on a Friday when he got home from work. He froze as he heard his wife coming down the stairs, the heavy suitcase hitting every step. He waited in the kitchen, dreading the moment she would depart from the house, leaving him for good. He loved her so much; he had from the first moment he saw her working on that farm outside the prisoner of war camp. She came into the kitchen and stood there staring at him, not believing that at a time like this he could calmly make a sandwich.

'You bastard,' she said and turned to go and get the other suitcase and fetch Lucia from the bedroom. He stood there, not knowing what to say or do. She came back in.

'*Ti amo*,' he said weakly. She laughed at his pathetic attempt at talking her out of this. She moved towards him.

'You're pathetic – do you think that just saying you love me is supposed to make me want to stay? I hate you,' she said, and slapped him across the face. 'You make me sick,' she screamed into his face. And he felt her spit hitting his cheek.

It happened in a flash; all the years of pent-up rage exploded in one terrifying moment.

The next thing he knew she was falling to the floor. It was all happening before him in slow motion. He later remembered punching her in the face, an old reaction returning to him, and then he looked at the bread knife he was holding – thick blood covered the long, sharp blade all the way to the handle.

Her eyes were wide open, staring at him as she had slumped down against the kitchen wall. He looked at her chest – yes, the two wounds were clearly visible by the blood. Two stab wounds to the heart, just as he had been taught in the naval *Comando Supremo* back in 1943, the elite unit he had been with during the war. No need to check – he knew she was dead, just like the numerous Allied soldiers he had dispatched the same way before his capture. He didn't know how long he had stood there just staring at her, then he heard a car pull up outside. He ran to the window. It was her taxi. He ran back into the kitchen, rinsed his hands under the tap and answered the door at the third knock.

'Sorry – my wife managed to get a lift with a friend,' he told the elderly man who stood there. He opened his wallet and handed the man a ten-shilling note. The taxi driver's eyes lit up and he went away a happy man. Giuseppe closed and locked the door.

He looked again at the lifeless body, her unblinking eyes still staring at him.

'*Ti amo,*' he said again. Then he went to check on the children.

Sunday 15 June 1986 10.10 hrs

Bryn sat in the office, trying once again to motivate himself to do some work, but it was Sunday after all and he had had such a lovely day yesterday, except for the slight hiccup on the bridge; he felt it hard to get going. It wasn't that he didn't have enough work to do. He had been joined by Lenny.

'Fancy some breakfast?' he asked.

'Sure,' replied Bryn who had left Heather in bed so had missed eating.

They went to a local cafe and Bryn ordered the fry-up with all the trimmings. Lenny only ordered brown toast, 'I'm on a keep-fit kick,' he said, Bryn just shook his head and wondered what the modern British police force was coming to. As they ate, Lenny asked Bryn to update him on the mummy case.

'Have you thought about revisiting the house and taking another look around?' asked Lenny, as he sipped his orange juice.

Bryn suspected Lenny must have read this in the *A to Z of Being a Policeman* book, but it seemed like a good idea, and he would do anything to avoid actually doing any work so when they returned to the station, Bryn telephoned the owner of the house, who told him that he had left a set of keys with a neighbour. Then he and Lenny made their way to the house and within minutes they were using the large key to unlock the back door.

Both men stood in the hallway and looked around. The house was very cold, despite the bright sunshine outside. Bryn gave an involuntary shudder.

'Any ideas what the hell we are looking for?' asked Bryn, now doubting the wisdom for this exercise.

'No – but let's just have a look around, you never know,' Lenny said as he walked down the hall and into the kitchen, which Bryn noticed was exactly the same as when he was here several evenings ago – the glass of water the lady had been drinking was still on the table and the open tin of red paint on the wallpaper table: the paint on the brush now solid. They appeared to have left in a hurry.

'Who could blame them?' he muttered to himself. 'They must have shat themselves when they found it.' He thought back to his action on seeing the mummy and smiled to himself.

'What?' asked Lenny.

'Nothing – just talking to myself,' replied Bryn with a smile.

'They can lock you away for that, you know,' said Lenny as he moved into the lounge.

Bryn went upstairs and gave another involuntary shudder as he walked into the bedroom. I must be getting soft in my old age, he thought as he looked at the still-open doors to the alcove, fingerprint powder covering almost the whole surface. He peered in. He was joined by Lenny. 'This was where they found her,' he said. Lenny moved quickly away.

The rocking chair was still there. The room smelt musty. He remembered Heather telling him that it was the dryness that had preserved her so well. There was nothing to see in there, even the floor seemed to have been swept. He came out of the room and looked at the partly stripped walls of the bedroom. He noticed something; a part of a letter painted in white on the once-yellow painted walls. He carefully peeled back the wallpaper. Revealing the letter 'J'. He called the station and asked if the scene of crime officer could meet him there. While they waited, they looked around the other rooms but there was nothing else to see.

An hour later they were joined by Karl. Bryn directed him to the bedroom and pointed to the letter. Karl photographed it. He couldn't get fingerprints from paper so he picked up a wallpaper knife and slowly started to remove the rest of the paper – it read 'JENNY AND GUS'. The 'A' had a very distinctive loop on the bottom. Karl photographed it, then left.

'That could be any of the owners back all the way to the reign of Queen Victoria. When was that?' said Lenny, obviously not putting much value to the find.

'1837 to 1901,' said Bryn, 'but I think this house was built late in her reign. At least by getting it photographed it shows the fucking bosses that I'm doing something.' He nudged Lenny, who smiled at his mate. He liked Bryn – he was what Lenny thought of as 'an old-style copper', more interested in 'thief-taking' than paperwork and sucking up to the bosses. This was something he knew he would never be.

It would be something for the next report. He now knew that all the wallpaper would have to come off the walls. How lucky for the owners to have the job done for them for nothing – not that they would give a damn for Bryn suspected, rightly as it turned out, those owners were never going to return to this house.

When he got back to the station, he telephoned the owner to say what they were about to do.

'Do what the hell you like with the bloody place. You can set fire to it if you like – you won't see us there again.'

Bryn wondered if he could afford to buy it – he could get it cheap – no, he quickly realised, not with the number of outgoings he had from his pathetic salary. He started to curse his ex-wife again.

He telephoned the chief superintendent to tell him he needed a load of bobbies to do some wall stripping. He listened to his boss make some remark about getting his own house decorated at the force's expense – Bryn didn't respond. He found this man's sense of humour about as funny as toothache.

At 5 p.m. that afternoon Bryn took the ten uniformed bobbies to the house and told them to strip all the wallpaper from every room. They gave him a look of disgust, but set about the work using scrapers Bryn had to buy with his own money. He sat quietly in the kitchen – he no longer felt the camaraderie that he was once part of when he was in uniform. Perhaps he was growing up – but he doubted that.

It took four hours and all the paper had been removed from the walls. The place was tidied and the uniforms left. Bryn and Lenny surveyed the results. Nothing was found written on the walls downstairs, but upstairs in one of the smaller bedrooms they saw: 'LEONARDO', this time in white paint. It too had that distinctive loop on the 'A'. There was that Italian connection again.

'It could just be a nickname for someone called Leonard,' said Lenny as he studied the wall. Bryn nodded but he didn't think so. He radioed to the station to get the SOC man back to get yet another photograph.

It was nearly midnight when the two detectives got back to the station. Lenny said goodnight and left and Bryn pulled Sophia's file to him and looked at his list to which he added:

Poss. names - Jenny and Gus

Poss. child - Leonardo.

Still not a lot to go on. He switched off the light and went downstairs to the control room where he was handed several messages, two from Laura, two from Heather who used the pseudonym 'Sally' which was her middle name and three that actually applied to work. He put them in his pocket for tomorrow and walked back to his flat – tonight he would have to try and sleep without the aid of any pills or sex. He still had his booze though and that would have to suffice.

CHAPTER EIGHT

Friday 8 February 1952 13.50 hrs

Having checked that Leonardo and Lucia were still asleep he went back into the kitchen and picked up Jenny's body and carried it upstairs to their bedroom. There was only a slight swelling to her lip though he knew he must have punched her with some force. He placed her lovingly on the bed. He tried to close her eyes but they wouldn't stay shut. They remained staring at him. He turned and closed the bedroom door and went back and stood at the foot of the bed trying to think what to do.

Just then the door opened and in walked his son, rubbing his eyes. Giuseppe jumped and snatched the boy up in his arms and carried him quickly out of the room. The little boy was so shocked that he started to cry until his father started to move him about, calling him '*aeroplano*', so the boy stuck out his arms and they went downstairs, the lad laughing fit to burst – the father in a blind, breathless panic.

It was after eight before the two children had settled in their beds again and he could go back into his bedroom and once again confront the corpse of his dead wife. He tried again to close her eyes and this time he succeeded. He sat on the bed with his head in his hands. He had no idea what he was to do but he knew one thing, he was not surrendering to the British – he had been a prisoner of theirs for over twelve months and he would never be so again – he would rather die first. That was when the idea of using the alcove came to him. He went over to the door and opened it – it was a windowless space that went back about five feet. The family had used it to store junk. He immediately set about clearing out the space, leaving nothing in there whatsoever, and when it was finally completely empty, he took the old rocking chair from the spare bedroom, put that in the alcove, then gently lifted his wife into the chair, kissed her now cold, dry cheeks and closed the door. He looked at the bedspread – not a drop of blood had leaked from her body. The *Comando* had taught him well.

He was just about to leave when he remembered her rings, especially the engagement ring. The diamond alone must have been worth a small fortune – he thought back to how he had taken it from some old Jewess in Rab, who was being deported from the camp. The stupid old Jewess had tried to use it to save the life of her daughter. He took the ring, and then shoved the woman and the child on the transport. He argued that if he hadn't taken it those fucking Germans would have.

He went back to the body and, trying not to look at her face, he forced the ring from her finger. The wedding ring was on too tightly – he tried for a while but it was just damaging her flesh. He would have had to cut her finger off to get it. He had no wish for that so he left it where it was, closing the door on his wife for the last time.

Monday 16 June 1986 10.27 hrs

Bryn called the admin office at his force headquarters asking if there was any chance that they might have archived two missing person reports going back to the late 1940s.

'Believe it or not, we do,' said a clerk, 'but we are slowly destroying them now – they are taking up too much space.'

Bryn went to see his boss and arranged to go over to the headquarters. He would have to stay a couple of days, or perhaps one of the others on the team of investigating detectives on the case could go, he thought but didn't say. His boss reluctantly agreed. Bryn then telephoned Heather and asked if she could take a couple of days off. She said she could even though she knew it would be difficult to arrange cover at such short notice – but she wanted desperately to be with him. He told her where he was going and she said she would meet him there tomorrow. She said that she would arrange a hotel for him. She knew his taste in places to stay and it did not match hers.

Bryn drove the forty miles to his headquarters; a large newly built building on the sea front. He showed his warrant card to the receptionist and went to the lift. The admin section was on the fourth floor where he met with the clerk he had spoken to earlier

'All the old records are in the basement, but as I say we are disposing of them, bit by bit. But you might just be lucky.'

After a cup of disgusting coffee in the canteen, Bryn made his way to the basement, and when he opened the door he saw boxes of old records – he opened one, the report on top was a stolen bicycle report from 1944. Crime of the fucking century, he thought, but if 1944 is still here then we might be in luck. He took off his jacket and started on the first box.

It was a fairly straightforward thing he was pleased to see, as all the different categories were filed together – crimes, general reports, and the things he was looking for – missing person reports.

By 9 p.m. he had had enough – he was up to 1950 and nothing from his area that was remotely similar to his lady, so he called it a night. He put on his jacket and closed the door and made his way to the hotel that Heather had booked. To his amazement it was the same hotel he had stayed at with Fiona all those years ago. It had changed its name. He remembered that he was a young uniformed policeman, sent to headquarters to attend a motorcycle course in 1976 – he had secretly spent the week with her, cocooned in that small hotel room – how he had loved her.

He checked in and was given the key, but he asked the receptionist if Room 27 was available? It was, so they changed the reservation and Bryn made his way to the room – the room he had shared with her. He let himself in and stared at the room – it hadn't changed much. He lay on the bed and was asleep in seconds.

He was awakened at about 6 a.m. by the door opening – he was still dressed. He was just about to shout something at the housekeeping staff, when he saw Heather peering around the door. Without too much being said, they quickly undressed and got into bed where they made love, but it wasn't Heather he was making love to – but his Fiona.

Over a late breakfast in the dining room Heather asked if she could help him with his search. He didn't see why not. The more hands, the better. They made their way back to the grotty basement with only a slight sideways glance from the receptionist who was wondering why a Home Office pathologist was interested in old files.

By one o'clock, they were into 1952 and just about to take a break for some lunch when Heather looked at a file:

'A woman, aged 34, went missing in February from that house, reported by her sister.' She handed the file to Bryn.

'This is it – thank God.' He kissed the file then put his lips to Heather's cheek, leaving a dirty mark. He took the file out into the light and read:

Name – Jennifer Salvino née Armstrong

Born 3rd January 1918

Reported missing 16th February 1952

By sister Emily Taylor née Armstrong – address 17 Kings Avenue, Quayside

Married to Giuseppe Salvino 1948

He disappeared February 1952

Also missing Lucia 3 months old.

Other child Leonardo seen with father around 12th February 1952 by mother-in-law

'We found these names painted on the walls of the house – all except Lucia's,' he told Heather, who was pleased to see him so animated. This is one in the eye for Lenny, he thought as he sat down to read the file fully.

Bryn looked at a faint handwritten note on the bottom of the file; it read:

'X ref. Dec. 1957 file D/187/57'

Bryn went to the other boxes and looked for the 1957 files. He took out the missing person ones – how neatly they were bound and how orderly they were – we could take some lessons, he thought as he went through the bundle until he came to no.187. He started to read:

Missing Samuel and Edwina Armstrong

Born 1881/1882

Reported missing by daughter Emily Taylor – same address

Never returned from a trip to Italy

Missing

Daughter and Granddaughter (Jennifer and Lucia) reported MFH 16 Feb. 1952 X ref. D/67/52

Bryn took that out too and returned the rest of the files to the box. As he did so, he wondered how many of the others named in those files were murdered. He knew of at least one other – Fiona Henley in the 1976 box – murdered by that bastard of a husband of hers but he was never able to prove it, not that he had tried that hard; in fact, he had deserted her when she needed him most – he shuddered at the thought. He then realised too that, if all the facts of that case came out, he would have been in prison for quite some time.

Heather and Bryn returned to the hotel where he rang his boss and said he had a few more boxes to go through and would finish tomorrow, 'It was a murder investigation after all,' he added. He put the phone down and joined Heather in the bath. How she relaxed him.

CHAPTER NINE

Monday 11 February 1952 04.20 hrs

Gus Salvino finally finished painting the new skirting boards on the false wall. He was knackered. He had hardly slept all weekend. He washed his hands with turpentine to remove the paint and went to make himself a strong cup of coffee. He returned to the room several times to see if the wall looked okay – it did. He was sure no one would be able to tell. He sat on the couch and tried to think what to do now. He decided that he would take the day off sick; after all he had a lot to prepare for the two days since his wife's demise had been taken up with the kids, and his nights, constructing his wall. As he sat there, he started to doze. He was so very tired. He heard Lucia starting to cry – he wearily went up to her and brought her down. He made her a bottle – but still she wouldn't stop crying. He cuddled her and rocked her but still that awful, nerve-jangling crying just wouldn't stop. It went on for nearly two hours, and then suddenly it stopped. He looked down at the lifeless body of his daughter; his hand still over her mouth, for all he really wanted was a moment of quiet. He laid the body on the couch and stood up – he began to moan uncontrollably. He knew hell was already waiting for him for what he had done during the war but now with what he had done to his own family...

What kind of man can do this? he thought as he stared at

the small lifeless body. He had done some awful things during the war, including murdering unarmed prisoners of war and innocent civilians– but this, murdering his family. He sank to his knees and tried to pray but he knew no God would hear his pleas now. He began to sob uncontrollably.

Wednesday 18 June 1986 09.20 hrs

Bryn sat at his desk back at the CID office and re-read the old missing person reports. He listed his plan of action:

Locate Giuseppe Salvino

Locate children Lucia and Leonardo

Speak to Emily Taylor

Visit 17 Kings Avenue.

Where in Italy did the parents go?

He had a bad feeling about the fact that the baby had been reported missing too when the young lad had been seen with his father, by the mother-in-law shortly before they went missing. But where was the baby girl?

He picked up his attaché case containing some statement forms and signed out. He needed some air so he walked the two miles to 17, Kings Avenue. This was in the poorer area of the town which was saying something in a shithole like Quayside. He looked in the gardens of the houses he passed – each one filled with junk – old cars, prams, broken toys – crap of every description everywhere. It seemed every house had the shell of a Ford Escort up on bricks. And dogs – what was this fascination the poor had with ugly, bad-tempered bloody dogs? He had no idea. Number 17 was one of the worst. It took some effort to avoid the dog crap that littered the path. He knocked. The door was answered by a large unshaven man in a filthy string vest. The stench from inside was awful. Bryn identified himself and explained the nature of his visit. The man shrugged his shoulders and closed the door without a word. 'Thanks for your help – you fucking moron,' Bryn muttered under his breath. He turned to go next house when the door to number 17 re-opened and a lady, who looked old before her time, came running out.

'Excuse me, officer – you're looking for Emily? She used to live here but she died a couple of years ago.'

'Oh, thank you.'

Before he could say another word, the woman continued, 'Her daughter lives in the next street, 8, Queens Avenue, I think.'

Bryn thanked her again and watched the woman return to her hovel. He wondered how people could live in such squalor – then, with some embarrassment, he thought about his dingy flat. He walked quickly towards the next street.

The woman had been close but it was at 12, Queens Avenue that Bryn found Vera, Emily's daughter. If Bryn thought the other house was dirty – in this house you had to wipe your feet as you left. It was with some reluctance that he sat on the ripped and stained couch as the girl, who was wearing the shortest dressing gown Bryn had seen in a while, sat opposite him, and as he related, over a glass of Scotch, to the others in the office later, 'Her beaver was winking at me'.

Bryn took out his notepad and asked, 'What can you tell me about the disappearance of your mum's sister and parents?'

'I know they went missing before I was born. My mum told me that my grandparents went to Italy a couple of years after Auntie Jenny disappeared. They went to try and talk to her husband who I think was called Giuseppe.' Bryn could tell that this girl wasn't the sharpest tool in the box.

After an hour and several 'come ons', he left. If she was a bit better looking, he might have been tempted to shag her but she was too common, even for him. He had gleaned very little further information but had managed to secure a picture of the girl's grandparents. He wrote down her statement anyway. Bryn was disappointed that she didn't have a single photograph of Jenny and, as her only surviving relative, she couldn't even be used to identify her.

He returned to the office and collated into his list what he had elicited from the young scrubber:

Emily died two years ago – never got over parents' and sister's disappearance

Giuseppe went to Italy at time of disappearance

It is believed he took Leonardo (mother saw him a day or two after Jenny's disappearance)

Giuseppe said Jenny had left him for another man and taken Lucia.

No idea what happened to Leonardo but was seen with father at time of disappearance

Parents went to Italy to find Giuseppe not known when or where – never came home

Emily went to Italy in the late 1960s but couldn't find Giuseppe

Not known where in Italy but thought it began with 'B'

Bryn put his pen down and looked at his growing list. He laughed when he thought he might get an all-expenses paid trip to Italy.

'Fat fucking chance,' said Noonan.

You fucking waste of space, thought Bryn.

The missing baby continued to bother Bryn, so, still having the key to the house, he went back there for another look. This time alone – he needed time to think, away from the others, away from the negativity that seemed to hang over the whole office. He had a feeling Lucia was dead, and had died with the mother but why then hadn't the killer, who now seemed to be Giuseppe, put the baby in the same place as Jenny? And what had happened to Leonardo? He went into every room and tapped the walls – even though this had been done several times before. They all seemed sturdy. He checked the floorboards – they too had not been moved since the house was built. He went to the only other place he could think off, the back garden. He stood there in the bright sunshine, willing some inspiration to suddenly burst forth but nothing came. It never did when he needed it. He was just about to give the whole thing up as a bad job when Noonan joined him in the garden.

'Sorry I've been such a tosser lately, Bryn, and not been much help – just got a lot on – you know how it is?'

Yes, Bryn knew and it was only the early stages of the divorce for Noonan – just wait a while – it will get a lot worse, he thought but didn't say. 'That's okay,' he said and they both went back inside the house.

'What can I do to help?' Noonan shouted as he went towards the kitchen and switched on the kettle and spooned coffee into two mugs.

Bryn explained the story from the beginning, hoping the more experienced detective would come up with something he hadn't thought of.

'I'd reckon that the baby, if it was killed, was done in after he had gone through all the trouble of boarding up the lady – so we need to look elsewhere.'

'My guess then is outside,' Bryn said, not really relishing the prospect of what he would now be setting in motion.

Noonan nodded. 'I'll call the troops,' he said with a wink and picked up the telephone and dialled the station. Bryn looked at him – he seemed like a new man.

Two hours later, over a dozen uniformed officers were methodically digging up the garden. Once again, they weren't too happy – for it had started to rain.

Bryn and Noonan remained inside – one of the perks of being a detective, Bryn didn't do the manual stuff.

They were quite settled when the chief superintendent arrived and started questioning what was happening – Bryn had never been so pleased to see the press arrive, for the boss left them alone to go and update them on the enquiry.

'Thank Christ,' Noonan whispered. 'I worked with him when he was a P.C. – he was a twat then too.' They both stared to laugh. The two detectives settled down with another coffee, and waited for the uniforms to do their stuff outside.

It was a couple of hours later, as Bryn was going through his notes with Noonan, when a very wet uniformed inspector came in. 'Bryn – you need to see this. We've found something,' he said, a slightly disquieting look on his face. The two detectives went out and looked into a trench and saw the top of what appeared to be a skull protruding from the earth.

'I'll call the pathologist,' Bryn said and went to the telephone. He called Heather at her office – she arrived twenty minutes later – she looked all business but it was clear from the looks he was getting that it was common knowledge to every officer there that they had a history. He smiled – his reputation enhanced once more.

It took a further couple of hours for the remains to be excavated from the ground, but now, there they were laid out on a piece of clear plastic sheeting – they were the bones of a very small baby. He popped out occasionally – he enjoyed seeing Heather so engrossed in her work.

'It's a girl, only a couple of months old too. No physical signs of any injury – but hopefully I'll know more when I've done the PM,' said Heather as she washed her hands in the kitchen sink.

Bryn went out as the remains were packed up for transportation to the mortuary. 'Hello, Lucia, I hope you can tell me something,' he muttered, feeling the sadness he always felt when he witnessed children who had been abused in any way. He turned back into the house. He saw Noonan smile and nod at him – he knew he was feeling it too but it didn't help.

Later that evening he sat outside the mortuary once again and waited for Heather to finish her examination of the set of small bones that were laid neatly on the slab.

He had been joined by Lenny, who should have been off duty hours ago. 'Just thought you might need a hand or at the very least some company,' he said as he sat next to Bryn and handed him a cup of stewed tea, 'Sorry, it was the best I could do,' he smiled. It didn't matter, it tasted strong and wet, just what he needed.

'No injuries – not strangled. My thoughts are that she was suffocated but I can't be definite. The soil was very wet so the bones are in a very poor state.' Heather looked at Bryn and answered his unasked question, 'Been in the ground around forty years, I'd say.' She handed him a small piece of blue fabric in a plastic bag. 'I think it was a blanket she was wrapped in,' she said. Then she passed over a large crucifix on a thick chain: 'This was inside the blanket. It was around the child's neck.'

'It is Lucia?' he muttered to himself. Heather smiled a sad smile and gave a nod that was almost unperceivable.

He looked at the chain – it was far too big for such a small child. The killer had placed it around the child's neck – that much he felt sure of. Was it the actions of a penitent father? he thought. He placed both items in plastic evidence bags.

'Can I take a look at the body?' asked Lenny.

'Sure. Be my guest.' Bryn walked over to Heather and making sure he couldn't be overheard he whispered – 'Your place in about an hour?'

Her face lit up. 'Don't be late – I'll have the bath run.'

He smiled, then Lenny came out; he looked upset.

'You okay?'

'Yes – just seeing kids, it always gets to me.'

Bryn winked at Heather and they left.

Almost exactly one hour later Bryn was sitting in a hot bath, sipping a Jack Daniels on ice, staring at a woman who was quickly becoming very important to him.

CHAPTER TEN

Monday 11 February 1952 05.10 hrs

Gus thought it still dark and quiet enough to dig the small grave in the back yard. He picked a place close to the large privet hedge, even though his house wasn't overlooked by any of his neighbours. He dug down past the roots, and then he hit something solid. He had no wish to make too much noise so he was forced to settle on that depth for a grave. He went inside and took Lucia's body out of his wardrobe. Her little body felt cold and stiff, her little lips were quite blue. He wished he had got to know his daughter – but Jenny had kept her all to herself in the couple of months she had been with them. He removed the cross from around his neck and placed it over the child's head, then he wrapped her in the blanket from her cot and took her outside, softly placing her in the hole. He covered the body over, and then placed a large flagstone on top of it to cover the newly-turned soil.

He couldn't think of a single thing to say over the body of his child so he went back in, opened a new bottle, and poured himself a large glass of his wife's gin; he sat at the table and finished it in one swig. He felt chilled to the bone. His hands were trembling terribly. His mind was unable to hold a single thought – but he knew he was crying.

Thursday 19 June 1986 12.10 hrs

Bryn stood facing his chief superintendent, who had never liked him ever since he heard him taking the piss out of his name; but who in their right mind would name a child Dick when his surname was Curry? He questioned him again about what he knew about the double murder, because the finding of the child's body had suddenly sparked a media rush and Bryn was sure his boss saw an opportunity for national exposure in the press. He again told him what he knew, the boss taking copious amounts of notes, then Bryn was dismissed. 'Wanker,' he muttered, the remark receiving a disapproving look from his sergeant who was just coming out of the squad room.

To get away from his so-called colleagues for a bit, he drove over to Heather's office to pick up the report on the child, not that it would give him anything he didn't already know, but he just wanted to see her. She invited him for lunch. Bryn radioed the station and told Penny that he was going to interview the mother-in-law. Lenny looked at the telephonist who calmly said, 'He's going to The Boot pub.' Lenny smiled all the way back to the squad room.

They had one drink then left to go back to his flat. They made love and then talked for a while. He spoke about his family and especially his daughter, Sian. She felt his unhappiness and vowed to herself that she would help him rid himself of it. As they got in their cars to return to their places of work she watched him – he was starting to open up to her and it felt so good.

Later that afternoon Bryn called a meeting of all three detectives who worked out of that office, together with his sergeant. He brought them up to speed on what he had and asked for suggestions as to how to move forward. He allocated enquiries about Jenny to Lenny, Noonan was going to take Leonardo and Bryn kept Giuseppe for himself.

He called the Imperial War Museum again and this time a very obliging young lady was only too pleased to be asked to help with a police enquiry. Bryn left her the details and she said it might take a while but when she had something she would call him back, which she did less than an hour later.

'Yes – we have the records of three Giuseppe Salvinos captured during the war and who were detained here in the UK. One was housed in a camp in Kent, and then shipped to Canada; one in Scotland, and one in Carmarthen in Wales. The first two were repatriated in 1946 but the other was granted leave to stay here on compassionate grounds – that usually meant they met a local girl and wanted to marry. The microfiche is a little smudged but it looks like the fiancée's name is Jennifer – does that help?'

'It certainly does – does it say where he was captured and what regiment he was with?'

'It says North Africa – he was listed here in the 39th Bologna Infantry regiment, but was captured as he tried to blow up a fuel dump so I reckon he was a commando of some sort.'

'Would the Italians have recruited locally for their regiments?' Bryn felt himself getting excited for this could set him on the trail of the killer.

'In all likelihood, yes, and him being an officer, I am fairly sure he would have come from the area around Bologna.'

'What rank was he?'

'A captain – he was decorated a number of times for bravery. It says in his record he received the *Medaglia d'Argento al Valore Militare* – it is a silver medal for bravery, one of their top awards. Ernest Hemmingway won one as an ambulance driver during the First World War.' Bryn could tell she was trying her best to give him all the information she possessed.

Bryn thanked the helpful young woman and made a note to send a letter of thanks to her boss. He sat back in his chair, commando eh? Useful with a knife – interesting.

He went downstairs for a cup of coffee. He liked to mix with the uniformed lads when he could and they respected him for it. He talked about the case when one of them said, 'Well the best record keepers would be the taxman,' while another said,

'What about parish records?'

'What about a local radio appeal?' Penny said, looking up from her crossword. These were great ideas that Bryn had overlooked. He said his thanks and went back upstairs. He immediately put a call into the investigation branch of the Inland Revenue, then he thought about parish records and as Mr Salvino was an Iti, he rang the local Catholic church first.

'Do you have marriage records going back to 1945?' he asked the priest once he had identified himself.

'Our records go back to the year 1717, young man,' was the rather snooty Irish reply.

Bryn arranged to call over straightaway to examine the records.

The priest turned out to be most helpful and guided him through the parish books.

Bryn couldn't believe it – a hit on the first try, for there in beautiful copperplate handwriting was the entry on the 17th April 1946, the date of the marriage of Giuseppe Salvino, born 6th June 1912 and Jennifer Jane Armstrong, born 3rd January 1918. It listed his occupation as solicitor, and hers as a secretary.

He returned to the office just as Lenny was putting down the telephone. 'Jenny was a land girl during the war,' he said with a smile.

'I bet she was based somewhere in Carmarthenshire,' Bryn said as he opened the file to add the info he had gleaned from the church.

'How the fuck did you get that info?' he said, slightly deflated.

'It was where Giuseppe was locked up as a prisoner of war – that was where they met.'

Bryn looked at his watch, it was 10.20 p.m. He looked over to Lenny and said, 'Fancy a beer?'

'Sure.' Lenny didn't drink but he could have one lemonade and besides, he didn't want to disappoint Bryn more than he already had.

They left the station and went to a local club that was a favourite of the local constabulary. They never had to pay for admission and usually their drinks were free too.

He was so drunk when he got home he had difficulty in getting the key into the lock. It started to look like another night in his car when finally, he got the door open. He wasn't too drunk to realise that he was in no state to negotiate the stairs, so he curled up on the couch and passed out.

The front door remained open all night.

CHAPTER ELEVEN

Monday 11 February 1952 09.10 hrs

Giuseppe hadn't been able to sleep much; he had gone out into the garden as soon as it was light to view last night's work. He had done another good job. The large slab had covered the whole of the grave – he put a couple of plant pots that now contained only dead plants on it to give it a reason for being there. Now he waited for the shops to open. He had rung work to say he was sick – he knew they believed him, and more than likely feeling sorry for him, thinking he had probably suffered another marital attack.

During that morning, Giuseppe had searched the house, and collected all the money he could find including the few shillings that were in the children's money boxes. He found his wife's bag and as he pulled out her purse, he noticed the small bankbook in one of the pockets. He opened it. He looked in awe at the amount – knowing full well that he was going to be unable to get his hands on all that money – money that would have helped no end. He put the book in his pocket – somehow he would get that money – but right at that moment he had no idea how.

He dressed his son for the cold and put on his only winter coat and ventured out. It was a lovely crisp morning, their breath visible in the cold air. As he walked close to his son's school, he saw his mother-in-law across the road. It was clear too that she had seen him. He had no wish for a conversation so he hurried into a side street and when he was out of sight of her, he picked Leonardo up and ran into the neighbouring street – it was with a sigh of relief that he realised that he had avoided that particular meeting.

It was just before ten when he arrived at Thomas Cook's travel agency, which stood at the other end of the High Street from his place of work. He bought two train tickets from Quayside to Bologna. It took the young girl an age to work out how to do it. She got so confused, the manager had to come over and complete the transaction. The tickets cost him most of the cash in the house, but he realised that this way it would take a couple of days to reach his destination. But Giuseppe had a deep-seated fear of flying, a reminder of his commando days, parachuting out over enemy territory, so the train was really the only option.

As he returned home, he reviewed his plan. He would leave at 2.20 p.m. on the 15th – he picked that date for two reasons, the first being he could collect his pay packet in the morning and secondly, it was the day of the King's funeral. He knew that the whole population of this shitty country would have other things on their mind, rather than asking too many questions of an Italian with a young son.

He just needed to stay out of sight until then. He checked the food cupboards. He was pleased that his wife had shopped just before he…

He quickly closed the cupboard doors, ran to the toilet, and vomited.

Friday 20 June 1986 09.30 hrs

Bryn was hung-over again – he had thrown up a couple of times that morning, and the light streaming into the office was excruciatingly painful. He needed to recover quickly as he was on local radio at 1 p.m. He rose from his desk again and rushed to the toilet, bringing up the coffee and the little red tablets that were supposed to make him feel better. It was while he was rinsing his mouth that he heard Lenny calling him to the telephone:

'It's the Inland Revenue Investigation guys,' he said. His eyes seemed to be mocking him but Bryn couldn't have cared less.

'Detective Lawton, my name is Mitchell; I am a senior investigator here at the Inland Revenue. I believe you are interested in Giuseppe Salvino, born the 6th of June 1912, is that correct?'

'Yes – I want to interview him in connection with the murder of his wife. It appears to have happened some time ago.'

'So it would seem – the last record we have of him is from the 1951 to 1952 year, but since then nothing.'

'I think he went to Italy then – do you have any record of where he worked?'

'I am afraid not – those records seem to have been destroyed.'

'Then you do destroy some things – there's hope for us all.'

His joke was received with stony silence from the other end of the line, and then he heard, 'Good day, Detective Lawton.'

'Humourless twat,' Bryn muttered as he put the phone down.

'You shouldn't take the piss out of those people, they can really mess with you,' said Lenny from the other side of the room.

'Fuck 'em,' said Bryn, adding that little bit of information to the file.

He sat there with his head in his hands, trying to keep the glaring sun out of his eyes, and he tried to think how he could get some information from the Law Society, for if Salvino was a solicitor he would have to be registered with them, but he had had dealings with them before and it proved so long-winded, they really were a bunch of jobworths. He needed to think of a way to circumvent the whole system – who did he know? Certainly not any of the crooked shysters in this town. He had already pissed off the majority of the local solicitors over the years he had spent in the town. Then it came to him, Jeremy Simpkins, the solicitor Fiona had used all those years ago and had recommended for his discretion. It was a long time ago – he wondered if he was still practising.

He telephoned directory enquiries. He put the phone down. Well at least the firm is still in operation, he thought as he dialled the London number.

He identified himself to the receptionist and was put through to Simpkins. He identified himself again and made reference to Fiona Henley or Carol Josephine Makepeace, which was the name he may have remembered her by. He also reminded the solicitor of the time they met over ten years before.

'Yes, I remember – you were a uniformed policeman in those days in a small village and she left you a package.'

He was right, he had a good memory; the package that led to a lot of money but he didn't want to dwell on the subject for it was still too painful for him.

'So – promotion, eh?' he heard the man say in his posh English accent.

Why did everyone think that becoming a detective was a promotion – it wasn't, but Bryn just acknowledged it. He explained to Simpkins what he wanted and he said he would see what he could do – Bryn remembered he was a Mason so he cordially invited him to his lodge should he ever come up this way. Simpkins thanked him for the invite and Bryn ended the call. He knew 'the brotherhood connection' would always help.

He then went to see his boss.

'It looks like our murderer skipped the country in 1952, shortly after he killed the wife and daughter. I believe he took the son with him. It's more than possible he went to Italy, probably Bologna, and when the parents of the wife went to look for him a few years later – they disappeared too. My thoughts are that they too came to a sticky end at his hands. I think I might need to go to Italy – what do you think?'

His boss's reaction surprised him – 'A holiday at the taxpayer's expense? Your job, your trip. You get confirmation he went there and I'll get you the trip. You'll need to draft a convincing report though and I'll push it through.'

Bryn was surprised at the boss's reaction to his request so he hurried back to his desk and, despite the headache, started drafting the report that would secure him a trip to Italy while he awaited Simpkins' call, which he received forty minutes later.

'He worked as a solicitor's clerk at a firm called Bryant and Maypole in a place called Quayside in Wales. He tried to pass the solicitor's examination three times but failed miserably every time. There is no trace of him after 1952 according to the records.'

'I am stationed here in Quayside and I have never heard of that firm.'

'Not surprising – they got taken over in '56, then again in '62 and '68. Both Messrs Bryant and Maypole are deceased.'

'Can I ask another favour?'

'Of course – I always like to oblige the police, if I can.'

Bryn knew there was a hint of sarcasm in his voice. Nevertheless, he asked if he knew how to access information about the Italian Law Society, if indeed they had one, and the solicitor said he would try.

Bryn went into the other room and called Heather at work and asked if she was free to meet for a coffee. She wasn't, but once again, she made the time. They agreed to meet in thirty minutes at a quiet public house near to the hospital. 'I'm off to do some trainspotting,' he said to Lenny and Noonan.

'Trainspotting?' asked Lenny after he had left.

'He'll be at The Railway pub if we need him.'

Lenny wondered how many more pseudonyms Bryn had for the town's drinking establishments.

He couldn't face any alcohol so he ordered lemonade for himself and for Heather, a glass of white wine. Then he went and sat in a booth at the rear of the lounge bar. He knew that this time neither he nor Heather wanted this relationship to become public knowledge. He watched her drive in and walk across the car park. He had to admit she was a beautiful-looking woman – and someone way out of his league in so many ways. He had no idea what such a woman saw in him. When she had settled at the table and had the first sip of her wine, he said, 'I might be able to swing a couple of days in Italy soon – do you fancy coming?'

'Is the bloody Pope Catholic? Of course, I would love to go. Any idea when?' She had often told him how much she loved Italy.

'No. Soon though.'

'Is it the Sophia case?'

'Yeah – it looks like her hubby did her and the baby in. He went missing with the four-year-old son in 1952. It seems he went back to Italy, possibly Bologna, and might have bumped off Jenny's parents when they went out to find him a couple of years later.'

'Christ – we'll be chasing a bloody serial killer.'

Bryn hadn't thought of it like that – he smiled at the idea and also her use of the word, 'we'.

'How old will he be now?' she asked.

'He was born in 1912 – that makes him, what...? Seventy-four, if he is still with us, and the son will be thirty-eight, if he hasn't been snuffed out too.'

'You're so callous. You bloody policemen have no soul.'

She smiled and kissed him on the cheek. He could tell she was excited, but the statement about 'we'll be chasing the serial killer' started to worry him a bit. He suddenly wished he could take her back to his place and make love all afternoon but both of them had work to do so it would have to wait until later.

'I can see you tonight, can't I?' he asked. It was the first time he had asked her in that way. She was pleased and simply nodded.

'What time?' she asked as she finished her drink.

'I am finishing at five on the dot – I have worked enough unpaid bloody overtime this month.'

'I won't be finished until at least seven.' She handed him her front door key, 'Make yourself at home; I'll be there as soon as I can.'

They kissed at the car then drove off on their separate ways.

The office was empty when he got back but there was a telephone message on his desk. It was in Lenny's writing and it read:

From Jeremy Simpkins
Re: Giuseppe Salvino.

He was registered as a solicitor with the

CONSIGLIO DELL'ORDINE DEGLI AVVOCATI
(Italian Law Society) 1937–1940 and 1952–1957 During
this time he had opened his own company in Bologna.
His home address is 17 via Santa Croce, Bologna 1952–1957
His office address is 34 via Ugo Bassi, Bologna
Nothing further recorded

So that confirms it – he had gone back to Italy and now, most importantly, he had to ensure he got the trip.

At 1p.m. Bryn sat nervously in the studio seat at the local radio station. He gave his rehearsed spiel about trying to find Giuseppe Salvino or anyone who knew him in the early fifties. Bryn steered clear of calling him a wanted person – he just said that he wished to question him in connection with the death of his wife. To his surprise, the fifteen minutes on air went very quickly. The DJ surprised him by asking if he could play a song – there was only one that sprang to mind – 'I am a Rock' by Simon and Garfunkel, a song he had listened to with Fiona years before.

When he got back to the office there was a message on his desk. It was from Noonan; it read:

Mrs Mary Collins

She worked with Gus Salvino in about 1950 at a local solicitor's office.

'Wow – the power of radio,' he muttered as he dialled the local telephone number and arranged to go straight over and speak to Mrs Collins.

'Yes, I knew Gus. He was Italian. Came here as a prisoner of war, a lovely man though terrible hen-pecked. She used to beat him you know.'

'Who used to beat him?' Bryn asked, trying to hold the cup of tea, poured into Mrs Collins' best china. He was also conscious of the hole in his sock as Mrs Collins had made him remove his shoes at the door.

'His wife – he would regularly come to work with bruises. He would give some excuse but we all knew who had done it.'

'Where did he work?'

'Bryant and Maypole, solicitors. He was a clerk. I was a secretary to Mr Maypole. He told us he was a solicitor back in Italy but he just couldn't pass the exam here, the poor dear.'

'Do you remember when and how he left the firm?'

'It was just before Mr Bryant died; it must have been early in 1952. The old King had just died. I remember he came in for his wages, which was unusual as he had been off sick that week but he collected the money, and I remember him telling me he felt much better and would be back on

Monday – but he never showed up. Mr Bryant sent me to his house by taxi to make sure he was alright but when I got there, I saw that the house was up for sale. We never saw or heard from him again.'

'Can you describe him?'

'I can do a bit better than that, young man. I have a photograph of him here, taken at a retirement party I think, just before Christmas 1951.' She handed Bryn a large black and white photograph, 'That's him there.' She pointed to a tall, thin, handsome man standing in the front row. For the first time Bryn now knew the face of the man he sought for the murder of two, possibly four, people.

'And that's his awful wife.' She pointed to a stony-faced blonde standing next to him. Now he saw the real face of the mummy. She was quite pretty in life. He asked for permission to take the picture, promising to take good care of it.

Once back at the station, he called Karl at the scene of crime office and asked if he could enlarge a photograph.

'I'll come over straightaway,' he said.

'Such service,' thought Bryn. It was nearing five so he left the photograph on his desk with a note and signed out. He had somewhere he wanted to be.

At 5.15 p.m. he let himself into Heather's house. He felt slightly uneasy being there alone. He made himself a cup of coffee in the immaculately clean kitchen and went to sit in the lounge. He put on the TV but within a couple of minutes he was fast asleep.

He was awakened by someone knocking on the door. It took several seconds for him to remember where he was. He got up and answered the door – Heather stood there, a big smile on her face. She enjoyed the feeling of coming home to him.

CHAPTER TWELVE

Friday 15 February 1952 14.22 hrs

Giuseppe was so relieved when, with great clouds of steam bursting out from the engine, the train finally started to pull out of Quayside railway station. He had been sick with worry all day but little Leonardo had been excited; now he sat quietly, looking out of the window, while his father closed his eyes with the relief. The strain of the last couple of days had been difficult to deal with and he felt it throughout his whole body.

In fact, the tension had caused him to be physically sick on several occasions especially after hiding from his mother-in-law on several occasions, when she came banging on the front door, and peering in through the windows and letterbox.

He and Leonardo had been up since early that morning. He had a lot to do before they left. For besides collecting his tickets, he went to the office to pick up his wage packet. He played the part of someone who was unwell to the max. His co-workers felt so sorry for him. He felt a slight twinge of guilt at his deception when he saw how much they all cared about him, and knowing he would never see them again.

What no one knew was the fact that he had already put the house up for sale, using a rival solicitor's office of course, and now life in Britain was behind him – he was heading home.

No one would ever catch him now.

Saturday 21 June 1986 09.30 hrs

Bryn was anxious to see his boss; he needed to secure the trip to Italy. Within an hour he had the 'go' from everyone right up to the chief constable – they had sanctioned five days in Italy. That's how long he had to catch this guy and get him extradited back to Britain to face a trial for two murders. He was to leave tomorrow, flying out from Manchester airport, and changing planes at Milan. He went into the control room and scribbled a message for Penny to send by telex to the police in Bologna to explain the reason for his visit. He went back into the office to try and finish off anything that was urgent – which he saw was most of the stuff in his in-tray, so he prioritised – but his mind wasn't really on it. He had a reply back from Italy before he left the station. Mario Fabrizzi, a senior detective of the Bologna *Carabinieri*, would be his liaison when he arrived.

He packed his evidence file and all the photographs and asked the inspector for the key to the evidence room so he could take the wedding ring and the crucifix. Bryn went into the room but they weren't where he had left it – he searched for quarter of an hour but was unable to locate them. He put it down to bad management, so returned the key to the uniformed sergeant but said nothing about it. It was something he would have to sort out on his return; he would have to make do with the photographs.

He had been given the rest of the day off to prepare – all four hours of it. Big fucking deal, he thought as he put on his jacket. He went straight back to Heather's and re-joined her in bed. She then spent an hour arranging cover and managed to free herself from work for the whole five days.

Her secretary made it clear she was not happy with her choice of travelling companion but she had even managed to book her on the same flight.

They spent a relaxing afternoon and evening together, most of the time, making love.

The following morning, they made their way to the airport for their eleven o'clock flight. They were both as excited as school kids as they boarded the plane for the three-and-a-half-hour trip. Once on board, and the wheels had left the ground – the only part of flying he hated – Bryn related the story of his very first flight:

He was nine years old and he was off to Spain on a family holiday. They boarded the plane at Manchester Ringway airport, but his father, Eddie, could see that his mum, Ellen, was worried. She had never flown before and to tell the truth neither had his dad, but he put on a brave face as he ushered his family to their seats – the wrong ones initially, but the right ones eventually. His mum had seen that the plane's layout had two seats on one side of the aisle and three on the other. Both his dad and Bryn noticed the very worried look on her face get worse as the aircraft taxied for take-off.

'What's the matter now?' asked his father, more out of exasperation than anything else.

'Surely there is more weight on this side of the aisle than that side.' She was convinced that the plane would fly lopsided. His dad explained things to her and her mind calmed and they settled down to enjoy the flight.

Heather was chuckling – it was also the first time Bryn had ever opened up to her and told her anything about his past

– she relished the opportunity to get to know him better.

Bryn continued his story:

Midway through the flight, somewhere over Paris, she whispered something to Bryn's father:

'I have been watching that light outside. It has been following us for well over an hour – in fact, all the way from Manchester Airport.'

'Yes, it's the wing light,' said her husband, 'can't you just read your magazine and relax, or better still, try and get some sleep, we'll be there soon.'

The greatest panic for his mother occurred when the pilot announced that the flight would be landing in Perpignan (pronounced Pepinyon) in twenty minutes. Ellen knew she was going to 'Per pig nan'. She had never heard the correct pronunciation. She was convinced that they were on the wrong plane. It took a while for his dad and a stewardess to calm her down.

'I wondered if I could in any way disown my parents. Through all the trials and tribulations, they did give me a holiday I would remember all my life,' he said, smiling with the memories.

'Sounds like a great family – mad, but great.' Heather kissed him.

Yes, he thought, that summed them up alright, and he hadn't even mentioned his older sister, Ellie – the raging alcoholic.

With the layover in Milan, it was nine thirty in the evening. by the time they got to Bologna and way past eleven when they reached the hotel – a small, smart, upmarket establishment in the nicer area of the town, chosen by Heather of course.

It was situated close to the most impressive medieval towers Bryn had ever seen.

'That's called the Torre Degli Asinelli,' said Heather, reading from the guidebook she had bought in the airport, and pointing to the taller of two towers, 'it is 98 metres high. It has 498 rickety wooden steps to the top.'

'98 metres. What's that in English? Over 300 feet?' Bryn would certainly take time out to view the city from up there.

Once in the room, Bryn telephoned the local *carabinieri* station and in very pidgin Italian, taken from a phrase book he had bought at the airport and had written in his notebook, he read:

'*Pronto. Io sono L'ispecttore Lawton della Gran Bretagna posso parlare con l'ispecttore Fabrizzi? Pou dire che io sono all' hotel Gabrielli, Via da Piazza il di Porta Ravegnana.*'

'I will put you through, Detective Lawton, Detective Fabrizzi is awaiting your call,' the telephonist said in better English than his Italian and almost better English than his too. The telephone was answered at the second ring. Mario Fabrizzi had the sort of accent that sent English girls into a swoon – he hoped he wasn't that Italian-type handsome. To Bryn's great relief his English too was perfect. They arranged to meet at the hotel at 8 a.m. for breakfast.

Despite the lateness of the hour, Bryn and Heather went out for a walk. They walked arm in arm through the quiet streets, and finding a small cafe still open, he bought two cappuccinos. His was gone in seconds.

'I have just paid for a cup of milk froth,' he said, licking his lips.

She smiled at him. He had innocence about him that she

loved. She couldn't wait to get him back into their hotel bed.

Bryn and Heather were eating their continental breakfast, when they were joined by Detective Fabrizzi. Bryn was pleased that his physical appearance didn't match his much-accented voice. He was small, not more than 5'7", balding and very rotund. They shook hands warmly and to Heather's total surprise Bryn introduced her as his fiancée. She positively preened herself as the Italian detective kissed her hand.

As Mario sat at the table, Bryn glimpsed the handle of his gun protruding from his hip – and even though Bryn was trained to use a firearm, they still caused him some consternation. He hoped they would not have cause to use it.

Bryn sipped his coffee while Mario ordered a triple espresso – that would have kept Bryn awake for a week – and while they waited, Bryn explained the case in more detail. Mario was very attentive and asked lots of questions. He seemed very impressed that the medical examiner was also sitting at the table.

'Since I received your message yesterday evening, I did a little bit of work – I went to 17 via Santa Croce – it is now split into flats but no one has heard of signor Salvino and the address on via Ugo Bassi is now chirurgia di dottore, a place a *dottore* works. They had been there over ten years. The place had been empty for years when they bought it.'

'Seems like a dead end all around.'

'No – I have located Giuseppe Salvino's sister. The family is, how you say, *prominente* here in Bologna. She lives on a large estate outside a small village about ten kilometres out of town. I have set up a meeting for us this morning.'

'Fantastic,' said Bryn brightening up.

He showed Mario the enlarged photograph of Giuseppe. 'That's our man; this was taken over thirty-six years ago, I am afraid.'

Mario studied it, then shook his head, as if disappointed that he didn't recognise the face, then handed it back.

Heather watched as the two detective officers relaxed in each other's company. It appeared that policemen can only truly relax when in the company of other coppers – especially detectives. The conversation eventually got around to their respective police departments and the usual gripes all policemen have then came to the fore – bosses, pay, working conditions, the public and so on. Heather excused herself – she was going sightseeing while Bryn worked. Mario stood and kissed her hand as Heather left the table – one thing you can say about the continentals, they have manners, he thought. Heather agreed not to go up the Torre Degli Asinelli without him. She nodded, smiled at the two men, and left them to their work.

'I have not been up there since I was a child,' said the Italian detective.

'You never appreciate what you have in your hometown,' Bryn replied but he was hard-pressed to think of anything worth seeing in Quayside.

'Can I take a look at where he used to live?' Bryn asked as they went out into the bright sunshine.

'Certainly – it is on our way anyway.'

They got into Mario's Alfa Romeo and headed out into the bustling city. There didn't seem to be any order to the traffic system as kamikaze scooter riders came at them from all sides. It took twenty heart-stopping minutes to reach the address. Before getting out of the car Bryn studied the old stone-built middle of the terrace house. He imagined Giuseppe and Leonardo rattling around in that big house, if it was large enough to have been split into three flats.

'I have been told that Salvino lived there from 1952 to 1957. I think it was here that he was living when he was being sought by his in-laws – is there any chance we can have a look inside?'

'We can ask,' said Mario as he walked up the three steps and banged on the large, impressive front door. He knew what Bryn was thinking without him having to say a word. Here is where the bodies of the two English tourists might be hidden, concealed somewhere in this building. Mario felt the rush of excitement at the prospect, for something he hadn't wanted to tell Bryn was that he had never been involved in a murder enquiry before, and the prospect excited him.

A very accommodating lady, Martha Sambrini, who turned out to be the owner of the property, showed them around. At the present time she was the only occupant as both the other flats were empty. Mario noted her telephone number – for it wasn't just British policemen that got divorced – it had just happened to him too. It seemed to be an occupational habit – worldwide.

Mario had a long conversation in Italian with the old maid – Bryn understanding none of it whatsoever, but he stood there, trying to look as if he did. He saw the old lady's colour drain from her cheeks.

He turned to Bryn, 'Her now dead husband bought the house ten years ago. It was he who turned it into apartments.'

'Is there a cellar here?' he asked Mario, trying to think of places that he wouldn't have had need to renovate.

'C'e' una cantina in casa?' he asked the elderly lady.

'*Sì – la voule vedere?*'

'She is asking if you would like to see it.'

'*Sì*,' said Bryn, reinforcing his poor language skills with a strenuous nod of the head. The old lady smiled. Mario giggled unsupportively. Bryn felt uncomfortable, but a wink and a pat on the back from Mario made him smile too.

The two officers went down into the damp cellar. They switched on the lights – it was now well lit and completely empty. He had never seen such a tidy unused cellar.

'It might have been here that Samuel and Edwina Armstrong came way back in the '50s to confront Salvino and, if what he did to Jenny was anything to go by, they might be still here.' He voiced what both of the policemen were already thinking. Bryn looked around the walls. Mario felt the chill of expectancy – if those people were still here, they would find them.

'We need to check to see if any of the walls are false – that's how he hid his wife – then we might have to dig up the back garden – in case they are there.'

'*Merda*!' he heard Mario say. Bryn knew enough about policemen to know a bad word in any language.

'I will make a call later and get some officers over here – they can do a thorough search.'

He went back upstairs to use the telephone and Bryn looked around the room – The hairs on the back of his neck bristled as something told him the Armstrongs were not too far away.

Bryn came out of the cellar as Mario was putting the telephone down.

'It will be tomorrow by the time we get the men assembled. I will go and explain to the old lady what is to happen then we must go to see his sister.'

From the raised voices coming from the lounge, it was clear that the old lady was not taking too well the idea of hairy-arsed coppers trampling through her house looking for long-dead English tourists and to be honest who could blame her. He stood quietly in the hallway and tried to picture Giuseppe and his son walking about here – but his imagination skills didn't stretch that far so he gave up. He opened the front door and stood outside in the hot sunshine and waited for Mario to extricate himself from the old woman who he could still hear, jabbering on.

Eventually Mario joined him outside.

'God, that woman could talk,' he said.

And that does say something, coming from an Italian, Bryn thought but didn't say – he didn't know his colleague well enough yet to extend his police humour that far.

The drive out into the Italian countryside was beautiful and the two officers took the chance to get even better acquainted with each other.

It turned out that they had joined their respective police forces at roughly the same time, but Mario had been a detective a lot longer. He was in the *Carabinieri*. Bryn would tell the story of how he and two other policemen friends of his were nearly arrested by the *Carabinieri* in Venice some years ago, following an unfortunate incident involving their hired speedboat and a Venetian gondola – but that too would have to wait until they knew each other a whole lot better.

The house they stopped at was magnificent but to call it a house was doing it a great injustice – it was a mansion. It was an Italian picture postcard mansion with a long tree-lined driveway. The two detectives were shown into the large library by the maid; this room was fantastic for Bryn loved books and here were literally thousands of them. His mind went back to the old squire's library in Dynas Dre – he wished he could get that bloody place out of his mind. While no one was looking he swallowed two anti-depressants – that should see him through until the questioning was over for the day.

They were joined a couple of minutes later by a frail old lady, who was accompanied and supported by a beautiful young girl of about twenty. Both detectives stood up as they entered.

The officers waited for the ladies to be seated then sat opposite them. Mario spoke first. He introduced himself and then Bryn. He explained to the two women the reason for their visit. He was interrupted by the young girl.

'My name is Gabriella, and so is my grandmother's. Since your phone call of yesterday, *Ispettore*,' – she spoke the most beautifully accented English Bryn had ever heard – 'we have been getting all the facts that are remembered. My grandmother has asked me to speak to you as she knows very little English and she wants to help all she can.'

She opened her notebook. Bryn noticed how small and white her hands were. It was very apparent that she hadn't done a hard day's work in her life – he smiled to himself, for come to think of it – neither had he.

They had prepared well, thought Bryn, pushing the vision of the young girl from his mind – this was going too well – he half expected some shyster solicitor to enter and give a 'no comment' interview.

'Before we start, can I ask if this is Giuseppe?'

Bryn produced the photograph and handed it to the girl, who showed it to the old lady, who nodded slightly, then put a small handkerchief to her eyes. The girl handed back the photo, 'That is *mio grande zio*, sorry, yes that is my great-uncle Giuseppe, my grandmother's youngest brother.'

The girl started reading from her notepad, 'My grandmother's brother Giuseppe was a clever fellow and became a solicitor in Bologna as his elder brother Guido was to inherit this estate. These were the three children. Giuseppe was a strong follower of Mussolini and when war was declared he joined the army as an officer and fought in Europe and North Africa, where he was captured by the British late in 1943. He was very brave and was decorated several times. He was taken to Britain, where he met a woman and married. My great-great-grandfather *rinnegato lui*.' She looked at Mario again.

'Disowned him,' he said to Bryn who was busy taking his own notes.

The girl continued, 'My grandmother secretly sent him money when she heard he had had a son and again a couple of years later when she found out he had a daughter.'

She produced a letter dated 25 August 1951.

'In this letter he asks to come home as things were not working out for him in Britain but my great-grandfather, who was on his deathbed, would not hear of it. However, sometime in early 1952 he returned with his son, Leonardo. By that time my great-great-grandfather had died.

'My great-uncle Guido was delighted that he had come home and bought him a house in Bologna and set him up with an office there as well. He returned to being a solicitor, but in about 1957 he disappeared without a word to the family and the last anyone ever knew of him was in Naples when he was spotted by a friend of the family. That was sometime in 1967.'

'Did he mention what had happened to his wife back in England?'

'He told the family that she had... *una relazione sessuale*,' she blushed and looked again at Mario.

Mario nodded to the girl. 'A sexual affair,' he whispered. Bryn nodded too – it was a very delicate situation.

'Then she left him for this man, taking his daughter and he came home with his son, Leonardo.' The young girl then slowly closed the notebook.

'Do you know if anyone from Great Britain ever visited him here in Bologna?' Bryn asked. The young girl spoke quietly to the old lady who looked at Bryn and shook her head.

'Did Giuseppe leave anything here when he left?' Mario asked before Bryn got the chance.

'No, nothing – he took everything when he went – he sold both the buildings in Bologna and vanished. I hope that has been of help.'

The old lady leaned across and whispered in her granddaughter's ear. 'Oh, I am sorry. My grandmother says that he did leave one thing – his son, Leonardo. He stayed here with my great-uncle to be educated.'

'Do you know where Leonardo is now?' Bryn asked but the old lady shook her head and whispered in the girl's ear.

'He left about nineteen years ago to go travelling – but he never returned,' she said in a quiet voice.

'Do you have any pictures of Leonardo?' Again, the old woman shook her head. Bryn thought this strange, for the house was littered with photographs, but he let it pass.

'Can I ask where Giuseppe's older brother is?' Bryn asked in a whisper.

'Guido died about three years ago – he had no family of his own so left the *proprietà di famiglia*.' She looked at Mario once again. She produced the death certificate dated 17th October 1983, issued in Bologna.

'Family estate,' he whispered to Bryn.

'Yes – family estate,' she went on, 'to my grandmother.'

'So, you have no idea what happened to Leonardo?' asked Bryn, as they were leaving.

'We had a letter from him about five years ago saying that he was fine and he would write again soon – he never did,' the young girl said.

'Did he say where he was?'

'No, but the letter was postmarked as being somewhere in France, I believe.'

Bryn was surprised that they hadn't kept the letter as they seemed to have retained everything else – but again he said nothing.

The officers thanked the ladies and left but as they reached the car the young girl ran up to them.

'Do you believe that he killed his wife?' she asked, a look of dread in her beautiful dark eyes.

'I believe he did,' said Bryn, 'and I think his baby daughter too.'

Bryn regretted saying that as soon as it left his mouth when he saw the girl's eyes fill with tears and she ran off into the house. Bryn hoped the frail old lady would be alright once she heard the terrible news.

'This will be a scandal around here if it is true – I hope they will be alright,' Mario said as he drove out of the large gateway.

'Me too,' said Bryn, and he meant it too – for they seemed very nice people.

Mario dropped Bryn off at the hotel for there was nothing more he could do until the search tomorrow.

'I will search out records to see if our man has surfaced anywhere. I will also speak to my counterparts in Naples – you never know.'

Bryn spent the rest of the afternoon, sightseeing with Heather. He had to admit that the view of the city from the top of Torre Degli Asinelli was unbelievable but that climb up those rickety wooden steps knackered him. He hoped he would have enough strength left for Heather later.

CHAPTER THIRTEEN

Monday 18 February 1952 16.52 hrs

It was already dark as Giuseppe and Leonardo walked out of Bologna railway station and he took his first look at his hometown, a town he had not seen for over thirteen years when, as a young lieutenant, newly appointed to the 39th Bologna Infantry Regiment, he was rushing onto the platform to join his unit shortly after *Il Duce* had declared war. Deep snow now covered the whole city. He hadn't realised just how much he had missed the place until now being here staring at the old buildings their lights twinkling in the falling snow.

'*Questa è la nostra nuova casa, Leonardo,*' their new home, he told his son – a place where they were safe, hopefully.

He took Leonardo by the hand and stepped out on to Piazzo Medaglie d'Oro. He walked over to a dilapidated taxi and gave the man the address. They settled back into the seat. It had been a long, arduous journey across Europe, and he was surprised how much war damage there still was, especially in Germany. The fucking Allies had done devastating work, he thought as he had watched the ruins drifting by – he hoped that Italy had fared better.

Leonardo was exhausted by all the travelling and immediately fell asleep on his father's lap. Giuseppe looked out of the window – everything was as he remembered. He was just worried about what kind of reception was waiting for him. He had burnt all of his bridges in coming here and he was now completely broke.

The taxi pulled up outside the gates of the country estate of his family, the driver refusing to go any further because of the deep snow. Giuseppe paid the man with the last of his cash, pushed open the large iron gates and started to walk down the long driveway. He saw that the snow was falling heavier now and lay very much deeper here. It wasn't long before they were both chilled to the bone. He picked Leonardo up and carried him the last hundred yards. He was relieved when he got to the door as his strength was leaving him. He composed himself, then knocked. He really had no idea how he and his young son would be received.

Tuesday 24 June 1986 07.25 hrs

The ringing of the telephone woke the sleeping lovers. Despite the heavy floral curtains, bright sunlight lit the room. He picked up the phone and was immediately awake when he heard Mario say, 'Bryn, we have found something – I have sent a car for you.' He noticed that Mario's voice was excited, Bryn looked at his watch. They start early in Italy, he thought. 'We have found a false wall in the attic. I will try to await your arrival before we go in. Hurry. Please.'

Bryn put down the telephone and quickly got dressed. By the time he came out of the hotel the police car was waiting. The smartly dressed *Carabinieri* officer was holding open the door for him as if he was some kind of dignitary which, by the looks he got from the people standing on the pavement, they obviously thought he was. The drive across Bologna was scarier than yesterday's with the police car, siren blaring, causing most of the confusion. The young Italian policeman talked continuously about England and paid no heed to any of the traffic or, Bryn suspected, any road signs. It was with a great sigh of relief Bryn got out of the car. He was met by a very irate Mario. 'My boss wouldn't wait. He is, how you say, "an anus".'

'We say 'arse'.'

'Yes, arse. Anyway, we have found two bodies behind the false wall in the attic, a man and woman. They are badly decomposed. Now I have a favour to ask, my friend. Do you think Heather would take a look at them? Our *il nostro patologo*… our police doctor, is not available, and won't be for quite a while.'

They went into the house and Bryn heard crying coming from the lounge.

'That poor lady,' Bryn thought as he dialled the number for the hotel that Mario had given him.

'Fancy doing a bit of work?' he said after getting a sleepy hello.

'Sure – what you got?' she mumbled.

'I think they have found Mr and Mrs Armstrong – I haven't seen them so I don't know what state they will be in but…'

'I'll be there, can you send a car?' she said without letting him finish. She even put the phone down without any goodbyes. He asked Mario to send the same police driver back to the hotel to pick her up. That'll teach her to put the phone down on me, he thought and chuckled to himself.

Bryn climbed the stairs to the attic and pushed past the

assembled uniformed *Carabinieri*, all trying to get a look at the remains.

'*Andate tutti al diavolo e uscite fuori da qui,*' the voice boomed from behind him and the uniforms quickly dispersed down the stairs. Mario winked at Bryn and gestured that he should go and take a look, 'How you say, 'privileges of rank'.' They both laughed.

The two bodies, now mostly bones in clothing, were lying on the floor, against the wall. A man and a woman. It was clear that the photograph he had in his pocket of the two people was not going to be of much use now. Mario handed Bryn a coffee, which a beautiful dark-haired policewoman had brought, which they sipped as they waited for Heather. He didn't quite know how he was going to explain her presence to his bosses once he got back home, but that was something to worry about later.

'Jesus – that was one scary ride, that driver is certifiable,' she said as she climbed the last flight of stairs and joined Bryn and Mario on the landing. 'Good morning, Detective Fabrizzi.'

'*Mario,* please, *donna bellissima,*' he said, kissing her hand.

Smooth twat, thought Bryn, and then caught Heather looking at him – she read his mind and smiled. He tried to.

'Well, what have we got?' she asked, suddenly becoming all business. Mario handed her a pair of gloves and she walked to the bodies.

'We can see that the woman's throat is cut and the man has what looks like a knife wound through his clothing but we have touched nothing,' he said as they all peered into the newly discovered attic space.

Mario called for the photographer to record everything and

the two detectives excused themselves and went back downstairs. They were just enjoying their third coffee when Mario's boss came in – a weedy, littler man with an officious nature. He spoke rapidly to Mario, and then with a nod to Bryn he left.

'My boss says that this is our job now so any help you can give us before you leave for England would be appreciated. He is, how you say, 'a horse's arse'.'

There was no way he was going home now without a result, even if he had to use up his annual leave to do it. Mario knew the look. He nodded – he was a bobby too – he understood.

It was nearly two hours before Heather joined them in the lounge – Bryn was wired on coffee. She handed Mario a plastic bag containing an old, black British passport. He glanced at it and handed it to Bryn.

'Samuel and Edwina Armstrong,' she said, accepting the untouched cup of coffee from Bryn.

He had found them but he was still a long way from Giuseppe.

'How did they die?' asked Mario.

'You were quite correct, detective. The man had two knife wounds to the chest; the woman's throat was cut – one cut, almost to the spine. That was a very sharp knife indeed.'

'Mario, please, if I can call you Heather,' he said with a smile. Bryn had heard how the Italians could turn on the charm – and here it was, right in front of him, and he could see Heather falling for it. He had a twinge of jealousy for he never had a way with the ladies – charm was something he just didn't possess.

In an effort to break his mood Bryn said to no one in particular, 'Both wounds in keeping with his training as a commando; just like Jenny's wounds back home.' The Italian detective was now deep in thought.

'That's not all – I found these in the inside jacket pocket of the male.'

She handed – again to Mario – another sealed plastic bag, containing papers. 'It seems to be a solicitor's letter.'

'I will get this examined and call you later,' said Mario as he stood up. He again kissed Heather's hand. He turned to Bryn whose face showed some concern, 'Don't worry, my friend, I will not keep you out of the loop – we are partners in this – I will let you know what I find out. I think you need to call home as you are going to need more time here in our beautiful city.' He winked at Bryn, kissed Heather's hand again and left.

'I like him,' she said as she sipped her coffee and watched him leave. Bryn said nothing but went out to watch the bodies being placed in the hearse for their ride to the mortuary. He had to admit – he liked him too.

They declined the lift back to the hotel even though it was a different driver from the one that morning, preferring the more relaxing walk across the city. They strolled arm in arm in the sunshine, deep in conversation and got hopelessly lost. They found themselves passing the railway station. While Heather searched in her large handbag for her *Tourist's Guide of the City*, Bryn said, 'Did you know it was bombed a few years ago?' He pointed to the station, 'About 1980, I think. It killed nearly a hundred people, if I remember right.'

'Who would do a thing like that?' she asked as she stared at the beautiful building.

'I don't think they ever found out. Some lunatic terrorists from either 'the right' or 'the left' I expect,' he said, taking her arm and moving off down the street, now heading in the right direction – thanks to Bryn using the map she had bought but couldn't use.

They ate a late lunch in a small cafe just off Piazzo Maggiore, and then spent some time exploring the Basilica san Petronio. Bryn wondered as they walked hand in hand over that holy ground, what the several priests he saw would think about what they had been up to earlier in the day.

By 5.30 p.m. they were in bed in the hotel, fast asleep – the vigorous shag they had just finished had finally sapped their remaining energy.

The phone was ringing somewhere in the darkness. Bryn tried to remember where the hell he was. Heather reached across him and picked up the phone. She handed it to Bryn.

'Bryn just a couple of things – you are staying for a few more days – I convinced my boss and he has sent a message to your boss so that is settled and secondly – this letter is from a solicitor here in Bologna; it's a sworn declaration from Giuseppe, issued by the Bologna court, granting his *petizione legale* that his wife is legally dead and getting her bank account money declared his. It was sent to a Midland Bank in Quayside. It gives instructions that the money, over six hundred pounds, should be transferred to his account here in Bologna straightaway.'

'That is a private document – I wonder how they got hold of it?'

'I will see you and Heather for breakfast tomorrow, *il mio amico. Buona notte.*'

'Good night.' He replaced the receiver – so that's how they knew where to find him, he thought, but how did they get that form from the bank?

He lay back on the bed his mind pondering that question until he felt Heather's hands move to his groin – when suddenly all his pondering stopped.

He quickly switched out the light.

CHAPTER FOURTEEN

Tuesday 19 February 1952 09.10 hrs

Giuseppe woke in his old bedroom in the villa. It was almost just as he had left it all those years ago, for even his old razor was on the washstand and his old clothes hung in the large ornate wardrobe that faced the window which looked out on the snow-covered lawns and the unused tennis court. He had always loved that view, and it was to this room, as a boy, he would run. Back into the arms of his old *bambinaia* Ginella. He knew she, his nanny, would always protect him. It was his only refuge from his father.

He could hear the hushed voices of the servants outside in the corridor but he was in no hurry to rise. He wanted to savour every moment of this feeling of contentment. He looked over at Leonardo who was asleep next to him. His son had refused to go and sleep in the nursery next door. It was understandable. It was a new environment for the little boy – but he would soon get used to it and in time grow to love his room.

Last night he had been more than a little surprised by the welcome he had received. He wept with unrestrained joy as he was taken back into the family without any reservation. Leonardo had been fussed over by family and servants alike. His brother Guido and his sister, Gabriella, were overjoyed to see him. They both kissed and hugged him and Leonardo all evening. All the disowning by his dead father was forgotten. The only one who showed any reservation about his return was his sister's husband, Fredo, but they had never got on, and besides he had no say in family matters so he put that out of his mind.

He rose quietly, trying not to wake his son, who he knew must be exhausted from the long journey. He bathed and shaved, relishing using his old shaving utensils. Then, leaving Leonardo to sleep, he went downstairs. The whole family was in the breakfast room waiting for him, without trying to give the appearance of doing so. It was obvious that they had been up long after he went to bed, discussing what they should do. Giuseppe kissed his sister and embraced his older brother and the embrace he received in return was encouraging. He sat down to a hearty breakfast and as he ate his brother was the first to speak.

'Giuseppe – do you have any plans?' he asked, hoping that his brother was now back home for good.

'I want to put the Britain thing behind me, brother, and take up where I left off. I want to provide a life for my son here in Bologna. I was wrong to have stayed away after the war – I should have come home.'

'Well, that is of no consequence – you are home now and welcome to share the estate as we three have always discussed.'

Giuseppe always remembered his brother telling him that no matter what – the estate was 'theirs' and not just to be inherited by him alone, 'no matter what Papa says.' Giuseppe had always loved his brother, and his sister too – it was his father that Giuseppe had always hated, with the feeling being reciprocated.

'No, Guido – I shall start my life again. I shall open a solicitor's office in Bologna and Leonardo and I shall move into the town – but thank you, my brother. I may need some help starting off.'

'We will do all we can, of course,' said Guido and kissed his brother on the cheek. He heard a loud sigh come from his brother-in-law, but he let it pass.

'If that is what you wish, we will go into town and look for premises this very morning,' said Guido with a smile. He was glad his brother had come home.

The mood lifted considerably when a servant brought the upset Leonardo into the room – they all fussed over him and soon he was back to his cheerful self.

Wednesday 25 June 1986 11.15 hrs

Bryn and Mario sat in the canteen of the hospital, as usual drinking coffee, while Heather, at the invitation of the Italian police pathologist, was busy in the mortuary with Mr and Mrs Armstrong. Bryn had taken to drinking cappuccinos, despite Mario's protestations, who laughingly called him a *'turista'*, but the espressos were giving him too much of a buzz – Heather had told him yesterday that 'he was talking faster than she could listen'.

Bryn had been up since 7 a.m. and had been in Bologna police station by 8 a.m. He sent a long telex to Quayside police station asking them to visit the Midland Bank on Church Street and see what they could find out about the letter. This was done to show his bosses he was making some progress here in Italy. He had called and spoken to Noonan direct, who said he would get straight on it as soon as the banks opened. Bryn had forgotten the time difference. He didn't have any high hopes about the bank enquiry but it was something to show he was working, not just on a 'jolly' from work and besides he should have been going home tomorrow but he had in his pocket a telex showing that Mario had given him another week. It was unfortunate that Heather had to leave tomorrow. He would miss her.

They both awaited Heather's arrival from the mortuary where she was in her element assisting the pathologist with the post mortem. Even coffee in the hospital canteen was strong, but Bryn was trying to get used to it.

Eventually she walked in. She was so excited.

'As I said yesterday, the man died as a result of double stab wounds to the heart, both blows hitting the heart; the woman, by having her throat cut.' She said this in such a matter-of-fact way, and the two men received the news in the same way; it suddenly struck Bryn just how callous about death in all its guises they had all become.

'Anything else you can tell us?' Bryn asked, knowing how Heather liked to slowly reveal what she had discovered.

'Yes. The lady was killed from behind and your killer is left-handed.' She sat back with that superior look on her face, and sipped her coffee, giving Bryn a harsh glaring look as she caught him staring at the backside of a passing nurse. Bryn looked away, embarrassed, not by looking but by getting caught.

'How can you tell this?' asked Mario, who was obviously impressed. Bryn tried smiling at her to stop the glaring.

She smiled back and shook her head. 'There was damage to the underside of the right jaw bone, consistent with such an attack,' she continued saying to Mario, who was oblivious to what was passing between them.

Both men were now seriously impressed. Bryn wrote on his pad:

Confirm if Giuseppe was left-handed.

'By the way,' Mario said as Bryn wrote, 'just in case – we have searched his old offices – there were no false walls and no garden to worry about.'

Bryn let out a heavy sigh of relief.

The Italian detective once again negotiated the Bologna traffic. They were on the way back to the police station, while Heather went back into the mortuary to work with her Italian colleague on the autopsy reports. She was so in her element, cutting up humans. He thought about it being a strange calling for a woman – then perhaps not. They had agreed that neither of them would not work past 5 p.m. for they wanted to spend their last night in Italy together.

'Your fiancée is a very beautiful woman. Intelligent too. You are a very lucky man to have such a woman, my friend.'

Bryn just nodded for he had to agree – he was very lucky. He still didn't know what in the world she saw in him.

'What of your wife, Mario. I know you are divorcing – do you have children?'

'Luckily, no – and that was the problem.' Bryn saw his looks harden and he could tell Mario wished to say no more so he rapidly changed the subject back to the case.

Bryn couldn't get over the fact that the Italians had armed

sentries at the entrance to the police station and they always seemed to view him with suspicion as he passed. He followed Mario into the detectives' office on the second floor of the Bologna Carabinieri office– a bustling place, filled with smoke and the obligatory smell of garlic and sweat. Mario took off his jacket and put it over the back of his chair. His desk was so tidy – not a thing out of place – it reminded him of Noonan's desk back home. He remembered that he had placed a sign on it saying 'A TIDY DESK IS THE SIGN OF A SICK MIND' – well, he thought it was funny. He made a mental note to send Mario one when he got home. He then thought back to his desk and how it would now be overflowing with unattended paperwork and messages, most of them probably from Laura – the moaning bitch. He will send her a postcard – that should piss her off a bit.

His thoughts were broken as Mario sat down with a weary sigh – he looked tired. He checked his messages.

'This is interesting – a call from a detective in Parma. Eight years ago, a body of a woman was found in a house, she had been walled up behind a false wall – found during some *restaurazioni*... house *rimodernamenti*.'

'Ah – renovations.'

'Yes, house renovations.' Bryn had noticed how frustrated Mario got with himself when he fluffed his English – but he pretended not to notice; besides, coffee had arrived.

Mario called the detective in Parma and Bryn called the Salvino residence and asked to speak to Miss Gabriella. He waited a couple of minutes for her to come to the phone. He introduced himself and he could hear the trepidation in her voice as she spoke. Even when she sounded nervous, she had the most beautiful-sounding voice.

He asked his question and she excused herself. She re-joined him a couple of minutes later – 'My great-uncle was left-handed – we all are. It is a... *tratto di famiglia*.' She put the phone down without another word. Bryn could tell she was crying. Once again, he hoped he wouldn't have to trouble them again, but he knew that was a forlorn hope. He took out his notebook and added:

Giuseppe WAS left-handed (family trait)

He sat and listened to Mario – he could understand nothing of what he was saying – he felt so inadequate. He heard Mario giving his thanks and as he put the phone down, he turned and smiled at Bryn.

'Could be our man – lady had her throat cut but unfortunately the report doesn't say how. We can drive over there this afternoon if you like.'

Mario saw the look in Bryn's eyes, 'Perhaps tomorrow would be better,' he said quickly, realising his mistake. He winked at Bryn as he picked up the phone to re-arrange the meeting.

As the clock approached five o'clock, a beautiful police civilian came into the office. Her skirt was so tight Bryn could clearly see the outline of her knickers, and her blouse had one too many buttons undone. It seemed an Italian trait that all women, particularly the more beautiful ones, wore blouses one size too small. The detectives in the office started the wolf-whistles but the girl just laughed and to Bryn's delight she came over to Mario's desk. She handed him a telex, smiled at Bryn, which he felt in his groin and walked out, though how she managed to walk at all in those heels was a mystery, a mystery that he was still thinking about as Mario nudged him.

'It is a telex from a Detective Noonan – it is for you.'

Noonan had been to the bank and an unusually helpful bank manager had been in contact with their archives and they had found the letter in a long-dead file. All the paperwork was correct and the money had been transferred to a Bologna bank. Noonan had noted that the file had been handled at the Quayside branch by a Gillian Armstrong. He had checked with Vera in Queens Avenue and she said she had an Auntie Gillian who had worked in a bank, but she emigrated to Canada in 1970 and unfortunately died in a car accident in Calgary in 1978.

'Well at least we know how the Armstrongs got the letter; a letter that proved to be their death warrant.' That was one little mystery out of the way.

At 5.20 p.m. Bryn let himself into the hotel room. Heather was packing as her flight was at 6 a.m. the following morning. Mario had arranged for a car to pick her up at 4 a.m. Bryn really didn't want her to go but he tried to hide it as he walked over and kissed her. They fell onto the bed and made love – not their usual frantic, mildly perverted sex, but slow, passionate, deeply emotional sex that left them entwined long after the actual act was over.

Over dinner, in a small intimate local restaurant on Piazza Galvani that Mario had recommended, Bryn posed the question that had been on both their minds. Is this the time to go public about their relationship? They both agreed that it was – Heather was delighted. She leaned across the table and kissed him. This was the first step – now to get him to commit to her – that was a bigger problem.

The two lovers got no sleep whatsoever that night, neither wanting to waste a minute of their remaining time together, but 4 a.m. came around far too soon for both of them. She didn't want him to come to the airport, she wanted them to say their goodbyes in the room, so they did, and she left.

He watched out of the window as she got into the police car – she looked up at the window – he didn't think she could see him but he waved anyway.

Suddenly Bryn felt very alone and within half an hour he was searching his suitcase for his pills. He washed them down with a mouthful of Jack.

CHAPTER FIFTEEN

Monday 7 April 1952 09.00

That morning Bologna had a brand-new firm of solicitors open its doors for the first time. Guido had not only bought the office premises in Giuseppe's name, but also a nice house for him and Leonardo not too far away. He had even purchased a small Fiat car for him. He was overjoyed to have his younger brother back, and so pleased to watch him open the doors for the first time. It had been a rush to get things completed but they had done it – for in Bologna the Salvino name meant something. After a celebratory glass of wine, Guido took Leonardo by the hand for uncle and nephew had become very close in that short time, and they went home – via a toy and sweet shop, Giuseppe suspected – leaving his brother and his new secretary, Maria Gambrelli, to start the firm off.

If Guido was a happy man, then Giuseppe was far more so, for now he could put everything behind him and start again, for after all, he was part of a much-respected family and he was something of a war hero so he knew success was assured. He was so looking forward to the lodge meeting tonight – he hadn't attended a Masonic meeting for years for his wife had frowned upon such things – he hoped he would remember all the rituals after all this time.

The telephone started ringing almost immediately – Guido

had been very busy ensuring that his friends knew of the new firm, and to ensure they put some business his way – which they were sure to do.

Thursday 26 June 1986 08.10 hrs

There was a telephone ringing in the distance once again and the more awake Bryn became the louder it grew. He picked it up and mumbled something into the receiver.

'*Buongiorno,* my good friend – did you sleep well? Hurry – we are off to Parma. I am downstairs so I will order breakfast for us.'

Bryn had always hated people who were cheerful in the morning. Mario, he thought, could represent Italy in being cheerful, no matter what time of the day. He dragged himself out of bed and into the shower. He downed a couple of his pills before leaving the room and put several in his pocket for he knew he would need them later. In just twenty minutes he was sitting with his friend, enjoying a hearty breakfast, discussing their trip.

'We will miss Heather – I think. No?'

Yes – he certainly would miss her – it was a feeling he hadn't felt in a long time and he didn't know if he liked it. The thought of another human being having any sort of hold on him was more than a bit frightening for him. He now regretted telling her that they should let people know they were 'an item'.

It was another beautiful sunny day. Bryn was wearing the expensive Ray-Ban Aviator sunglasses and Italian-style jacket that Heather had bought him yesterday. He felt very smart, almost Italian. Fifteen minutes into the drive, Mario stopped the car and pointed to the building across the street. 'There, my friend, is the scene of another infamous murder that happened over seventy years ago.' Bryn looked at the name on the side of the building, via Mazzini. 'It was there that Count Bonmartini was stabbed to death, by his wife I think, but she got away with it anyway. It was a... how you say... something of a sex scandal at the time – a lot of very prominent people involved. It was a big conspiracy with lots of depravity, including *incesto* if my memory serves me – everything we Italians love.' He started to laugh. 'Perhaps our murderer will put us in the history books. If not, then we will write it ourselves,' Mario chuckled to himself as he drove off.

'That is something to consider,' Bryn thought – for he always kept copious amounts of notes but he didn't think there would be any '*incesto*' in this story. He was thankful for that small fact.

They drove out of Bologna on route E45 and, once they had cleared the bustling city, the volume of traffic eased; Bryn settled down for a snooze – Mario understood why his friend needed to sleep. He remembered back to the early days of his relationship with his soon-to-be divorced wife. Heather seemed a very passionate woman. He envied his friend. Since his separation from his wife, who had been the love of his life since his college days, he had felt lonely – he wasn't the type of man to spend a lot of time on his own, nor was he one to have one-night stands – he always craved companionship.

He woke Bryn an hour later as they drove into Modena. Mario hadn't taken the ring road, but had chosen to drive through the town. He was proud of his country and wanted his visitor to see what he could in the short time they had left together. They drove passed the large Duomo. Mario pointed to the tower that he named The Torre Ghirlandina. Bryn noticed that the tower leaned quite precariously.

'You think only that shithole Pisa has a leaning tower?' he said with an element of pride.

They stopped at a roadside cafe for a bite to eat and some coffee. This time the caffeine helped. He needed it as Heather had certainly sapped his energy last night. The perversions she was bringing out in him were now starting to concern him, and it was only during his more rational moments that he considered it but – he had never been sexually violent towards women. He had of course slapped Laura about a bit early in their marriage, but that was when he was drunk, and that had almost stopped when she had Sian but his slapping of Heather during sex had started to become more aggressive. But she didn't seem to care and that really started to concern him too. Mario stared at his friend, wondering what he was thinking about – he seemed so distant all of a sudden. He threw some money on the table, the noise of the coins waking Bryn from his worrying thoughts. He looked up and smiled at Mario, who saw sadness in Bryn's eyes, but he said nothing as they both rose from the table and walked back to the car.

They took just under two hours to drive the fifty or so miles to Parma, yet another wonderful city that Bryn hoped to have a little time to explore before going back to Bologna, but in his heart, he knew he wouldn't. He made a mental note to return with Heather on his next annual leave and do some exploring. He understood now why people fell in love with this country

– for it was starting to occur within him too. Despite the rush of the traffic there was an underlying tranquillity to the place that he liked.

They showed their identification to the officer on the main desk and were directed to the detectives' squad room where they were introduced to Detective Alessandro Sacchetti. Once again, he spoke perfect English and how glad he was that Heather wasn't with him this time for he looked like the sort of Italian you see in the movies – God-like handsome, jet-black hair, olive, unblemished skin and wearing designer clothing right down to his underpants, no doubt. Bryn wanted to hate him but his easy manner soon won him over. He suggested that they left the noise of the squad room and adjourned to the cafe across the street where they could talk. Alessandro looked at Bryn as if he had made an indecent suggestion when he asked for only a single shot in his espresso.

He handed the old dog-eared file to Mario and sat back and sipped his coffee and he too quizzed Bryn about England. He didn't correct him even though it always grated on him that foreigners referred to England when they meant Britain. Bryn was Welsh and proud of it, but he let it pass.

Eventually, Mario closed the file and explained to Bryn what he had read:

'The woman was found eight years ago and, according to the autopsy report, she had been killed about five years before. Her throat had been cut and she had been put behind a false wall in a cupboard in the kitchen. She was identified as Mrs Ambra Salvati; her *nome da signorina* was Tomaselli. She was forty-five years old, a schoolteacher, who had recently married her husband, Giovanni Salvati; all that is known of him is that he had worked in a law firm in Padova. There was no record of him working here in Parma.'

'Husband's initials – 'GS', that's a good start and the law thing. Does it say if she had any relatives or any other witnesses we could speak to?'

'An older sister,' said Alessandro, with a confident smile, 'I have spoken to her and she is free today, if you want to interview to her.'

The two officers certainly did.

It was a fifteen-minute walk to the home of Miss Carla Tomaselli on Strada della Republica. Bryn relished the chance to view the city, basking in the hot sun, the heat seemingly bouncing off the buildings as they walked. As they made their way through the crowded streets Bryn wondered at the number of graffiti everywhere. He had noticed it in Bologna too. It seemed that most of them were political slogans but they did detract from the beauty of the very old buildings. It was something he couldn't understand – why desecrate such beautiful buildings with spray paint. He remembered back – it was only a few days ago – when he was looking at that graffito in Quayside with his name and the word 'BASTARD' mis-spelt. He wondered if the artists of Italy were as illiterate as the ones back home. However, it would take an awful lot more than the removal of a bit of graffiti to make Quayside look any better. It is a complete fucking dump, he thought as he walked through the bustle of this Renaissance city. Then he remembered that was the day that all this started; the day he first met Jenny Salvino, and began the chase for Giuseppe.

He was about to mention all the graffiti to Mario when suddenly they turned into one of the very narrow streets just off a large square. They stopped almost immediately outside a huge, blue door. The local detective buzzed the intercom, Detective Sacchetti identified all the officers, and the door was clicked open.

Miss Tomaselli was waiting for them at the top of a curved staircase and ushered them into the apartment before her neighbours could see. The whole conversation was conducted in Italian with Mario taking the notes this time.

After about half an hour, it became clear to Bryn that the interview was coming to a conclusion so he looked at Alessandro and said, 'Can I show her the picture I have of Giuseppe? It was taken back in 1952.'

The Italian detective explained the photograph to the old lady.

Bryn opened the file and handed Mario the enlarged photograph.

He heard the lady suddenly take a deep breath, and then she let out a scream that only seemed to shock Bryn. It seemed they had a hit and he smiled inwardly as he experienced the Latin temperament – this nation was not averse to showing their emotions – he liked that but it was something he found almost impossible to do.

'*Si – conosco Giovanni. Il Bastardo.*' From her reaction there was no need for a translation.

Later, as the three officers sat back at the cafe, Mario explained and this time it was Bryn who took the notes:

Ambra Tomaselli, born 1926

Married Giovanni Salvati, 1970

She was a schoolteacher

He had a son – Leonardo (who he spoke about often but was never seen).

Said he came from Padova

Was a solicitor

Said he was a 'vedovo' (widower)

Met and married within a month

House only rented

She had a large legacy left by father

Both people disappeared about 3 years after marriage.

Nothing further heard from them until body found at house.

Miss Tomaselli identified Salvino as husband.

Bank account cleaned out March 1973 – the equivalent of £10,000.

After Sacchetti had left, the two remaining detectives discovered that they were hungry and as the *Carabinieri* were paying, Bryn ate the most delicious lasagne he had ever tasted, followed by a large glass of Chianti.

'The report on Ambra Tomaselli is very poor – the investigation was badly conducted. All they did was circulate a description of the husband and left it at that, then after six months it was filed as unsolved. We were very, how you say, *incompetente* back then.' Bryn noticed a touch of embarrassment in his friend's voice. 'How many more do you think there are out there?' Mario asked.

Bryn shook his head. 'Well, there is a large gap between 1957 and 1973. Where was he and what did he live on – and now 1973 to 1986. He had a lot of money from Jennifer and the sales of the buildings in Bologna – then Ambra, but that won't last forever. 'Why do you think he mentioned Padova? Is it far from here?' Bryn had no idea of the geography of Italy.

'It is about 100 kilometres north of Bologna – about 150 kilometres east from here.'

'I think we need to ask for some help there to see if Signore Giovanni Salvati or Giuseppe Salvino is known there. We also need to speak to the bank – they might have some information about him too.'

They finished their meal in silence, both detectives deep in thought. Just how many other dead women are out there waiting to be discovered? Worse still – how many women would they never find? It was that question that bothered the policemen the most.

During the drive back to Bologna, even armed with the file on Ambra Tomaselli, neither man discussed the case. Women, football, and gripes against their bosses and even Bryn trying to explain the rules of cricket, filled the conversation – in fact anything that would keep their mind off Giuseppe Salvino and the possibility of more dead women.

Mario dropped Bryn off at the hotel and once again returned to his police station to set in motion enquiries, this time in Padova.

Bryn ran a very hot bath and sank slowly into the water, and waited for the promised telephone call from Heather, which woke him forty minutes later, the bath water now cold and him rather wrinkly.

CHAPTER SIXTEEN

Wednesday 18 September 1957 17.25 hrs

Once again Giuseppe was standing back, admiring his DIY skills. This had taken him a lot longer than that time in Britain; trying to get the materials was difficult and cost him a small fortune. But that was of little consequence for now he was a very successful solicitor; his clients, the rich and famous and in some cases, infamous, of Bologna and beyond. With the help of Guido and the brotherhood they had flocked to him – his name and status saw to that. He was after all one of them. His reputation for discretion was now well known.

But, thanks to the British once again, his peaceful live was disrupted and he was forced to flee his new cosy life again. It had all happened so quickly too.

Two days earlier, he had received a couple of unwelcome visitors from the past in the shape of his in-laws, all the way from Wales. They had surprised him by walking unannounced into his offices early that morning. He had no idea how they had managed to trace him after so long, then he cursed his arrogance at thinking now that he was back home his past would not catch up with him. His first reaction was that his wife had been discovered, then he relaxed – it would be the police who would have turned up on his doorstep, not these two idiots.

He was anxious that his lover and secretary, Maria, should

not be made aware of his true history. He also knew his mother-in-law had a violent temper, which was of course where her daughter had inherited it from but her husband was a quiet, hen-pecked man, just like he used to be. Giuseppe greeted them warmly, working hard not to show the shock and anxiety he felt inside. The British pair seemed very wary of him and remained distant. He immediately suggested that he take them to his home, where they would be far more comfortable.

He got them settled in his home. He saw in his mother-in-law's eyes, as she examined the fine furnishings and paintings in the large, comfortable lounge, that she was unimpressed by the opulence of his home here compared to the squalor in which he kept her daughter back home. He made the excuse that he was required in court for a couple of hours but would return later that afternoon and tell them what he could about Jenny. He knew they would search the house while he was out, but it didn't matter – he knew there was nothing incriminating there. He had briefly explained to them, as he conveyed them to his home, that their daughter had left him for another man, taking Lucia with her but the rest of the story he would explain later, including the name of her lover. He couldn't tell from their manner if they believed his story – and that un-nerved him, but in all honesty, it made no difference – he had already decided that they would not be returning home anyway.

He went back to his office, and without saying a word to Maria he closed the door. He tried to think of how to do it. Was he really capable of committing murder again, his initial bravado quickly leaving him? He felt sick to his stomach, which he had continued to try and hide whilst in the presence of the British couple, but now he felt he needed to vomit. He rushed to the toilet and was violently sick. Maria could only watch as he went back into his office, his face white as a sheet. He sat at his desk and tried to think. He supposed in his heart of hearts he knew this day would come but the further away from the murders he got, the easier and more relaxed his life had become – now it was on him and he had to do something quickly, or he was doomed to face the British gallows – but what was he to do? Was this the only way? He knew it was.

After half an hour Maria became anxious and called through the closed office door but she got no reply. With more than a little trepidation she slowly opened the door and entered his office. She saw him sitting behind his desk with his head in his hands – he appeared to be crying. She moved towards him but without looking up he shouted her away:

'*Vai Via*!' She left immediately. She had never seen him like this before – in the five months they had been together he had never so much as raised his voice to her and certainly never ordered her out of his office.

A little after 3 p.m. he very reluctantly returned to his home, and although he now lived with Maria, he asked her to give him some time before coming home. He needed to talk to the British couple alone. He told her that he would come and get her when they had finished their business. Maria felt a little left out for she knew all about his wife leaving him and taking his daughter. How could she do such a thing to this gentle, sophisticated man was a constant thought for Maria, for she longed to be the next Signora Salvino and to have his children. She could see the emotional state he was in so she sat at her desk and tried to get on with some work.

When he arrived back home, he found his in-laws were sitting quietly in the lounge, holding photographs of Leonardo. He entered, and without any pleasantries, his mother-in-law asked about their grandson.

'He spends a lot of time with my brother – he goes to his house after school, and then he brings him home for tea. They are very close. He will be home about six and will be overjoyed to see you. He asks about you often,' he lied in an effort to disarm these people – people who could send him to the executioner back in Britain. He spoke slowly and was surprised how quickly he had forgotten the English language. He knew Leonardo could not meet these people. 'Let me make you some tea and we will talk.'

He stood up and went into the kitchen. He put his head in his hands – he became resolved to what must happen. He knew now what he had to do. He quickly went to the cutlery drawer. He chose his knife carefully, not that it really mattered for he always kept all his knives very sharp. He remembered the mantra of the commandoes' drill instructor: 'A dull knife is a useless knife.'

'Have you heard anything from Jenny since she left me?' he shouted from the kitchen. The British pair just looked at each other but said nothing. Mr Armstrong could tell his wife was about to explode, and that did not bode well for the Italian. Giuseppe felt the deafening silence emanating from the lounge. His breathing slowed as he watched the kitchen door, and his senses bristled.

He just knew that they suspected something – he just knew it but that was their problem and they were his – but not for much longer.

He called for Edwina, to ask if she could help him bring in the tray. He stood behind the door. He knew this woman was brash enough to just rush into the room. He knew she needed to confront him. He listened to her heavy footfalls quickly covering the distance to the kitchen.

He was quite calm. All commando now... as the whole world slowed down.

She entered; he quickly and silently stepped behind her, put his right hand over her mouth and sliced. The blood spurted across the room and as he laid her quietly on the floor it pooled on the old, uneven flagstones. He moved back to the door, picked up a coffee cup from the table and dropped it. He shouted. He heard Samuel get up and start to walk slowly across the lounge floor, the old board creaking as he neared the kitchen door. Giuseppe watched the door handle slowly move. He grabbed the handle and quickly pulled the door open, thrusting the knife twice in rapid succession into Samuel's chest. The look in the dying man's eyes seemed to say, 'Now I have all my answers.' Giuseppe stepped back and slipped in the blood of his first victim, almost falling. The man fell in the doorway – Giuseppe's aim was as perfect as before. He now had to work fast for Guido and Leonardo would be home soon. It took him over twenty minutes to carry the bodies up two flights of stairs and into the attic. He had bound Edwina's throat with a towel to stem the blood. He then set about cleaning the kitchen floor – he was glad he didn't have a squeamish nature. It took over ten buckets of water to clean up the mess and even when he had finished it was clear something had happened there. He had already worked out a story for Maria, about a piece of meat leaking blood everywhere.

He was just drying everything up when the kitchen door opened, scaring the life out of him – he looked up, it was Maria. She looked at him on his knees, doing woman's work, a thing he would never do. She saw blood-soaked rags on the table. She asked him what he was doing, and where were his in-laws. He said that they had gone to a hotel and he would see them tomorrow. He quickly made some excuse about them having brought some papers relating to his divorce that required his signature. She remained in the doorway and asked why the kitchen floor was so wet? He was becoming angry with all her questions but he forced himself to stay calm – he told her the tale of the meat – from her reactions, it was clear to him she didn't believe him but she said nothing.

Then, to his relief, his brother brought Leonardo in and Maria went to greet them. Guido, who had very old-fashioned attitudes, was not happy with his younger brother's living arrangement as far as it concerned Maria, but he saw that she loved Leonardo, and the boy needed a mother so for now the situation would have to do but he would continue to push his Giuseppe to marry her, even though she was way below their social standing. Any real hostility he felt towards Maria had been worn away over the months and now they were becoming friends.

That evening it was clear to Maria that Giuseppe had no wish to discuss this afternoon's meeting, so she sat quietly and read her book, while he just stared into space. She had never seen him like this and she was beginning to think he might be ill.

That night, during their lovemaking, Giuseppe was very aggressive and hurt Maria several times – another thing he never did. He was usually so gentle with her but again she thought it best that she didn't say a word.

Friday 27 June 1986 midday

Once again, they were sitting outside a small cafe. The sun warming his neck, Bryn was holding the telex in his hand – it was from his boss back in Wales. It had been arranged that he was to fly back to Britain on the 2nd of July – he was to leave the rest of the enquiry to the Italian police and come home. He had four more days left to find Giuseppe – it seemed a forlorn hope. Mario brought over some ice cream for Bryn in an effort to brighten his friend's mood – and delicious though it was – it didn't help. Mario had told him that no one by either of those two names was known in Padova, so they sat there, both drinking their fourth three-shot espresso of the day, both of them feeling somewhat helpless. Giuseppe was winning this game of cat and mouse and neither policeman liked that.

'I know this is a long shot but what about his initials, 'GS'? Perhaps we could try that,' Bryn said, licking the last of the delicious ice cream off the spoon. He tried to keep the hint of desperation out of his voice but his colleague picked it up.

'It is worth a try.' Mario stood up and waited for Bryn to finish. They both knew they had to do something – anything – to keep the enquiry alive.

They went to the police station and Mario rang the police in Padova again, enquiring about anyone with those initials coming to light during that period. They also contacted the Italian law Society asking them if, in about 1957, anyone with the initials 'GS' tried to register – or started working as a clerk. The two officers sat back and waited.

The Law Society came back to them within the hour.

'Nothing,' said Mario as he replaced the receiver and settled back with a newspaper that was three days old.

Bryn went back to creating his list. He wanted to keep collating all the facts for the idea of them writing a book still resonated with him. Now that would be one in the eye for Mrs Pownell, his old English teacher, he thought, for like all the other teachers in his school, she never thought he would amount to anything – which, to date, he hadn't.

Suddenly Mario stood, waking Bryn from the reverie he had fallen into. 'We have nothing better to do, and an open ticket from my boss, so let me show you Padova.' Mario picked up the car keys.

He stood up. Yes, thought Bryn, there was nothing else to do. He excused himself and went to the bathroom, splashed some cold water on his face and took a couple of his anti-depressants – he knew he was falling into that black hole of depression and that was the last thing he needed right now.

The A13 out of Bologna was busy with holiday traffic, but Bryn was enjoying the sights, and his friend was good company.

'We have a couple of hours to kill, so now I think it is time that you tell me the story of you being arrested in Venetia.'

Bryn laughed, took a deep breath, and started his story.

'My friend, Dave, another policeman, knew I'd got dumped by my girlfriend Enya... so to cheer me up...'

He went on... The 'dumping', necessitated a call to Dave's mother, a travel agency, and a few weeks' later three world travellers made their way to Manchester airport and in a few hours were in Venice.

'Let's at least try and stay out of trouble this time,' said Bryn, looking forward to a weekend of culture, and not spending a night in the cells, as had happened a couple of months earlier in Barcelona. 'But that's another story,' Bryn said to Mario, who got the feeling that that story would not be told. 'This time I was looking forward to the galleries and museums of that beautiful city.'

The first afternoon they took a gondola tour through the canals. It was so picturesque. All Bryn could think about at the time was how Enya, his ex-girlfriend, and the first real love of his life, would have been if she were with him in such a romantic setting. The spell was broken when Alun, the other member of the trio asked:

'Do they sell Lucozade here? I only brought a few bottles with me and they're nearly empty'. Alun was addicted to the yellow health drink.

During the blissful ride Dave and Alun were taken with the motorboats they saw speeding around the lido.

'Now that's more like it,' said Dave.

Oh shit, thought Bryn.

The following day, after a fantastic lunch in St Mark's Square, they trooped off to locate the motorboat rental facility. Unfortunately for them all, Dave found one, and twenty minutes later they were whizzing along at breakneck speeds with Dave driving and Alun shouting encouragement, as if he needed any. He ignored Bryn's plea to slow down as he was breaking the speed limit in certain sections of the canals and also going where motorboats were prohibited. At one point, he even saw the wake of the boat entering someone's house.

The end came as he swung around a blind ninety-degree corner like something out of a *James Bond* film, and hit a gondola coming in the opposite direction. Luckily it was unoccupied by any tourists and no real damage was done, but it was a very irate gondolier that was left in their wake as Dave zoomed away.

'Sure enough, two *Carabinieri* officers were waiting on the jetty as we docked. I could almost hear the handcuffs jingling in their pockets.'

He saw his friend laughing.

'Here we go again,' muttered Bryn as he approached the uniformed police officers who had already opened the back of the van for the offenders.

Bryn played the *'GET OUT OF JAIL FREE'* card, telling the officers that they should have known better being policemen themselves. Once again it worked. The officers proved to be great tour guides, ferrying them around in both cars and motor launches, showing them all the sights. 'It saved a great deal on taxi fares and admission costs,' Bryn said, turning to his friend.

Tears were running down Mario's cheeks – well at least he thought it was funny and it kept them away from thoughts of multiple murders and the murderer they couldn't catch.

'Well, as Padova is only about fifty kilometres from Bella Venetia – perhaps we can pay it a visit and you can re-live old times and maybe I can find the officers and reprimand them for not doing their duty. *I turisti di Englist condannati.*'

Before long they arrived at their destination and they walked into the police station, both seeming to sense the 'air of doom' they were collecting around them.

The detectives here were not as friendly as Bryn had been used to here in Italy – for nearly everywhere in the world there was a special camaraderie between policemen – and especially detectives – but it seemed not here in Padova. They were shown into a small waiting room that smelled of piss and unwashed bodies. They were told to wait. Mario, who seemed to be taking this blatant snub in his stride, sat on the thin bench that was chained to the wall, while Bryn, who was quietly fuming at their treatment, stared through the bars of the window out into the sunshine and the very busy street called via Brigata Padova. He only knew that because he could see the name on the building opposite. He mused about how different things looked; softer, more tranquil in the sunshine then thought, Christ, Lawton, get a hold of yourself. Don't turn queer. He smiled but continued to look out of the window.

A couple of minutes later they were joined by someone who appeared to be a senior officer, for Mario showed him due deference. Bryn couldn't have cared less. The man took no notice of Bryn whatsoever and spoke in Italian throughout. He laid two files on the table and without another word he left.

'*Bastardo!*' Mario declared – Bryn thought that there was no need to translate that. He knew the sort only too well, for there was enough of that type of boss in his own police force.

Bryn went over to the two grubby files on the dirty, sticky table and opened the first one. It related to a small-time thief. The picture was taken in 1958 but bore not the slightest resemblance to their man. Mario got up and opened the second – Bryn saw his face light up. He slowly turned the picture to Bryn and there was the face of Giuseppe staring back at him.

He had put on weight and grown a moustache but it was unmistakably him.

'It seems he had been arrested following a disturbance at his home in February 1958. It says that there was a complaint from one of his neighbours about late-night noise – he had then assaulted the arresting officer.'

'Giovanni Salatzzo.' He handed the file to Bryn.

'What did he get for that?' asked Bryn, throwing the other file back onto the filthy desk.

'Nothing – it appears he was let out after a couple of hours. No explanation why. Not even any record of an interview. This is interesting though – there is a note here saying that he paid for a telephone call to Bologna.' Mario noted the number.

'Got an address?'

'*Sì – 137 Cavalcavia Borgomagno.* It is Apartment 2.'

Mario put the file in his briefcase and both detectives left the police station without a word to anyone. Bryn bought a map of the city from a street vendor and they sat in a cafe and tried to find the Cavalcavia Borgomagno. Bryn needed his three-shot espressos now for he found the caffeine worked well when combined with his anti-depressants.

'Here it is – right by the railway station.'

They returned to their car and set off into the afternoon traffic – it was worse here than in Bologna but Bryn was getting used to driving Italian style; he was glad though that he wasn't actually doing the driving. He just sat back as Mario calmly negotiated past everything that the city threw at him. Twenty minutes later they drew up outside the address. They got out into the bright sunshine. Bryn was starting to get used to this too – he really didn't want to go home in just a couple of days' time – back to that depressing, gloomy shithole that was Quayside.

Mario rang the bell to Apartment 2 and it was answered by a female voice. He heard Mario introduce himself and the door click open.

The two men ascended the stairs in silence for the echoing of their footsteps on the stairwell seemed to increase their anticipation – Bryn wondering if Mario was thinking the same thing… was another woman decaying here? He looked at his friend and realised that that was exactly what was going through his mind.

They knocked on the apartment door and it was opened by a mini-skirted young girl in her mid-twenties. Her long, blonde hair cascaded over her face as she moved. Mario introduced Bryn and they both showed their identification. They were asked inside and offered coffee, which both men accepted.

'*Per il benifit del mio partner – lei parla inglesi?*'

Bryn knew by now what he was asking. He tried not to look embarrassed.

'*Si* – a little,' said the girl, who told them her name was Matilda Bettendorf. They both looked at her as she said this. She smiled as she told the officers that she was a German student, studying at the University.

'Miss Bettendorf…'

'But please call me Mattie,' she said with a very friendly voice.

Bryn sat quietly, and more than a little uncomfortable, for here were people who spoke several languages to his one. Those twenty-two miles of water called the English Channel had a lot to answer for in keeping the British so insular, he thought as he opened his notebook.

'How long have you lived here?' Mario asked as they sat with their coffee.

'I am in my third year here.'

'Have you lived here all that time?' Mario could see out of the corner of his eye that Bryn was more concerned with her shapely legs.

'*Sì* – yes. My family owns the place.'

'What? The apartment?'

'No, the whole building. My father owns several properties all over Europe.'

'This may seem like a very odd request but can we take a look around. We are investigating a very old case and one of the people involved used to reside here.' Bryn still couldn't take his eyes off her – and she knew it.

'No, please go ahead. I am studying law so I might be able to use this in my dissertation.' She had the most beautiful smile. Bryn was captivated until his partner hit his arm and woke him from a very naughty fantasy.

'How long has your family owned the building?' Bryn asked as he stood up, more in an effort to hide his embarrassment.

'I think about twenty-five years – but you would have to ask my papa.'

'Would you be able to call and ask – it is important and please ask him who he bought it from?' Bryn asked as he left the room.

He heard the telephone being dialled and her German voice begin speaking.

'Nice, eh?' Mario was looking at him with a knowing look.

'Okay – if you like that sort of thing,' Bryn said without

looking in his direction.

'And I can see you do like that sort of thing my friend.' He slapped him on the back and they entered her very tidy bedroom, the smell of perfume thick in the air.

When she got off the telephone Mattie was surprised to see the two men walking around her bedroom tapping on the walls and stamping on the wooden floor.

'I am sorry for being so long, but I got my papa's secretary to check the files. My father bought this building in 1959 – it had been empty for about twelve months – the previous owner was Giovanni Salatzzo. My father's secretary remembers it so well because unusually it was all done through a firm of solicitors in Bologna called Menoltti, or something like that, and the sale was delayed for some reason.' She handed Mario the paper she had made the notes on.

The two officers looked at each other – Mario nodded. Bryn felt the hairs on the back of his neck bristle.

'Does that help?' she asked, knowing by the policemen's expressions that it did.

'Thank you, Mattie, yes – it helps very much,' Bryn said, this time without looking at her.

Nothing untoward was found in the main rooms but in a small cupboard under the stairs Bryn found a false wall. He called Mario and as he stood at the door, he tapped the wall to confirm it. The empty noise was ominous.

Mario knew that he was breaching all protocol but he asked the girl if she would give them permission to look behind the wall. He knew he should have handed it over to the locals but... Mattie knew enough about the law to know that they would do it anyway, using a warrant if they had to and besides, her interest was aroused now and she wanted to see if anything was hidden behind there. She brought back a claw hammer and a chisel, and handed them to Bryn.

'Your boyfriend's?' asked Mario nodding to the tools.

'No – I have no boyfriend – I am too busy with studying.' Bryn felt Mario nudge his leg.

It was Bryn who made a hole in the plasterboard large enough to get his hand in. The wall was about 18" beyond the false wall. He reached down. 'There's something in here – it feels like a roll of carpet.'

That was enough for Mario – he called the local *carabinieri* office and awaited their arrival. All the time Mattie was asking questions of the pair and taking notes.

Within a couple of hours, the rest of the wall was removed and the woman's body in the roll of carpet was removed to the mortuary. Bryn watched the heated conversation between Mario and the unfriendly senior officer. He knew a 'chewing out' when he saw one; after all, he had had more than a few in his time too.

While that was going on, Bryn took the opportunity to talk to the girl, who was so calm about the whole thing. 'I thought you were just after some stolen property,' she said, 'but a body – that's so cool.' Bryn just smiled. 'It must be fascinating being a policeman, but a little unsettling with all the things you must see.'

'You get used to it,' he said, giving his stock answer.

'This is so cool,' she said again, and went out to watch the activity. The younger generation was rapidly becoming a thing he didn't understand. He thought about Sian, then realised that this was the first time he had thought about his daughter since he had come to Italy. It was a realisation that he was not proud of. Then he had an awful thought: I am turning into my father. He certainly needed to change that.

They said their goodbyes to Mattie and Bryn was very quiet during the drive back to the *carabinieri* office, but they didn't go straight in.

'Well, he is going to get me fired,' Mario said as they sat in a small cafe across the street.

Bryn laughed. '*Bastardo!*' he said and they chinked coffee cups. Mario started to laugh. 'Fuck him, the arse,' he said.

Bryn and Mario went into the office and sat in a small vestibule on the second floor, outside the office of the commander of the Padova Carabinieri. There was definitely a complete change of attitude to the two officers from the Padova Carabinieri who had been instructed directly by the Comandante Generale in Rome that all assistance was to be given to Mario and the officer from England, and so they waited for a city-wide search to be made for missing persons in 1959. By 8.30 p.m., it was clear that this would not be a quick task so they found a nice hotel and booked in, for after all the *carabinieri* were paying.

Bryn had thought about calling Mattie to ensure she was alright following the ordeal and to invite her for dinner, for he had made sure he had asked her for her telephone number, seemingly as part of the enquiry, but then thought better of it – the fewer complications in his life, the better. Instead, he called Heather from the lobby payphone then went to bed. He swallowed a couple of anti-depressants, and he was asleep within minutes.

It was almost midnight when Bryn was awakened by the knocking on his door. He opened it and saw Mario, fully dressed, car keys in hand.

'They have something.'

Bryn hurriedly got dressed and met his friend at the car.

'They have a match – a woman who went missing in 1958, Quorra Calvelli, she worked in a solicitor's office in Bologna of all places. She had been sent here to see a client and never returned – the client went missing too and I think you can guess the name of the client?'

'Giovanni Salatzzo.'

'*Correggere!*'

Bryn was invited into the meeting of the detectives but he excused himself for most of them didn't speak English and, as his Italian was still almost non-existent, he thought that discretion was the better part of valour. He sat in the small room and took out his notepad, turned to a fresh page and wrote:

VICTIMS

Name	Location	Date	Name
Jennifer Salvino	Quayside	1952	Giuseppe Salvino
Lucia Salvino	Quayside	1952	" "
Samuel Armstrong	Bologna	1957	" "
Edwina Armstrong	Bologna	1957	" "
Quorra Calvelli	Padova	1958	Giovanni Salatzzo
Ambra Tomaselli	Palma	1975	Giovanni Salvati

How many more, he wondered once again as he stared at the list for there were quite a number of large gaps in the dates, and how many have we missed? That was the thought that haunted him most.

At the conclusion of the detectives' meeting, Mario slumped down on the chair next to Bryn – he smiled a very tired smile.

'You know how you mentioned that you hoped you wouldn't have to bother the Salvino family again? Well, I have had one of our friendly Padova colleagues check with the telephone company – it took a while to get that old number checked, you know; the one he called from the police station.'

Bryn nodded.

'It was registered to Guido Salvino. It appears that his brother was still in touch with him even then.'

'And continued to help the bastard,' said Bryn, suddenly coming to life again. 'I think we need to pay another visit to *Il Salvino di Famiglia*. For I think we have been the victims of a closely guarded family secret.'

CHAPTER SEVENTEEN

Thursday 19 September 1957 09.35 hrs

The following morning, after Maria had returned from taking Leonardo to school, Giuseppe suggested that they take the day off – they had worked nonstop, and they had earned some free time. Maria loved the idea. She tried to push yesterday's awful thoughts out of her head. He seemed back to his old self. She asked if they went out for the day, when he would meet with his British visitors.

'I have arranged it all. We will all have dinner together later. We shall pick them up at their hotel at seven and you shall pick the *ristorante*. They said that they cannot wait to meet you, and they are glad that I have found happiness at last,' he said this with a warm disarming smile. She loved him so much. This pleased Maria for it proved to her that he had nothing to hide from her and, as she went into the kitchen, she started to mentally admonish herself for thinking so badly of him yesterday. How could she have been so stupid?

For the next forty minutes she busied herself preparing their picnic basket. When Giuseppe had loaded the car, they drove out of the city heading south. At the small village of Sesso Marconi, they stopped for a coffee. How she loved to be with him – she never thought in her wildest dreams that she would capture such a man. He was so relaxed as they chatted about the future. She was so happy.

Giuseppe turned off the main road and drove into the small car parking area of Parco Regionale Storico di Monte Sole. It was a large country park that he used to come to as a boy. He stopped the car in a secluded place amongst some tall fir trees. He helped Maria out of the car and took her to view the magnificent lake – it was so very romantic. She was so excited for a thought had been with her ever since he had mentioned the trip – perhaps he was, at last going to propose to her. She stood, admiring the view. She heard him approach, his shoes crunching on the pebbles. She didn't want to turn. She was filled with excitement.

She was unable to shout out as the sharp pain struck her in the back; his hand across her mouth had stopped that. He pulled the knife out of her back as she slumped to the ground. He hadn't wanted to slit her throat, in case the blood spurted out and somehow got on his fresh clean clothes. He threw the knife as far as he could into the waters of the lake. He looked around again but all was silent. He picked Maria up and carried her body into the thick undergrowth and the lee of a fallen tree, where he laid her down and covered her with rocks. He wished he had remembered to bring a shovel but then again that might have proved a little suspicious. He smiled at the joke. He stood back from his work – no one would find her, especially when the ferns and other plants regrew, and of course when the wild animals that must roam this vast park had finished with her.

He washed his hands in the cold waters of the lake and went back and sat in the car and ate some of the picnic. He would certainly miss her cooking.

He started the car and drove slowly back to Bologna – he was quite calm for he knew that Maria was an orphan with no siblings so there would be no one on her side to mourn her passing. His family was another matter – he spent the whole journey trying to concoct a viable story to mask Maria's sudden disappearance to everyone else, especially Guido, who, ever since childhood, could tell when Giuseppe was lying.

On his way home he called in to see his brother and asked if Leonardo could stay for a couple of days as he had some things to do at home – Guido was delighted.

Giuseppe carried the pieces of timber into the house and started constructing the wall in the attic to house his in-laws, who, even after such a short time, were beginning to smell. He knew he would also have to find something to mask that too – but what...

Saturday 28 June 1986 10.35 hrs

Once again, the plain, blue Alfa Romeo police car stopped outside the large front entrance of the Salvino family villa and, as the two officers emerged, the large wooden door opened and there stood the young Gabriella, as pretty and well turned out as before but her face showed the signs of concern. She greeted the two officers with politeness but it was clear she was now very wary of them, especially Bryn. She directed them into the library again and then went to fetch her grandmother. The plan was that Bryn was to lead the interview this time for, despite the language problem, Mario thought he would provide an unknown quantity for the family.

It took over ten minutes for the two ladies to return to the library. This gave Bryn time to go over the notes he and Mario had made the night before. Bryn never believed in going into any interview unprepared; besides he always loved playing 'bad cop' – he hoped Mario was as good as the 'good cop'.

The two ladies sat demurely on the couch, the elder looking genteel and aloof, the younger seemed to be growing more apprehensive by the minute.

'I believe you have some more questions for us?' the younger one spoke first, trying to show confidence that was clear to all she did not possess. She looked at Mario and seemed surprised when Bryn spoke:

'We wish to ask your grandmother some more questions about her brothers. I know there are things you have omitted to tell us,' he said emphasising the last couple of words.

'Then ask your infernal questions, *Ispettore*.'

Bryn was surprised to hear an older voice reply – the family matriarch stared at him, defiance in her cold blue eyes. This wasn't going to be as easy as he and Mario had originally thought.

Bryn thought of a way to turn this to his advantage:

'So, *signora* – what else have you kept from officers of the law? We need to know ALL about your family's dealings with your brother Giuseppe since he left Bologna in 1957. Whatever you tell us will, of course, remain in the strictest confidence but if we have to find out the hard way then I cannot answer for the scandal that may come your way.'

Bryn saw the older woman swallow hard but remain composed, and he took the looks of pure hatred from the young girl without flinching. He was quite used to those kinds of stares – in fact, he relished them for it showed that somewhere he had hit a nerve.

'Now it is up to you, Signora Gabriella.' Bryn sat back and let the words marinade for a while – for in some cases, especially during interviews, silence really was golden. He could see Mario itching to say something for the Italian temperament seemed to hate silence – Bryn looked over to him and shook his head, trying to keeping his colleague quiet.

After a couple of minutes of the heavy silence, the old lady got to her feet, pushed away any support from her granddaughter and walked out of the room. Bryn noticed that all pretence of frailty had gone.

'Are all Englishmen so ill-mannered?' the young girl shouted at Bryn.

'Not all – just British policemen who are tired of being lied to by people who really should know better.'

He saw Mario smile slightly. The young girl sat back and waited. Bryn was sure she wasn't used to people talking to her in that tone but she didn't know what to do about it.

The elderly lady returned with a large box and placed it on the coffee table. Bryn tried to hide his impatience to get at its contents. He looked at Mario; he could see he was in the same state.

'I think we need some coffee before we start,' said the old lady, her voice calm and very controlled. She rang the bell and immediately a servant entered with the coffee and biscuits. Young Gabriella poured and her grandmother slowly lifted the box's lid, as if she was about to reveal a priceless piece of art.

'You are correct, *ufficiale*. My brother Guido was in contact with Giuseppe since about 1957 or '58 – here are his diaries.' She handed one to Bryn with a knowing smile – he handed it to Mario who opened it and started to read. 'Guido loved us both very much – but I do not think he knew of any *malefatte*,' she looked at Mario.

'Wrongdoings,' he translated.

'Yes – wrongdoings of Giuseppe.'

Bryn had his doubts and by the look on Mario's face – so did he. The old lady's face remained inscrutable.

'I am seizing this box and its contents as evidence in a murder enquiry.' Bryn knew he was overstepping the mark as he had no jurisdiction to do so, but he hoped Mario had, if they complained.

The old lady looked confused. He heard the younger Gabriella translate – *'Io sequestro questa scatola e il suo contenuto per fissure usata come prova nelle indagini dell'omicidio.'*

The old lady nodded and turned her head away. She waved her hand as if it was of no consequence. Bryn put the lid on the box and stood up.

'Is there anything else we need to see?' Mario asked in Italian.

The old lady, with tears in her eyes, shook her head and waved the officers away as if she was swatting flies.

No one bothered to show them to the door.

CHAPTER EIGHTEEN

Friday 11 July 1958 15.25 hrs

Giuseppe Salvino loved Padova. He had arrived here purely by chance; it was the destination of the first train leaving Bologna. He was just getting settled in the city and was now eagerly awaiting the arrival of the solicitor that his brother had hired to bring him some more money and the documents he needed to finalise the sale of the properties in Bologna and the purchase of a house here. He was anxious to get the matter out of the way and cut all his links with that city. The lawyer was due to arrive at three – his lateness started to prey on Giuseppe's mind.

At last – he heard the knock on the front door, he opened it and there, to his surprise was Quorra Calvelli, a female lawyer from Bologna, who he had worked on many cases with over the years, both before the war and a couple since. She was surprised to see Giuseppe standing there, then realised that the matter was being conducted on behalf of his brother so... Giuseppe cursed his older brother's stupidity in not ensuring this sort of situation wouldn't happen. He realised his brother would need some guidance in the future.

She was very surprised to see Giuseppe but greeted him warmly and asked if Signore Giovanni Salatzzo was at home.

Giuseppe immediately started to feel the panic rise inside him. His new identity was blown before he really had the chance to get used to it. He invited her in. She made herself comfortable in the house, which bore all the signs of someone just moving in. As she sat awaiting her coffee and the arrival of Signore Salatzzo, Giuseppe went into the kitchen to think. He quickly realised that there was really only one way out of this situation and once that decision was made, to his total surprise, he calmed down. Then he remembered – that was how it was with him during the war, how he was with the others – he was always calm when killing was to be done.

Over coffee he asked, in a flirtatious way, when she needed to be back in Bologna, and he inwardly sighed with relief when she replied, equally flirtatiously, that she didn't have to be back in the office until Monday. She had always secretly admired Giuseppe and saw a chance to further that here, away from her elderly lover back in Bologna who had become so possessive over her of late.

He went back into the kitchen and took a dishcloth from the drawer; he had learned how far blood can shoot out of the body following the killing of his mother-in-law. He took the bread knife from the wooden knife block. He always kept his knives razor sharp, and then he called Quorra to come into the kitchen and see the view. He heard her get up and hurry into the room – once again, he picked his spot behind the door. In one quick, well-practised movement, he stepped behind her and with one slash her throat was cut. He was also very quick with the cloth to stem the flow of blood. He was impressed with himself for very little sprayed out of her, or drained onto the floor.

He left her on the floor and then searched the apartment. He knew what he was looking for. The small cupboard space under the stairs was ideal for the storage of the body.

He sat quietly and completed the paperwork and tomorrow he would mail them direct to his brother, with a note explaining 'almost' everything.

He brought the wood into the house and began to construct his wall, losing all track of the time in the process. It was dark when he heard a loud rapping on his door. He looked out of the window and saw a police car parked outside. His blood ran cold for Quorra's body still lay on the floor outside the small cupboard and the wall was far from ready. He hurriedly pushed the body into the small cupboard. He didn't have the time to move the blood off the floor though.

He opened the door to the two police officers.

'We have received a complaint from one of your neighbours about the noise at such a late hour.' It was the taller of the two who spoke.

'They are always complaining about something,' was his reply. He just couldn't get on with the people next door.

'Can we come in and see what you are up to?'

'No – you will not. I refuse to let you in – unless you have a warrant that is.'

'Calm down – we are only doing our job,' the smaller officer said.

'Why don't you fuck off and pester someone else.' He knew he had to stop them entering so he took a swing at the officers, hitting the smaller one on the side of the head, his cap rolling into the hallway and down the stairs.

He was handcuffed very quickly, manhandled down the stairs and placed in the police car. He was driven away at speed. He saw his neighbours looking in disbelief, but he needed to keep the officers out of his house.

At the police station he was placed in a small room. He shook hands with the senior officer, ensuring he gave the 'third degree Masonic handshake'. The officer looked at him and nodded. Giuseppe was given access to a telephone. He called Guido and explained what had happened.

About a quarter of an hour later the police captain received a telephone call from a prominent senior police officer and was ordered to release Signore Giovanni Salatzzo immediately, without charge. The police even took him home – such was the power of the Italian Masonic brotherhood.

He let himself in but waited until the morning to finish off his wall – Quorra remained in the cupboard while he gulped a large glass of wine. His stomach was still in a knot with nervousness.

Saturday 28 June 1986 21.35 hrs

Bryn sat in his hotel room. It had been a waste of time being in the police station while Mario and a team of detectives went through the papers and diaries that he had seized. He began to feel a tad useless. He had taken a walk around Bologna – what a beautiful city. He stood and admired the two medieval towers again – this made him miss Heather all the more. He had enjoyed his time with her, here in Italy. Away from everything. He returned to his hotel room – he felt the depression, it never really left him but now it started to intensify. He took a couple more of his pills and had a gulp of Jack, emptying the bottle. He hoped that would at least postpone the inevitable. To take his mind off it he started to compose a report for his and Mario's superiors, collating what they knew so far of the case against Giuseppe Salvino. He tried to be as polite as possible in his writing.

To: Detective Superintendent Curry, Quayside CID

cc: Comandante Generale, Carabinieri, Rome

Sirs,

I wish to report the following:

The following person is suspected of several murders both on Quayside, Wales, and several cities in Italy:

Giuseppe Salvino b. 6th June 1912 at Bologna.

Suspected alias: Giovanni Salvati (Parma), Giovanni Salatzzo (Padua).

The investigation into these matters is not yet completed so this must be treated as an interim report.

The suspect arrived in Britain as a prisoner of war in late 1943. He was an army captain and had been captured in North Africa. He had enlisted in the 39th Bologna Infantry but it is now believed that, for at least some of his time in the military, he was a commando.

During his captivity at a camp in Carmarthen, Wales, he met Jennifer Armstrong, who at the time was working as a land girl. They married in 1948 and had two children, Leonardo (1949), and Lucia (1951). They settled in a large Victorian house in Uplands Common, Quayside, Wales and the suspect worked as a solicitor's clerk at a firm called Bryant and Maypole (no longer in existence) until he suddenly left in 1952. This has been confirmed by a work colleague.

On Wednesday 11th June 1986 a telephone call was received from the owner of 7, Uplands Common, Quayside. He had found the mummified remains of a woman behind a false wall in the master bedroom. Subsequent investigations revealed that this was the body of Jennifer Salvino, née Armstrong, b. 3rd January 1914. A further examination of the grounds revealed the body of a three-month old girl, buried in the back garden – this is thought to be the body of Lucia, b. 11th November 1951.

The suspect returned home to Bologna, Italy, shortly after the disappearance of his wife and child (which was reported to the police by Jennifer's mother) and he set up as a solicitor in the city, where sometime in about 1957/58 he was visited by his Welsh in-laws Samuel and Edwina Armstrong. They didn't return home and once again the suspect fled. On the 24th June 1986, following our investigations, two bodies were found behind a false wall at 17, via Santa Croce, Bologna, which were subsequently identified (by a passport and paperwork in the pocket of one of the bodies – copies attached) as Samuel and Edwina Armstrong. The address is known to have been the domicile of Giuseppe Salvino at the time.

Enquiries were sent throughout Italy resulting in a report being received that a body of a young woman had been found in 1976 in Parma, Italy, walled up behind a false wall. The lady was identified as Ambra Salvati, née Tomaselli, 45 years, a schoolteacher, who had recently married her husband, Giovanni Salvati. A photo of Giuseppe Salvino was shown to the deceased's sister, who confirmed that it was the suspect.

Enquiries were conducted in Padua (Padova) as the suspect had mentioned coming from there and as a result a file was discovered for Giovanni Salatzzo of 137 Cavalcavia Borgomagno. It is Apartment 2. A search of those premises revealed a body of a woman *who was subsequently identified at Quorra Calvelli, a solicitor from Bologna. (This matter has not as yet been investigated).*

Enquiries are still continuing here in Italy and in Quayside.

It has recently come to light that the suspect's older brother had been assisting him since his disappearance, and a large quantity of paperwork was seized today and is currently being examined by detectives of the Carabinieri.

As and when further information comes to light, I will forward that immediately.

Signed: Bryn Lawton Detective Constable No 856, Mid Welsh Constabulary.

Mario Fabrizzi Detective Appuntato Selto, Carabinieri, Bologna.

He would let Mario read it in the morning and add anything they might find tonight. He put the pad on the bedside table and switched off the light but he knew he wouldn't be able to sleep. He was thinking about getting up and searching out the town to buy another bottle of Jack Daniels.

Just before 11 p.m. the phone rang – Bryn picked it up before the second ring. They must have found something and he was needed back at work.

'Is that Detective Lawton?' It was a young female voice that Bryn couldn't quite place.

He hesitated.

'It's Mattie Bettendorf – you came to my flat the other day – I hope you remember me.'

'Oh yes, Miss Bettendorf. Of course. What can I do for you?'

'I hope you don't mind me calling. I spoke with Detective

Fabrizzi – he gave me your hotel number. He was sure you would not mind my calling you.'

'Not at all. How can I be of help?'

'I was wondering if I could ask you some questions about the investigation – for my thesis of course and in return I will buy you dinner, for I have come all the way from Padova to speak to you.'

An hour later Bryn was sitting in Piazza della Mercanzia, opposite a very beautiful young girl, eating a delicious pizza and trying to be as macho, mysterious, and interesting as he could.

Bryn told her what he could about the case, which as it turned out wasn't very much, but Mattie didn't seem to mind. Then she quizzed him on policing in general.

At the end of the evening, he invited her back to his hotel and to his surprise, she readily accepted. It hadn't bothered her in the slightest that a decaying body was the reason for their initial meeting, in fact she seemed to revel in it.

She made the first move, which Bryn followed and they made love, which was over very quickly – his fault entirely.

During the early morning, lying there on his hotel bed after Mattie had left, Bryn felt the twinges of guilt about what he had done, his betrayal of Heather for something that, to be honest, hadn't really been that good but the thought of him aged thirty-seven having sex with someone in their twenties did go a long way to cheer him up.

CHAPTER NINETEEN

Saturday 24 December 1960

Giuseppe now was using the name of one of his old teachers, Guillermo Sabatasso. He had been in the capital since February and during that summer it had been easy to hide away in the crowds who thronged to the Olympic Games. He had even secured a job as a security guard, but now the visitors had gone so it was a bit more difficult to hide away. It had also turned very cold.

He walked briskly past the Christmas revellers; he was never the most gregarious of people and soon tired of saying '*Buon Natale*' to those who passed him. He did enjoy looking at the city all dressed up in its Christmas lights. He also liked the fact that he was anonymous here in this big city. He went to the *ufficio postale* on *via Monte della Gioie* to pick up his mail, and thankfully it included the cash his brother had sent him – he also noticed he had a Christmas bonus. '*Buon Natale, Guido – L'amo. Noi tutti il colpo mancato lei.*' He did truly love his big brother and missed them all too, especially Leonardo – but he comforted himself in knowing that his uncle adored the boy almost as much as he did.

He had first made contact with Guido a couple of years before, mainly to try to explain his sudden disappearance from Bologna. He made the lame excuse that he had suffered a mental breakdown after Maria had suddenly left him and had not wished to be a burden to the family. He told his brother that he had signed himself into a sanatorium in Rome to cure him of his melancholy. He knew his loyal brother would desperately want to believe him.

So he returned to the dingy flat he was staying at on the outskirts of the city. He shared it with an old whore who went by the name of Genevieve. He knew it was not her real name but he really didn't care that much. It was somewhere to hide and be anonymous and he had the company of someone – that was enough for him at the moment.

He had met the whore during the early summer as she plied her trade in the city centre. He had discovered her bent over a car bonnet, having sex with a client around the back of the main Olympic Stadium, so in his security guard role he had scared the man off and, in payment for not moving her on, she let him finish the job, after all it had been paid for. They met several times over the next few weeks and when his job ended, she suggested he move out of the YMCA hostel on *via Varese* and move in with her and they could share the rent. He thought it was an ideal stopgap, while he sorted out his next move. He scanned the papers daily for any signs that any of the bodies had been discovered and that he was a wanted man, but so far all was fine.

He came back to the flat that night, his cold hands holding some wine, cheese and bread and he sat and waited for Genevieve to return home from her evening's work. Now that her looks had faded, and the vast army of Olympic tourists had gone home, she was back once again plying her trade at the bottom end of the market along via del Borshetto.

When she got back home, she quickly obliged him with some oral sex, then they settled down to eat. He liked her conversation – she was an intelligent woman. He didn't know why he was surprised that a whore could have intelligence, but he was. She had once tried to tell him her life story but he really wasn't that interested.

A strange noise awoke Giuseppe. It must have still been very early as it was still dark outside. He found himself alone in the small bed. He turned over and saw a light shining under the wooden door with the occasional shadow moving quietly in the only other room in the drab little flat. Genevieve didn't usually bring her punters back to the flat. He got up as silently as possible and opened the door slightly. He saw the naked whore emptying the envelope that contained Guido's money. He went back to bed and soon Genevieve slipped back under the covers. He rolled on top of her and started to fuck her. He became rougher with her and at first she accepted it but it started to get worse even though this was out of character for him. He started to really hurt her so she tried to resist. As he reached his orgasm, he put the pillow over her face and held it there. She fought violently for air but she was no match for his strength. All her struggling was over within minutes. He removed the pillow and looked at the lifeless whore, her thick lipstick smudged across her face. He got out of bed, dressed, and packed his meagre belongings. He opened her handbag and removed her evening's taking, paltry though it was and also the money she had stolen from him, and left the place, locking the door behind him. He felt quietly confident that nothing would be said to the police when the body was eventually found, for this was the underbelly of the city – an area that kept itself firmly to itself.

As he walked over the bridge that spanned the river Po, he discreetly dropped the key to the flat into the water then made his way to the railway station. As usual he would let fate decide his next port of call; he would catch the first train out – wherever it was heading. It was a long walk right across the city but the cold air seemed to dull his brain and kept the thoughts of what he had become out of his mind.

The following day he called Guido on his private number at the villa to wish him a merry Christmas and, despite the extra cash he had received, he asked for more. He spoke to Leonardo, who was at the villa for the holidays, for Guido was paying for him to go to a private school in Milan. Their conversation was strained. He hated that thing had got so awkward between them, but he knew he was better off with his family in Bologna than with his murdering father wandering all over Italy looking for something – salvation perhaps, or just a place to hide.

Later that morning he boarded the train and headed south.

Sunday 29 June 1986 10.20 hrs

The two detectives sat in a small cafe not far from Bryn's hotel. Bryn was thinking about just how much he had spent on coffee, when he saw his Italian counterparts flash their ID and get it for nothing. He could tell Mario was desperate to ask about his meeting with Mattie last night but Bryn, out of sheer devilment, kept talking about the case

'*In nome di Gesu, Giuseppe e Maria* – what the hell happened last night? Did you...?'

'A gentleman never tells – but *ha fottuto come un coniglio*.' He had been practising this phrase all morning. She didn't really 'fuck like a rabbit', in fact he hadn't really enjoyed it all that much but his friend was expecting gory details, like most of his male police friends would, so he had to embellish the facts – for a policeman telling a sex story, that was mandatory.

Mario burst into laughter and slapped Bryn hard on the back.

'Thanks for giving her the number.' He wanted to keep up the pretence that he felt no guilt but Mario saw through that.

'I am sure you will do the same for me one day, and let me tell you, my friend, as our American cousins say, "What happens in Italy – stays in Italy."'

Ah, the policeman's creed, alive and well and living in Italy too, he thought as he sat back and sipped his coffee.

'Now back to work I think,' Mario said as he opened his briefcase and produced his notebook. Bryn ordered more coffee and waited for Mario to disclose what he had discovered, his notebook at the ready to record all that his friend said:

'We went through all the diaries *con un bel pettine di dente*.' He made a movement like he was brushing his teeth. It took Bryn a couple of moments to realise what his friend was up to – then it dawned on him – 'with a fine-tooth comb'.

Mario grinned and Bryn saw that he was storing the English phrase away for future use.

'Yes, exactly,' he continued, 'and found monthly payments to someone recorded as 'GS' and the locations are given...'

Bryn recorded in his book:

1958–1959	*- Padua*
1960	*- Roma*
1963-1965	*- Taormina, Sicily*
1965–1970	*- Naples*
1970–1973	*- Palma, Italy*
1973–1976	*No entry for payments*
1976–1980	*- Turin*

'There is an interesting entry just before the location of the payments changed,' said Mario as he turned to a relevant page and read, '"*L'ha fatto di nuovo – quando farà ferma? L'amo ma non so se posso portare così tanto più lungo*" which says he must have known what his brother was doing for it means: He has done it again – when will he stop? I love him but I don't know if I can take this much longer. What are your thoughts?'

'It certainly sounds like he knew all right. Now we need to clear up what we know of this killing first before we travel around the country like a couple of nomads – we need to find out about what happened to Quorra Calvelli, our solicitor from Bologna. Let's clear up the loose ends – yes?'

'*Sì* – I think your young 'rabbit' means Menotti's. It is a very old and highly respected firm of lawyers here in the city – let's see if we can get a lawyer to work on a Sunday.' He began to laugh as did Bryn when he thought that lawyers must be the same the world over.

Following a couple of telephone calls, they were in the office of Signore Alfredo Menotti himself, the great-great-great-grandson of the founder. It truly is a family business, Bryn thought as he sat in the sumptuous oak-lined office of a very dapper, middle-aged man. His suit and shirt must have cost more than Bryn earned in a year.

Once again, for Bryn's benefit, the conversation was conducted in English, and once again, he felt the embarrassment rise within him, but the other men didn't seem to mind.

'I believe you wish to know about Quorra Calvelli – she was my grandfather's protégée. I think there was something more too but the less said about that, the better I think.' He smiled and winked at the officers and they smiled back the way men of the world are expected to do. He had a file in front of him – the pages slightly yellow with age. 'She was sent to finalise the sale of some property here in Bologna and the purchase of some in Padova and also to complete some other business with a Signore Giovanni Salatzzo. The file only says my great-grandfather was given instructions for a letter to be delivered to Signore Giovanni Salatzzo from Guido Salvino, who is now *deceduto*.' He nodded to Mario.

'Guido is now deceased,' he said to Bryn who simply nodded.

'So the family Salvino are clients of the firm?' Mario asked, both officers taking notes.

'*Sì* – since the firm opened in 1810, we have looked after the affairs of that family, along with most of the other families of prestige here in Bologna.' Signor Menotti said this with some considerable amount of pride.

'Is there a note of the exact date when she was sent to Padua?' Bryn asked, looking up from his notebook.

'Eleventh *luglio*, sorry – July 1958. She was reported missing when she failed to return to work on Monday 14th.'

'Do you know what enquiries were made?' Bryn asked.

The lawyer looked up from his file and took off his very expensive glasses, 'Well that is the strangest thing – and this is in the strictest confidence you understand – my father told me that my grandfather was on the phone constantly with the authorities both here in Bologna and Padova, urging more action to find her, then following a visit to the Salvino estate, he suddenly dropped all enquiries and it was like Quorra never existed. He never spoke of her again, and insisted others didn't either.'

'Do you have any further record of Signore Giovanni Salatzzo?' Mario asked.

'No.'

'Do you know who Signore Giovanni Salatzzo really was?'

'No.' It was clear from his manner that he was lying but there was little they could do for he had been unusually helpful for a lawyer.

They all stood and shook hands. Bryn's Masonic style was reciprocated by the lawyer. They both smiled.

As the two officers left his office the lawyer said, 'If I can be of any further help especially in corroborating anything, please let me know,' and what surprised both Bryn and Mario, he genuinely seemed to mean it.

CHAPTER TWENTY

Monday 3 May 1965 18.15 hrs

Giancarlo Saccento walked slowly up the hill towards his house, his jacket over his shoulder and his shirt stained with sweat. As he stepped through the small wooden gate, he performed his daily ritual. He stood and looked at the blue Mediterranean Sea and the Bay of Giardini Naxos far below him, then he turned to his left and saw the tip of mighty Mount Etna. He wondered how long it would be before she blew again. He felt like he could stand and admire this view all night for, no matter how stressed he felt, it always had the power to relax him.

He had lived on the outskirts of the small fishing village of Taormina on the island of Sicily for two years, having moved around the toe of Italy since fleeing Rome. He had never in his life been this far south – always reading how backward and corrupt it was down here with the Mafia running everything, but in reality, it was a lovely, peaceful place to live. In fact, it was the Mafia who saw to that. It was them, not the law, who kept things in order and as long as you realised that and paid a tribute everything was fine. Being a member of the lodge helped too. He ensured he never missed a meeting.

He was now working as a tour guide, showing tourists around the many ancient monuments that were in abundance in the region but his main area of expertise was the Greek amphitheatre – the finest example outside Rome and something he had wanted to see since he had read about it as a child back in Bologna. Now he was there every day. And every day it had the power to captivate him.

He pulled himself away from the view and entered his small house and was greeted at the door by his wife, Carlotta, a young girl he had met while dining alone at a beachside cafe. She was his waitress, who had told him when she knew him better that she had run away from home in Naples. She told him this to elicit better tips, but that information drew her to him – for she too had no ties either.

He was glad to be back at work after the winter break – Carlotta was pretty and obliging enough sexually but he had had weeks of her inane conversation and it was driving him mad.

He was already starting to plan his escape from her. He had been saving his wages for he had a pleasing way with the tourists so he did well for tips too and the money he got from Guido was still arriving every month; this was an income he had always kept from his young wife. Carlotta still worked as a waitress in the summertime but the cafe was closed for the refurbishment so she was home under his feet all the time and besides all that, she was becoming broody – wanting a baby, which he certainly didn't want, so sex between them was always very careful. The time had definitely come for Giuseppe to make another move.

His supper was ready as soon as he walked through the door, so he washed his hands and sat at the table in their little dining room and Carlotta served him spaghetti bolognese – she was not the world's best or creative cook but she knew the basics so that would have to do. He was hungry and when he had cleaned his plate, she handed him a large glass of red wine and he sat back a very contented man, if only for the moment.

'*Sono incinta,*' she blurted this out so as to give herself no chance of stopping. Her voice several notes higher than usual.

Pregnant! He looked at her in disbelief. How could this be? He had been too careful for this to happen. Then he remembered – New Year's Eve – that drunken sex they had had; that must be it. The bitch had tricked him. He was furious, more with himself than her at that moment but that very quickly changed. He wanted to slap the stupid bitch – it was lucky she had already cleared away the cutlery, otherwise his knife would have been between her ribs.

He continued to stare at her – she could tell by his fiery look that he was not happy but she was sure he would come around to the idea when he had time to think on it. She knew about his first wife who had left him a few years ago and had taken his baby girl. He had told her all about it when he was drunk, shortly after they had met. She was sure that, given time to adjust to the idea, all would be well.

'How long?' he asked, his voice strained with the tension he felt somewhere deep in the pit of his stomach. He was so angry he had difficulty getting the words to come out.

'Four months – I saw the *dottore* last week. He told me everything was fine.' She hoped that this would calm him, make him proud of her but she started to feel scared of him.

'And you have waited this long to tell me about this – why?' He could feel his temper rising once again. He felt her was about to explode. He looked at her stupid, imploring face – he could willingly have smashed it in with a rock.

'I wanted to tell you – but I knew you would be angry with me for letting this happen. I wanted to have your baby.'

He stood up without a word, the old wooden chair falling back onto the floor. He walked to the door and without looking back left the house, slamming the door behind him, the sound reverberating around the small cottage. Carlotta collapsed on the chair and began to weep uncontrollably. Giuseppe stood outside the door and listened. He realised what he had to do to that stupid fucking bitch.

As he walked towards the village, he thought about why he was cursed when it came to women. Giuseppe tried to think if there was another way – but he realised that there wasn't. He knew he didn't want the child and Carlotta had become a troublesome burden – there really was only one thing to be done and he would do it tonight. And once again things became clearer when that decision was made.

With this heavy burden of knowledge of what was to come, he knew it was going to be a very long evening. As he sat in a small trattoria near the beach he started to plan where he could hide her stupid body.

Monday 30 June 1986 09.50 hrs

As they sat in the airport Bryn asked his friend about the Mafia in Sicily.

'Simple, they rule everything from the politicians to the drug trade – anything they don't like, they kill. It is as simple as that, my friend.'

'So the stuff in *The Godfather* films is true?' He felt a little naïve after he said it.

'Very little happens in Sicily or indeed the whole of Italy that they don't know about and/or have a hand in. They kill, if you cross them and it doesn't matter who you are – politician, judge, or policeman – hell, they even had a war between themselves a few years ago, over drugs. So let me tell you this, we are there to investigate a murder case – that's all – leave the Mafiosi out of it and I am sure they will leave us alone. I don't think Giuseppe is mixed up with them – Masons yes, but not them – but if I am wrong and something proves he is...' His face changed as he shrugged his shoulders. 'By the way, one of the clans they formed was called the *Corleonesi*.'

He opened his newspaper and said nothing more – Bryn knew that particular conversation was over. He also knew that the mere mentioning of the Mafia to Mario gave him some cause for concern.

On their arrival they were escorted out of Palermo airport and taken to the main *Carabinieri* office, following the short flight from Bologna. They breakfasted with several senior officers. The two detectives updated them on the extent of their enquiries, before setting off for the drive to Taormina, a small fishing village on the east coast of the island. Mario had decided that they should take the more scenic route along the Sicilian coast rather than the slightly more direct route across the centre of the island. It was decided that Bryn should drive for a change, as the traffic was a lot calmer here than on the mainland and up to now Mario had had no time to update his partner fully on something else he had discovered. He quickly opened the envelope that one of the senior *carabinieri* officers had handed him on his arrival in Sicily.

'As we know, Guido died in 1982, but the diaries only go up to 1980 – it would appear that the last one is missing, no doubt kept back by Signora Salvino so that we don't know where Giuseppe was last seen. I have also received his military record from 1939–1943. He moved swiftly up the ranks – family influence and his Masonic connections, I think. From mid-1943 there are a lot of references to 'Rab' in the paperwork as it related to Giuseppe's duty during the war – I have just found out that Rab was a concentration camp on an island in the Adriatico and was initially used to detain Yugoslav partisans and later, Jews. The main man was a guy called Mario Roatta, a *Bastardo* by all accounts – his second-in-command was one Captain Giuseppe Salvino. I have his army record here – he was only there a short time and was transferred in September 1943 to North Africa, just before Italy signed the armistice. It says nearly 2000 people died at that camp and when it was taken over by the Germans, those that remained – mostly Jews – were transferred to Auschwitz. The island now belongs to The Republic of Croatia.'

'I have never heard of Rab Concentration Camp.' The Second World War was a favourite topic for Bryn to read about.

'Nor me – but it was one of the largest island concentration camps in Europe and housed 15,000 prisoners.'

'Were there any investigations in Italy after the war to find those involved in war crimes?' Bryn asked.

'*Sì* – nothing like Nuremberg of course but well over 1000 people were indicted for war crimes but...'

'What?' He saw his friend turn a little grey.

'Because we changed sides, Rab was considered, and I quote,

"a footnote to evil". Bryn we, the *carabinieri*, the 14th battalion – were involved at Rab. I can't believe it.'

Bryn could tell that this news preyed heavily on his friend's mind so he remained silent for a while. After a couple more miles they stopped at a cafe – they both needed a drink.

They arrived in the small, beautiful coastal town of Taormina in the late afternoon. The sun was blazing down and everyone seemed to be indoors, except for people who were obviously tourists. They located the *carabinieri* office, but then went on to book into a small hotel in the centre of the town and have a late lunch at a cafe on the sea front.

'First things first – isn't that what you English say?'

Bryn nodded to his friend as they both chomped their way through a large plate of delicious spaghetti. Mario seemed more relaxed.

They went back to Piazza Vittorio Emanuele II, where they showed their identification to the officer on duty and were directed to the detectives' room.

'*Michael Reali.*' The only detective there introduced himself without getting up, a thing he may not have been able to do anyway for, to Bryn's surprise, he was one of the fattest men he had ever seen. His first thought was where he could possibly have found trousers with a waist that big?

They introduced themselves to Ufficiale Reali, who suggested they went across the road to talk over a bite to eat.

It was with some relief that Mario explained that the officer's English was not too good, so he said he would take a walk for an hour while they chatted.

The town proved enchanting with many ancient sites dotted

everywhere – he hoped that this time he would get some time to explore before they moved on to who knows where. He remembered as a kid reading *Hansel and Gretel* – that was how he felt following Salvino's breadcrumb trail all over Italy. Not far from the police station he saw the beautiful building called Palazzo Corvaia, which, according to the guidebook he just bought, was built in the fourteenth century. It was beautiful. He would have liked to tour the nearby Duomo but he knew he didn't have the time. He also knew he had to get back to work, as his time in Italy was rapidly running out. Now this was a place he would come back to with Heather.

When he returned to the cafe, Mario was alone. He saw his friend was deep in thought and Bryn startled him as he sat down.

'Jesus, Mary, and Joseph, that man could eat! I kept my hands in my pocket in case he started eating my fingers.' Bryn started to laugh and hoped his friend was returning to normal. 'Anyway, tomorrow he will assist us in checking the records for anyone with those initials who might have come to their notice between 1960 and 1965 – he said it wouldn't take too long and he will arrange for us to go to the town hall and with the mayor's permission get the property records checked – now that might take a while.'

They returned to the hotel and said their goodnights, but Bryn went back down to the lobby and called Heather. He still felt guilty about screwing that young girl and began to feel even worse as he spoke to her especially when she told him how much she missed him. She couldn't believe it when he told her that he was now in Sicily. He told her about the beach and the bright blue sea and all the archaeology.

'I am so jealous – it's pouring down here,' she said, her voice quite animated, 'if you are still in Italy next week – do you think it would be alright if I re-joined you there for a couple of days, say over the weekend?'

'It is unlikely that I will be here – the boss back home is screaming for me to return.'

'Oh, what a pity – I was looking forward to joining you there – still, perhaps we could make a holiday of it. I have a couple of weeks of my holiday time left.'

Unfortunately, Bryn had used the last of his holiday time to attend Fiona's funeral a couple of weeks ago but he didn't mention that – he didn't want to spoil the mood.

They said their goodnights and he put down the telephone and went out into the town – it was so picturesque. He walked down to the water's edge; a gentle balmy breeze blew off the water. He saw the lights of the fishing boats on the horizon. He took off his shoes and socks and paddled in the warm Mediterranean Sea, he had a delicious cappuccino in a small beachside cafe, and retired to bed and for the first time in a long time he hadn't needed the aid of his pills or a glass full of Jack to get to sleep.

The following morning, they presented themselves back at the offices in Piazza Vittorio Emanuele II. The squad room had several more officers milling about, and Bryn was viewed as a bit of a curiosity but no one spoke to him.

'Old mug shots,' one of the detectives shouted to Bryn as he leafed through a book of photographs of local criminals of the 1960s. He smiled, took off his jacket and opened the book marked 60–61. Mario wished him luck as he set off for the town hall – they thought it better he went alone as he had been told by Michael Reali that the mayor's family had suffered badly at the hands of allied bombing of Palermo during the war, with several members being killed, including his father and younger brother.

By lunchtime Bryn was still only halfway through the first book – he hadn't realised that these books covered all of the island of Sicily. Looking at the photographs, noting the '60s style his mind often wondered back to his home in 1960. He remembered the great music of that time, his older sister sitting in a bath of cold water, fully dressed in order to shrink her jeans, and he started to laugh as he remembered his seventh birthday, when his mother, never the sharpest tool in the box and eccentric as hell, bought some indoor fireworks to be lit after his birthday tea. If ever there were two words that should never be put together, it was them. His mind drifted back...

His mother had an innocence that transcended everything, but her actions did not always end with the desired outcome and most times, to his father's total despair, but with fantastically unbelievable humorous results.

On completion of tea. His father, who, after living with Ellen for so many years, really should have known better, set the pyrotechnics on the table, ready for the fiesta. He lit the first one, after ordering everyone back; it went off and destroyed the lampshade that was situated over the table.

Did he stop there and just clear up the damage?

No.

He set off the miniature Roman candle, which set fire to the tablecloth.

Did he stop there and simply put out the fire?

No.

He finished with the jumping jack that fired off the table and onto the carpet. Every time it landed, it scorched a small patch of carpet. The sight of his father doing a type of Highland fling around the dining room trying to stamp on the offending missile was fantastic. To a nine-year-old Bryn this was pure theatre.

He tried to snap out of this dreamlike state he had wandered into. He was glad he was alone in that squad room, because surely, they would have thought him mad as a hatter sitting there chuckling to himself.

Eventually he finished the first book but by now the faces were blurring into one. He got up and went outside to find a cafe and get some coffee, which of course he now grudgingly paid for.

He returned half an hour later, and wearily pulled the second book to him.

Just after five Mario walked in, his face lined. They were both very tired.

'There are seventeen men with the initials 'GS', who owned a house in the town at that time, but only five in the area around the post office where he received his money – so we will start there by showing pictures to the neighbours. It's a long shot but what else can we do?' Bryn looked up at his friend and shrugged his shoulders in agreement. This was becoming a bit of a mantra.

'We will, of course, start first thing in the morning,' Mario said with a smile. Bryn took his jacket and after a hearty meal, eaten mostly in silence, a short telephone conversation with Heather, and a long bath, Bryn finally hit the sheets and was asleep by half past eight. Tonight, once again, he was so tired he had no need of either Jack or his anti-depressants.

Unusually he was up before Mario, and already sitting having his breakfast as he came down. Bryn could see that the information he had discovered about the *Carabinieri* involvement at Rab Concentration Camp still prayed heavily on his mind. He remembered back a couple of months when he read of the involvement in the deportation of Jews by British policemen in the Channel Islands. That had upset him too at the time.

Bryn tried to put a brave face on it. 'It was war, my friend, and you and I have been lucky not to have experienced it like our fathers and grandfathers so... don't judge them too harshly. I am sure it was a shit time for everybody.' Mario nodded but said nothing.

They arrived at the office just as a team of four uniformed officers set off to visit the addresses, each officer armed with the 1952 photostatted blown-up picture of Giuseppe Salvino.

Once again, they found themselves with nothing to do but wait.

'You never told me how you come to be dating the beautiful Heather.' They were sitting in the police canteen their untouched meals still in the dishes before them.

'It was about twelve months ago when we first met. Believe it or not, it was over a dead body.' Bryn told the story:

He was called to a house near the river, where a small child of five years had gone missing. The uniformed lads were already there. He went and spoke to the very distraught mother and with the few officers available started a search.

He requested further backup to be sent straightaway. He just had a feeling this wasn't a case where the toddler would show up in a few hours, having been out playing with his friends.

Within an hour, more officers started to arrive and a full major incident was underway.

It became clear as the days progressed that the child had fallen into the river. Bryn contacted experts on the river. It was established where and when the child would turn up. Bryn was sceptical at the time but sure enough they were right.

Bryn went to the scene and was present when the small body was recovered and he attended the post mortem, although he only identified the body to the pathologist; he didn't have the heart to stay for the procedure. That was when he met Heather.

'I hate it when it is children involved,' Mario said, his eyes full of compassion for his fellow officer. 'Death has followed me throughout my career,' he said but he felt very different about this particular death.

'That evening I went home and saw my daughter, who was aged about seven years, playing with her toys. I scooped her up and held her. I held her so tight as I sat on the armchair in the lounge. I was just unable to let her go. I was totally unaware of the child crying in pain until my ex entered the room and pulled the now-screaming child from me.'

"For Christ's sake Bryn, what the hell is the matter with you? Let her go," she screamed.

'Later that evening Laura called me into the bathroom when she was giving Sian her bath saying, "Look what you've done to her. Look at her side," in a very accusing tone.'

Bryn had looked at his naked daughter and saw the imprints of his knuckles on both sides of her ribcage for he had held her so tightly.

Bryn was deep in thought when he finished his story. Mario knew what he was feeling – the things they had to deal with were the 'policeman's curse'.

'So anyway,' he said, shaking himself out of a little melancholy, 'that was how I met the beautiful Heather. I asked her out when I picked up the file on the dead boy. Lucky, eh?'

He omitted to say what an absolute bastard he had been to her during their first three-month relationship.

The call came through to them a couple of hours later.

When they met the search officers back at their car – Officer Reali was sitting on a low wall, sweating profusely with both the heat and the exertion of actually leaving the office and doing something remotely strenuous – like walking.

He spoke excitedly to Mario, who turned to Bryn: 'I think we have a hit. A neighbour identified him as Giancarlo Saccento.' He smiled as did Bryn who nodded to Reali who seemed very pleased with himself.

Reali gave Mario the address and directions to the house of the witnesses but made no move to go with them. To Bryn he looked like a heart attack waiting to happen. They decided to leave their car and walk the mile to the witness's house.

Bryn stood at the gate of the small cottage and admired

the view of the bay. He could even see the summit of Mount Etna. 'Nice place.' He looked at Mario who just nodded. He was still in a poor mood so Bryn took the lead. The door was answered by an elderly lady – Mario introduced them and they were asked inside, where an old man sat, smoking a long thin pipe. Mario showed the old couple the photograph and it was clear that they knew the man.

'*Ispettore – Lui era il vicino di casa E Vivera con sua moglie Carlotta, ma poi tutto di un tratto dono scomparsi. Una volta Carlotta disse a mia moglie che fra incinta ma vaeva paura di dirlo al marito.*' It was the old man who spoke.

Mario translated, 'He lived next door with his wife, Carlotta, but they left very suddenly. Carlotta had told my wife she was pregnant and was worried what her husband would say.'

'How long ago?' Bryn asked and Mario translated for the old man.

'*Quanto tempo fa?*' said the old man.

'About twenty years,' said Mario.

Bryn nodded his thanks to the old man, who just stared at Bryn suspiciously. As he looked around the room Bryn saw why – there above the mantelpiece was a small, faded photograph of *Il Duce* himself.

'There are still many fascists here in Italy, especially in the south – I think they are awaiting the Second Coming.' He started to laugh. Once outside Bryn stood again and looked at the view of the bay – he thought that this was a strange, beautiful country, full of contradictions, friendly people like Mario, fascists, Mafia, the very rich and the very poor and at least one mass-murdering war criminal leaving a trail of bodies behind him – then he thought about Peter Sutcliffe, the

Yorkshire Ripper, who over a period of something like six years had murdered thirteen women. He suddenly realised that there was no real difference to Britain or perhaps any other country in the world come to that.

They knocked next door and it was answered by a young woman, a young child on her hip, her olive-skinned face definitely once beautiful but now care-worn. She appeared very nervous once Mario had identified themselves. She invited the officers in. Once again Bryn felt like a spare part as they babbled away in Italian, with the lady becoming more agitated as the conversation went on. She picked up an ancient-looking telephone and started dialling.

'Calling her husband at work,' Mario whispered. Bryn just nodded – what else had he expected? Certainly nothing straightforward, not in this case any way.

As they sat and waited for the husband's arrival Bryn looked around the room – it was exactly as he had seen in old movies – an old, battered wooden table with some flowers in a vase, four chairs, each a different style, an equally old wooden dresser in the corner with what was obviously the 'best china' and several old sepia photographs of sturdy folks in their best suits, mixed in with several religious photographs and icons. They were not offered a drink. Bryn wondered why they were, what he termed 'anti-police'. What did they have to hide? Were they part of the Mafia perhaps? He shuddered at the thought.

Signore Ragusa arrived, eventually, and reluctantly allowed the two officers to look around the rest of his small, sparsely furnished house. He was surprised to hear them knocking on the walls and stamping on the floor. All the walls were solid, but in the kitchen, there were signs that the floorboards had been taken up and replaced. They called to Mr Ragusa who confirmed to Mario that he had never been under the floorboards in the five years he had lived at the house. Bryn looked at Mario – they knew they had no option but to go down there and check it out. They took Mr Ragusa to one side and explained their suspicion quietly, trying not to alarm him, or indeed his wife, unduly. He sent his wife to a neighbour. She seemed very glad to go. He then went out to his shed. He returned with a large bag of tools and he carefully began to remove the floorboards himself.

He was anxious to go through the small hole but Mario stopped him.

'*Questa è la mia casa.*'

Bryn understood. It was his house but...

'*Si, ma adesso e diventata scena del crime,*' Mario got in first. Yes, it might be a crime scene – Bryn couldn't tell if he hoped it was, or wasn't.

It was with great reluctance that he stepped aside. Bryn went down first, followed by Mario, using the torch Mr Ragusa had given them. They easily found Carlotta, or at least those parts of her that hadn't been eaten by rats and ants. She was wrapped in an old tarpaulin and placed against the back wall of the house.

Bryn sat outside in the warm evening sunshine as the forensic team, such as it was, went to work. How he fucking hated Giuseppe Salvino – but all he could do was follow him, and hopefully keep finding his long-dead victims until he could catch up with him. He prayed for the bastard to still be alive to face the consequences for all he had done. He wished Italy still had the death penalty but the people too, just like in Britain, had become too liberal and abolished it some time ago. He realised that this would have been a whole lot easier if they had the last diary – but the Salvino family would have ensured that that was well out of his grasp by now, so he sat on that low wall, enjoying the dying sun on his face, looking out over the bay. What a beautiful spot, he thought. He was beginning to love Italy.

'She was mostly just bones. The damage to the ribs suggests that she was stabbed twice in the chest. There was no knife found and the initial examination says she was pregnant.' Mario was pale and clearly as fatigued as Bryn. 'The neighbours remembered that Signore Giancarlo Saccento worked as a tour guide down at the old amphitheatre – shall we take a look as there is nothing we can do here?'

'Sure, but didn't they miss them when they suddenly disappeared?'

'This is Sicily, my friend. People have a habit of disappearing here, and neighbours know better than to ask questions.' Mario's face was deathly serious so Bryn left the subject there.

He needed something to take his mind off the carnage he was facing every day in this beautiful part of the world.

They left the house and began to walk down the hill towards the town. Both men could hear the cries of Mrs Ragusa, but they paid it no attention – for their minds were only concerned with the dead that Giuseppe Salvino left behind – the living could take care of themselves.

They spent a couple of hours viewing the sights of the town and when they saw an ancient monument they went and spoke to a couple of tour guides but unfortunately, they were mostly young men, far too young to have known Giancarlo Saccento all those years ago.

That evening – alone, in the quiet of his hotel room, Bryn added Carlotta's details to his growing list of the dead:

VICTIMS

Name	Location	Date	Name
Jennifer Salvino	*Quayside*	*1952*	*Giuseppe Salvino*
Lucia Salvino	*Quayside*	*1952*	" "
Samuel Armstrong	*Bologna*	*1957*	" "
Edwina Armstrong	*Bologna*	*1957*	" "
Matilda Calvelli	*Padova*	*1958*	*Giovanni Salatzzo*
Carlotta Saccento	*Taormina*	*1965*	*Giancarlo Saccento*
Ambra Tomaselli	*Palma*	*1975*	*Giovanni Salvati*

There were a lot of time gaps still to be filled in and he dreaded how many more names he would have to add.

He put the list away and called Heather for he really needed to hear her voice.

CHAPTER TWENTY-ONE

Monday 4 May 1970 14.40 hrs

Giuseppe called his brother to say he was leaving Florence and needed more money; Guido could tell from his voice why. He had hoped that his younger brother had settled down, for this was the longest Giuseppe had stayed in one place for nearly twenty years; and the reason – he had kept himself to himself and avoided women at all costs.

Using the name Goffrado Sanci and claiming to be from Bari, Giuseppe had found employment as a tour guide around the city – he had used his passion for Renaissance history and the knowledge of architecture he had gained amongst the many ruins of Taormina to secure the appointment. It was a job he thoroughly enjoyed and when he returned to his small attic apartment each evening, he felt a fulfilment he hadn't experienced for a long time. His English too was improving again but, whereas in Britain he endeavoured to rid himself of the accent, here it seemed to make him more interesting to the tourists.

Then six months ago he had met someone, a tourist from Birmingham, who he fell for, and she for him. She would be going back home soon so there was no chance of a long-term relationship. They met each evening in a small intimate tavern on the banks of the river Arno after he had finished work and, on his days off, he would take her to the Galleria dell'Accademia, the Duoma and Baptistry and the Uffizi – she thought him to be so knowledgeable and, despite her age, she swooned like a schoolgirl as she listened to his sexy accent. He would take her on long walks around the Piazza della Signoria and point out the many interesting features. She was captivated.

Over those ten days they became inseparable. Her name was Hilda Bradshaw. She was several years older than him. She told him she was a school teacher, but in reality, she was a nursery classroom attendant at a primary school in Halesowen, a Birmingham suburb. Their time together was over too quickly. He had mixed emotions as Goffrado saw her off from her hotel. He made his way back to his flat and convinced himself that he was pleased he hadn't taken the stupid step of asking her to stay.

Just after nine that night there was a knock on his apartment door – he opened it and in rushed Hilda – 'I have been thinking Goffrado,' she said as she held him in her arms, she not witnessing the look of absolute dread on his face, 'there is nothing for me back in Birmingham so I have decided to stay in Italy with you – what do you think, my darling?'

He knew it was a mistake but he let her stay and for the next couple of months things were fine until he came home one evening and saw Hilda standing on the small balcony of the apartment. He could see that she had been crying.

As he approached her, she backed away from him: 'Why didn't you tell me you were married?' She was holding a picture of him and Carlotta that had been taken on their wedding day. He could see the bay and the beautiful Mediterranean in the background – how he missed that view.

'Where did you get that?' He knew full well but wanted to hear her say it.

'I was cleaning our bedroom and I found the old suitcase at the back of the cupboard. Do you collect wives? You seem to have been married a few times, Giuseppe. That is your real name is it not, Giuseppe Salvino – it was on the British marriage licence. When were you going to tell me? Are you divorced; because I didn't find any divorce papers?'

It was clear she had spent some time rummaging through his private things, things he couldn't bring himself to dispose of, though he knew all along he should have done. The more she talked, the more he knew she was signing her own death warrant. It was happening again – he asked himself, 'When will I learn?'

Then suddenly it all became clear and calm – he realised he was having what he had heard called nirvana.

He walked over to her, held out his arms and he smiled disarmingly, and she relaxed, she had never seen him angry and she was glad that his rage was short-lived. He smiled and moved lovingly towards him – she wanted to make it up to him – she was sorry – she shouldn't have pried; after all what did it matter – they were together. He was hers, and that's all that mattered. In one rapid movement he grabbed her around the throat, choking off all of her air supply – she tried to scream but nothing would come out. She tried to fight but he was too strong. She remembered crashing to the floor with him on top of her, knocking what was left of her wind out of her body; she looked into his eyes — once so loving – now cold and emotionless, then blackness.

Giuseppe kept his hands around her throat much longer

than was really necessary. When he was satisfied she was dead, he stood up and looked at her lying there. 'Why did you have to come back? If you had gone home, you would still be alive. *Lei la femmina stupida.*' He felt sorry for her, then thought about her snooping into his private things and he began to get angry again.

It wasn't long before he was sitting on the railway platform – all his possessions in his suitcase – all that is, except all that old paperwork – very reluctantly he had thrown it into the river, in very tiny pieces.

Tuesday 1 July 1986 09.35 hrs

The two policemen sat drinking coffee, having eaten a very satisfying breakfast. Bryn studied the telex that Mario had given him.

'According to this, I must now be home by the 10th – I am required to give evidence in Crown Court in a murder case where the murderer is an ex-colleague, so we have only nine days left to solve this.' He smiled at Mario; he would be very sad to leave this beautiful country.

'Wow, my friend and colleague – you must tell me about it on our next adventure.'

Bryn smiled, 'Where shall we go to dig up a dead woman now?' He tried to lighten the mood but Mario looked at him over the rim of his coffee cup.

'Roma,' he said looking at the list of places Giuseppe had been, according to his brother's diary – Bryn was looking forward to going there.

It was a very short flight that afternoon into Roma

International airport, and once on the plane Mario was eager to hear about the murder involving Bryn's friend.

'I remember it was 23.47. It was a call from Tif. He was an officer I had known all his service, but never worked with. He had a little less service than me and had been promoted to sergeant about six months earlier. He was known as Tif, which were his initials, Terrance Ian Foulkes.'

'His telephone call said, "Bryn, thank God it's someone I know. My wife's gone missing."'

Bryn continued the story. Bryn knew his wife, Camilla, who was Latino and had that very volatile Latin temperament. He briefly recalled the argument they had had at a police Christmas dinner a few years earlier; Bryn had intervened and she had nearly hit him too.

'What's happened?' he asked, putting down the sandwich he got one of the uniforms to pick up for him as he hadn't eaten since breakfast and was starving hungry.

'We had a blazing row earlier this evening, over nothing really. I have checked with everyone I know. I can't locate her. I am so worried about her.'

'Does she normally storm out after an argument?' asked Bryn, who was continuing to make notes on his pad.

'No, she normally just goes to the bedroom and sulks for a while, then snaps out of it.'

'What time did she leave?'

'About eight, maybe eight fifteen.'

'How did she leave?'

'She took the car. I tried to stop her but there was no talking to her at all. She just grabbed the keys and ran out.'

'Where are the kids?'

'In bed.'

For a moment that struck Bryn as strange. He knew Camilla was obsessive about her children, but he made a brief note on his pad and let it pass.

'Get the kettle on, I'll come over. I'll be there in about fifteen minutes.' Bryn was now wishing he had left for home ten minutes ago. He had always hated domestic disputes, especially ones involving people he knew.

He walked into the control room and told them where he was going, just as the station officer was sending a police car to a serious road traffic accident.

Once again he thought, thank God I don't have to deal with them anymore, as he went out to the plain CID car. He drove out of the station yard. It started raining very heavily. He cursed as he didn't have a coat with him.

On route to Tif's house he heard the banter on his police radio. The officers had reached the accident; there was only one vehicle involved. From the conversation it appeared that the vehicle had left the road on a notoriously bad bend and travelled down the bank. He knew that piece of road well and this wasn't the first car to do this. He then heard the station officer relay the name of the owner of the vehicle to the officers at the scene, Terrence Ian Foulkes. Bryn changed direction and went to the scene of the accident.

On his arrival the rain was still very heavy. He realised he was going to get soaked. Sure enough, he could see that the car had left the road on a very bad bend and gone down the steep bank and hit a tree at the bottom, near the river. The person reporting the find was a fisherman on his way home, who Bryn saw sheltering under a tree.

'There is no one in the car,' said one of the uniformed lads, 'but we can't see too much down there.'

Bryn called the station on his radio and asked for some more help at the scene. He took a yellow reflective jacket from one of the police cars as some protection against the rain and then joined the others officers in making only a cursory search as it was pitch black.

'And get them to bring some big lights with them and get my coat from my office. Also call Tif and tell him I got delayed, but don't mention the accident yet.' He put the radio back in his pocket.

When the extra officers arrived and the area was better lit, they made their search. It was Stefan who found the body at the water's edge. He called Bryn.

It was Camilla.

He checked for a pulse. She was dead, and by the look of her, had been so for some time. She had severe injuries to her head both at the top and rear. Bryn returned to the car. He looked inside and although the windscreen was smashed there were no traces of any blood. The first officers on the scene confirmed that when they arrived the doors of the vehicle were closed. The fisherman too confirmed this.

Something didn't make sense. This 'scene' was just wrong to Bryn's experienced eyes.

Bryn was dispatched to tell Tif of the accident by the night duty inspector. He had mixed feelings about this; glad to be getting out of the pouring rain, but not sure how to handle this. This whole thing didn't feel right at all.

He drove to Tif's house which was on a new estate about three miles from the accident scene.

He opened the door as Bryn was hurried down the path, as the rain seemed to be getting heavier.

'Any news?' he asked.

Bryn entered the house and was directed into the sitting room. He told Tif to sit down.

'I prefer to stand,' he said nervously.

'We have found her, mate. She's dead.'

Bryn couldn't think of any way to tell him other than the direct approach. That was how he would want to receive such news.

'How?' asked Tif.

Bryn quickly played his friendship card.

'Come on, Tif. What the hell happened?' he asked, walking over to him and placing his hand on his friend's shoulder.

'What do you mean?' Tif couldn't look Bryn in the eyes. He knew he had supposed right.

'Look mate. The troops are going to be beating down your door any minute. I have seen Camilla and it doesn't add up. For Christ's sake, tell me what the hell happened tonight. I know she didn't die in a car accident.'

Tif looked down at the floor, and then he very slowly turned his face towards Bryn.

'I hit her with my staff, Bryn. I didn't mean to kill her, just frighten her. She was really having a go tonight. You know how she can get. Remember that Christmas do? I just lost my temper. I just couldn't take any more. I didn't mean to kill her, Bryn, honest I didn't. Christ, what am I going to tell the kids?'

This all came rushing out of his mouth like a torrent.

'Why did you have your truncheon in your hand, at home?' asked Bryn, not believing a word of it. He had interviewed too many offenders to believe this story.

'I always keep a truncheon in my riot gear bag that I keep in the garage,' he replied – his head in his hands.

'Where did this happen?'

'In the kitchen,' replied Tif. 'Do you want to see? I have cleaned up a bit though.'

'Not just now, mate,' he said, wanting to keep the crime scene as uncontaminated as possible.

Bryn arrested him and all he said was, 'I'll make you that tea you wanted.'

At the police station, when formally interviewed, Tif went back on all he had said to Bryn, saying that he had made it all up just to make himself look good.

The forensic specialists went to work and proved that the injury was consistent with a blow from an object similar to a truncheon, blood was found in the kitchen, and a passing motorist identified Tif as being the man he had seen walking away from the scene of the accident earlier that evening.

'It also came to light that Tif had an eighteen-year-old girlfriend, the family babysitter, who he was leaving Camilla for, a thing that her Catholic upbringing would certainly not allow.'

'That is some story – and this is in court next week?' Mario asked. He had been engrossed in the story.

'Yep – he is pleading not guilty – saying I made up everything,' he laughed and, picking up the in-flight magazine to indicate that the story was over, he said, 'But then again he isn't the first and he sure won't be the last.'

A short drive in the waiting *Carabinieri* car along the via Concordia saw them at the Holiday Inn. They checked in – then made their way to *Carabinieri* headquarters to brief the very senior officers on their progress so far. He could tell Mario was excited for he had never been to his headquarters before and it was clear he was relishing the prospect.

To Bryn's surprise they all seemed happy with the results of the enquiry, despite the fact they had not yet made a bloody arrest – and even though all they had managed to find so far were lots of decayed bodies.

They sat in a nicely appointed office on the second floor and waited for a secretary to being in the files on missing women in 1960 and when they arrived it amounted to seventy-six unsolved murders of women. 'Well, we did have the Olympic Games that year,' Mario said, looking apologetically at his friend.

It took them all the following day to go through the files, placing pins in the map of Rome to indicate the locations of the crime, and a big red pin showing the location of the post office where Giuseppe collected his money.

They discarded the files where the body was found outside, or where two or more, had died – that left fifty-five, but only twenty-two of those were located anywhere near the post office. Both detectives studied the files until their eyes began to go blurred.

'Nothing – It could be any, or none.' Bryn picked up the folder relating to a prostitute smothered in her flat by someone thought to be her pimp who was never seen again, or this one, an elderly lady stabbed and put down to a botched burglary. None were stabbed twice or had their throats cut.

'You seem to conveniently pigeonhole all your unsolved murders – pimp, botched burglary, this one jealous lover.' Bryn saw the disapproving look on Mario's face, 'Sorry,' he said, 'I'm just tired.'

Mario smiled but said nothing – Bryn hoped he hadn't upset his friend too much with his derogatory comments about their way of doing things here in Italy – not that it was that much different in Britain.

'Okay, there is nothing that is clearly our Giuseppe here – where to next, Turin or Florence– your choice?' Bryn was pleased that Mario snapped out of his reverie very quickly.

'Turin,' said Bryn, 'I have always wanted to visit that city ever since I saw *The Italian Job* and besides, I need more time in Florence – I want to visit the Uffizi.'

'What is it with you British and the Uffizi Galleria? It is one of the worst museums I have ever been to.'

'You're only supposed to blow the bloody doors off,' Bryn said in a very poor cockney accent.

Mario just shook his head and said 'It must lose something in the translation.'

Mario went to tell the *Carabinieri* office in Turin to expect them. While he was gone, Bryn looked again at the file on the prostitute named Genevieve, who was now buried, unmourned in some pauper's grave; no one knew her last name. He looked at the description of the pimp; it could match Giuseppe or indeed anybody else too. Perhaps he was just getting paranoid.

Bryn smiled sadly at Mario when he returned and then replaced the yellowing file on the top of the pile. He had arranged for the latest flight he could manage, just to give Bryn some time to wander around his capital city.

They put the files in a neat pile ready for the clerks to put them back into storage – this time probably forever, and then they left. They had a lovely meal close to the Colossseum. Once again, their conversation kept away from anything to do with Giuseppe Salvino and his victims, but kept to the subject close to a policeman's heart –women, for Roma abounded with beautiful women.

CHAPTER TWENTY-TWO

Friday 8 May 1970 21.20 hrs

At long last he arrived at Parma's railway station, for he had had to wait a long time for the money to arrive from Guido. He knew his brother was feeling the strain so he promised himself he would live quietly here. He had thought about moving to another country, but that too had its problems.

He didn't want to walk too far so he stayed at a hotel on the viale Bottego overlooking the river, a stone's throw from the railway station. He signed the register, Giovanni Salvati from Padova and told the landlady that he was a man of independent means and was taking some time to see this great country. She seemed impressed by his story and gave him her best room, one overlooking the river.

It took a couple of weeks but, through Guido's Masonic connections, Giovanni got a job as a clerk to a small firm of lawyers in the town. He left his hotel and rented a small furnished apartment on via Mazzini in the city centre, near the Piazzo Garibaldi. Giuseppe Garibaldi, that old Italian revolutionary patriot was something of a hero to Giuseppe Salvino.

It felt good being back in the law again and his aged employer, Signore Carlo Odella, had also been an officer during the war and had served in the army in North Africa. He had been lucky and avoided capture and later had been on the Greek Island of Kefalonia with the 33rd Acqui Infantry Division, when in September 1943, the Germans massacred almost his entire regiment following the Italian armistice – he had been hidden in the hills by a family of Greeks and had made his way back to Italy, along with several others in a small fishing boat. It was a story that fascinated and angered Giovanni and the two men soon quickly became firm friends and any misgivings Signore Odella had had about his new employee were soon dispelled, for not only did he come highly recommended by some senior figures in his lodge but he was also very good at his job, if not quite up to date with his legal knowledge – but he was sure that would come with time.

Each Friday evening Giovanni would spend a couple of hours away from the thoughts that kept troubling him by visiting the cinema. It was after about three months that he started to notice a very well-dressed lady who was also always on her own – she didn't seem to notice him, and she always sat in the front row and to the right of the stalls. He preferred the back on the ground floor. He always felt safer in the darkness.

It took him a couple of weeks to pluck up the courage to engineer a meeting but the evening he did, she didn't arrive, nor for the next two weeks; then to his joy she reappeared and went and sat in her usual place – Giovanni followed her in and sat a couple of seats away. During the interval he struck up a conversation with her about the film and he found that she too loved western films and she laughed when she coyly admitted that she had a crush on Robert Redford, so *Butch Cassidy and the Sundance Kid* was perfect – at first, she seemed reluctant to get involved in further conversation but eventually she relaxed with him. He noticed she had the most amazing smile – he was captivated. After the film he bid her a goodnight and they went their separate ways.

The following week he sat a little further away, acknowledged her as she took her seat, but ensured they left at the same time. In the foyer she stopped to put on her raincoat and he again initiated a conversation – this time about the weather and to his surprise she seemed in no hurry to leave and not just because it was raining heavily. He asked her if she would like to get something to eat and she accepted. After the meal he walked her home – he liked her but it always ended in tragedy so he tried playing it safe. He kissed her on the cheek and walked away. He wasn't to know that playing it safe only made him more desirable in her eyes. He respected her – she liked that.

The following week they met at the cinema and sat next to each other and later ate at the same restaurant. He asked her back to his apartment and she accepted. That night they spent the together and despite his better judgement he became smitten.

A little over a month later Giovanni, aged 58 years, and Ambra Tomaselli, aged 44 years, a school teacher, were married at Chiesa Cattolica Parrocchiale di Ognissanti, a small church across the river on Strada Nino Bixio. It was a poorly attended affair with their only two witnesses being Signore Carlo Odella and Ambra's older sister, Carla Tomaselli – who didn't seem at all happy with the marriage and told Giovanni so, in no uncertain terms, when they were alone together a couple of days before the service. She had also warned her sister about him, for she had the sneaking suspicion that he wasn't what he professed and she sensed a danger about this that she couldn't quite put her finger on but she could feel it and she vowed to watch him – but her younger sister took no notice and went ahead and married him anyway.

Ambra moved into the small apartment and settled down to her domestic life; she still continued to teach but at a school a lot closer to her home.

Giovanni had mentioned that he had a son, Leonardo, who he had been forced, for various reasons far too complicated to explain, to let live with his rich brother. He conveniently never mentioned where that was. He never really mentioned much about his past but she shrugged that off – it didn't matter. All that mattered to her was their future together.

Ambra loved children but as a result of a childhood injury, when she was knocked down by a car, she was medically unable to have any of her own. Giovanni professed to be upset but secretly was relieved. He never again wanted to go through what he had done in Taormina.

In the third year of their marriage, Ambra waltzed into the kitchen on his birthday – it wasn't really, it was just a date he had plucked out of the air when she had asked – and she was smiling so brightly. He was surprised that his present wasn't on the breakfast table, as it had been the last two birthdays.

'I have a surprise for you,' she said and she was positively beaming.

'Oh – what's that?'

'We will be having a visitor on Saturday who will be staying a while.'

'And who's that?' He had a terrible feeling of foreboding. He hated any sort of surprise, for he believed nothing good ever came from one.

'Your son, Leonardo, of course – he will be here on Saturday.' She hugged him lovingly as she said it.

'Leonardo – how did...?' he stopped himself saying anything else.

'I found his address on some old papers in your wallet so I wrote to your brother, Guido, and he wrote back with a telephone number and I asked him if Leonardo could come and stay and he said yes, providing you agreed. He seems such a nice man.'

He cursed himself – he thought he had disposed of everything that tied him to his old life back in Bologna.

'He is – I must get to work – we will talk about it tonight.' He had to get out – away from this stupid woman. He needed time to think.

'You are pleased, aren't you?' She was staring at him; he saw the look of disappointment on her face.

'I am very pleased – it was just a bit of a shock, that's all – who have you told about this?'

'No one – no one at all.' She hoped she had covered the lie as she had told her sister some of the story.

'I am very pleased – I can't wait to see him. We will talk about it tonight. We are going out for a meal to celebrate and discuss how to make his room nice for his stay.'

Ambra relaxed and started to smile again as she cleared away the breakfast things. She heard Giovanni put on his coat and went to the window and smiled as she watched him go through the gate. She knew everything would be alright for she saw him turn and wave to her when he closed the garden gate and set off down the hill to work.

She sat at the kitchen table as it would be ten minutes yet

before she had to leave for school. She thought about what she had done. He was pleased – she thought she saw him smiling as he closed the gate.

Giovanni was surprised and more than a little disappointed that he was not alone when he arrived at the office. Usually, he was the first in and had at least a quarter of an hour before the others arrived – but not today of all days. He cursed under his breath as he settled at his desk by the window.

It wasn't until past eleven that he had the opportunity to be alone and call Guido on his private number.

'What the fuck are you playing at, telling her Leonardo could come?' he shouted down the phone. He was so angry the words were drying in his throat. Don't you realise what I will have to do, because of what you have done? he thought, but couldn't say to his older brother.

He heard Guido take a sharp intake of breath and he was silent for a moment. 'What else was I supposed to do? She caught me by surprise when her letter arrived. I must have sounded stupid when she first called and mentioned your name – then I realised...'

'Does Leonardo know about this?' Giuseppe was starting to calm down – his voice became quieter.

'Of course not – what do you think I am? I would protect that boy with my life.'

Giuseppe knew that he would, for he was more Guido's son than his now. 'You have put me in a difficult spot,' Giuseppe whispered.

Guido knew the truth of it – he had put Ambra in a difficult spot too – one that she was unlikely to survive. Guido put down the phone and held his head in his hands – he felt trapped. He started to cry. He called a number in Bologna – he needed Father Colosomo's advice. He had been his priest since childhood and he was a fellow Mason – it was safe to talk to him.

Giuseppe put the phone down and tried to think what to do – he knew there was only one sure way out of this – he regretted it for he really liked her but she knew too much now – she had to go.

At a little after 5 p.m. he packed up his desk, secretly taking all of his personal things, for he knew he would not be back, then left the office. He felt very gloomy knowing what he had to do tonight. He got home before Ambra and tried to calm himself. He poured himself a glass of wine and sharpened the knife to a razor-sharp edge. He left it hidden but easily accessible. He poured another large glass of wine and waited for her return. He looked at his hand – it was shaking – he realised that for the first time he was having a reaction to all this killing. I am human after all, he thought.

Twenty minutes later Ambra came in – she was very excited. She ran over to her husband and kissed him. They immediately went into the bedroom and made love. He was rougher than usual, and hurt her several times but she put that down to him being excited about the news and she relaxed.

Giovanni had decided to use the tried and tested method of dispatching his wife. He got up from the bed and went into the kitchen to make the coffee – he called to Ambra and waited behind the door, towel in hand to stem the blood. Ambra, still naked, bustled into the room – he was behind her in a flash and with one slash he cut her throat almost to her spine. He certainly knew how to get a sharp edge on a knife. He quickly wrapped the towel around her and laid her dead body gently on the floor. He placed the body in the tin bath he brought in from the outside toilet. It needed to drain. Then he returned to bed. He already knew where her body was to be put.

The following day, with his wife still in the kitchen, he started on the wall. Before nailing on the plasterboard, he dragged her now stiff body and squeezed her inside. Once everything was back in the cupboard, it concealed it well – for he was getting a bit of an expert on this type of construction.

During the night he left the apartment, carrying just one case which he deposited in the left luggage office at the railway station and awaited the opening of the bank at 10 a.m. He called his employer from the telephone kiosk opposite a small cafe, and professed to be sick.

By 11.30 a.m. he was on the first available train that happened to be heading north. He had cleaned out Ambra's bank account and had the considerable amount of money stuffed in the suitcase on the luggage rack above him.

In Milan he walked to the nearest bank and deposited the money in an account in the name of Gianpaolo Scachetti. Once the bank transaction was completed by a very beautiful and extremely helpful cashier, and for the first time since yesterday morning, he started to feel calm. He hurriedly left the bank and seeing the cafe open he dashed across the road. He didn't see the Fiat truck. The sound of the impact was heard inside the bank.

He was taken to hospital. The doctor's initial reaction was that he wouldn't survive, not with such terrible head injuries. He remained in a coma for some considerable time – his life hanging by a thread.

Thursday 3 July 1986 09.10 hrs

'I wonder where Salvino was between 1973 and 1976?' Bryn asked, his lips covered in cream from a delicious cappuccino, a drink to Mario's way of thinking, that only a tourist would be seen drinking. It was proving difficult to educate this man in their ways and he liked working with Bryn but he saw a dark side to him – a side he would hate to experience first-hand. He had seen him secretly taking the pills but said nothing – he trusted his friend enough to know that if he wanted to tell him he would so he settled for that.

Bryn showed Mario his now famous list that he had been working on:

In prison

In hospital (Injured/ill)

Committed to a mental institution

Lost his memory

Hidden at his family home or by his family

In the army (French Foreign Legion) or other armed services

Returned to Britain

Left Italy for another country

'Can you think of anything I've missed?' Bryn asked as Mario scanned the list.

'No. You seem to have everything – I will ask if we can conduct enquiries to see what we come up with – looking for someone with the initials 'GS'.'

They were sitting in another well-appointed office, this time in the Turin *Carabinieri* office. They must have the same decorator, Bryn thought as he studied the same pictures on the walls. They were received like dignitaries for their reputation and the fact that the General in Rome was actively engaged in helping them as much as possible had preceded them.

While they waited Mario produced one of the diaries from his briefcase. 'I have been re-reading the entries and there is an entry here that I missed though, it was written on the 8th May 1973,' said Mario somewhat apologetically. He was holding open one of Guido's diaries: '*Nessun contatto – Mancare.*'

'What does that mean?' Bryn asked. He felt like all the leads had now run out and they were clutching at straws.

'No contact – missing. Even Guido didn't know where he was. So, we can scratch stuff relating to the family off my list.' He put a line through his writings with a little too much force – he ripped the page.

'And what date was the last payment? he asked, smoothing the torn page.

'27th April 1973.'

'What did it say at the time of the first payment after the break?'

'*Grazie a dio e'li. Ma non ha detto dove.*' – Thank God he's there – wouldn't say where he had been'.'

'And when was that?'

'18th April 1976.'

'Almost three years' gap. Secretive fellow, our Giuseppe – or ashamed to tell his brother perhaps. Lord knows why when he knew everything else – so what would he be ashamed of?'

'That gives us prison or mental home. There is a stigma to both here in Italy,' Mario said.

Just then two very pretty female clerks came in carrying with them the unsolved murder files for 1976–1980 in Turin, involving women victims – all sixty-two of them. They smiled at the two policemen.

'*Se c'è nient'altro possiamo fare per lei, niente a tutto chiama appena,*' the one with the big breasts said, looking at Bryn to whom she handed a piece of paper with a telephone number written on. Then they left.

'What did she say?'

'Anything we need, we just have to ask – I just might do that.' He took the piece of paper from Bryn, kissed it, and put it in his pocket.

Bryn smiled – he felt he needed a little light relief and the one with the big tits was just the sort of person who he would want to fulfil that wish. He looked at the files on the desk and sighed – he was a thief-taker, not a bloody admin clerk, but he picked up the top file and looked at the address. So he excused himself and headed for the toilet – Bryn realised his friend knew where he was going and to what purpose. He also knew he would say nothing about it.

I like working with this man, he thought, as he swallowed more pills.

There was something they needed right now. Mario asked for a large map of the city, which someone went out and bought and they pinned up. He then marked the post office on via Montebello where the money was paid in. They then set about the task of marking where the murders had taken place – this time in addition to multiple murders and those committed outside. They excluded any as a result of firearms and any where forcible sexual assault was involved. That brought the number down to forty-two.

'Ah – the ultimate answer to the ultimate question in life, the universe and everything,' he smiled at Mario who looked back, confusion written all over his face. 'Forty-two? Douglas Adams? The book – *The Hitchhiker's Guide to the Galaxy*? Arthur Dent? Zaphod Beeblebrox? No?'

'What? You English make no sense.'

'It's a... never mind.' Bryn picked up the first file. 'And I'm Welsh by the way.'

It took just over three hours to plot the forty-two murder sites. Twelve were located in the vicinity of the post office mentioned in Guido's diary; most of the others were dotted around the poorer end of town.

'We just have to work back from the post office – I'll go and ask for some more help.'

He returned thirty minutes later – 'We will have twenty-four officers tomorrow morning at 8 a.m. Until then we are free men – let's go and eat.'

Tomorrow? Another day wasted and another day closer to going home without a result. This thought depressed him – he went into the rest room before leaving and popped some more anti-depressants. He hoped they would work on him quickly as he felt his mood going into a rapid decline and his supply of pills was dangerously low. He had been taking these pills for some time now in ever-increasing amounts; he shuddered to think what would happen should he fail to take them.

It was gone six o'clock when they walked into a small intimate restaurant in the back streets. 'How did you get know about this place? I thought you said you have never been here before,' Bryn asked as they sat down in a booth at the rear of the dining area.

'It was highly recommended to me today,' Mario had a strange smile on his face. Bryn thought no more about it until ten minutes later when he saw the two female clerks walk in. Mario waved and they walked towards them.

'Remember what I said – what happens in Italy stays in Italy – my friend,' he whispered this as they stood up to greet their visitors.

Magda and Helena proved to be excellent company, made easier for Bryn by the fact that they both spoke passable English. And it was clear that they had decided how the men were to be divided. By the end of a sumptuous meal and a couple of bottles of the local red wine, Helena was all over Mario like a rash and he didn't seem to be resisting too much. Magda was more reserved and politely quizzed Bryn about England.

It was well past eleven by the time they left the restaurant. They were all invited back to Helena's flat on the outskirts of the town. It was obvious to all that Mario was very drunk. Bryn was pleased to see his friend thoroughly enjoying himself. They both needed to relax – it had been a trying couple of weeks.

Once in the flat, Helena and Mario excused themselves and disappeared into the bedroom while Bryn and Magda sat on the couch listening to music, but it wasn't long before they were kissing and once that happened Bryn just felt like a passenger as she took total control and within half an hour, he was a spent force, lying naked on the couch; the wine, sex and warmth of her body lulling him to sleep. He woke a couple of hours later. He was freezing and he quickly realised that he was alone. Magda had left. He got dressed, went downstairs, hailed a lone passing taxi and was in his bed in the hotel in thirty minutes.

He was awakened a little after seven by knocking on his door – he opened it to see Mario standing there. He looked terrible but the smile he had on his face, despite the increasingly difficult hunt for Giuseppe Salvino, would be difficult to remove.

Over breakfast in the hotel dining room Bryn asked if he knew what had happened to Magda. 'She wasn't able to stay all night. I think she had to go home to her husband.' Mario laughed when he saw the startled look Bryn's face, 'Oh *spiacente* – I am sorry, my friend, I thought you knew.'

Fucking hell, he thought, that was all it needed for that information to get back home. He finished his breakfast, the silence between them only broken by the occasional annoying Italian chuckle.

By 8a.m. in the exquisite briefing room the large group of very smartly turned-out uniformed officers were assembled. Mario addressed them and copies of Giuseppe's photograph were handed out. They were to ask in the vicinity of every murder if any neighbour remembered this man or remembered a neighbour who disappeared quickly, or had the initials 'GS'. They should work backwards from the latest murder and start with the murders closest to the post office and work outwards. They left the room in an orderly and very quiet fashion – it was then that Bryn remembered that this was a military organisation that policed. The last to leave was a large, muscular senior officer, who simply nodded to the two men.

'All we can do now, my friend, is sit and wait. Oh, and by the way, that big guy – that's Magda's husband.'

Shit – he's massive. With the size of him, he could kill me, Bryn thought as he watched the man strut down the corridor, his highly polished boots squeaking on the marble floor. Then another thought struck him like a thunderbolt– why use physical force? The *carabinieri* were fucking armed.

Throughout the morning Helena would come in to see Mario but there had been no sign whatsoever of Magda. Bryn wasn't sure if he was sad about that, or very much relieved.

By two o'clock both Bryn and Mario were getting antsy so they decided to take a look around the area. They were just about to leave when the phone rang. The telephone conversation made Mario even more animated that he was usually.

'*Finalmente*,' he said as he slammed down the telephone receiver. Bryn didn't need a translation – he saw what he needed on Mario's face. They grabbed their jackets and much to their relief they left the stuffy room, back on Salvino's trail: they walked down the corridor and Bryn noticed Magda sitting at a desk near to the control room – she saw him too and the shake of her head was almost unperceivable but he saw and understood so he left without a word.

The *Carabinieri* driver negotiated the afternoon traffic with consummate skill. Mario updated Bryn on the telephone conversation.

'18th September 1980 a 52-year-old woman, Dorotea Asaro,' Mario consulted his notes, 'she was found in an apartment on via Giuseppe Verdi. She had been suffocated. She'd been there a while before she was found – six months they estimate. The man who rented the flat disappeared. A neighbour thinks she recognises the picture. Dorotea had been a nurse at a local hospital.

Bryn sat back and closed his eyes – he realised he was so very tired. He woke up as the car stopped.

Via Giuseppe Verdi was a long street with beautiful architecture. The houses were big, most having been converted into apartments. They walked up the path to number 127. The door was guarded by a *carabinieri* officer who didn't even acknowledge them as they entered.

Mario spoke to the large senior officer and Bryn stood back – the less contact he had with this big guy the better – that was his way of thinking anyway.

'The murder happened in the upstairs flat. The lady on the ground floor is our possible witness – she is in a bit of a state. Do you mind if I speak to her alone?'

Bryn shook his head and went outside to get some air. He saw a small cafe across the road and went in and bought an espresso and sat in the window. He saw the big man come out and approach the cafe.

Oh fuck. He's built like a brick shithouse, he thought.

'Do you mind if I join you?' he asked after he had obtained a free coffee from the waiter – his English was not that good but understandable. It was clear he had been practising that bit.

Bryn smiled and pulled out the chair and for a couple of minutes they sipped their coffees in silence.

'I0 ho un *cugino*... a cousin in London – his is *il cameriere* in *un ristorante*.' Bryn got the gist, smiled, and nodded. He just wanted him to go away for he seemed such a nice man and here he was sitting at a table, sipping coffee with a man who, just a few short hours ago, had been fucking his wife. They sat there in an awkward silence and to Bryn's relief he saw Mario come out of the address. The uniformed officer directed him to the cafe. He was surprised to see Bryn's companion. He sat across from Bryn – their guest didn't move. The waiter brought Mario his free coffee.

Mario opened the file on Dorotea Asaro. 'Could be our man – the witness remembered his name, after a little pushing – Gilberto Solito. She remembered it because he had a name close to that of an old boyfriend she had in the 1940s. She thought the picture looked like him. She also remembered he had a very ugly... *cicatrice*,' he drew a line across his forehead.

'A scar?' Bryn was intrigued.

'*Sì*. A scar – very deep and stretching all the way across his forehead. He also had a bad leg – used a *bastone da passeggio*.' He performed some action.

'Ah – a walking stick. Could that be why he was missing for those couple of years?'

'Could be my friend – could be – and it says here that our Dorotea was just about to be fired from her job as a nurse. She was suspected of stealing drugs from the *farmacia*.'

'Would there be any way of tracking if any accident was reported to the police in March to June 1973 involving a male with the initials 'GS'?'

Mario spoke to the large man that sat between them, who hadn't said a word but whose presence worried Bryn tremendously. He was learning the language slowly but he could make no sense of their rapid Italian. To Bryn's relief the big man, whose name he discovered was Michael, got up, shook Bryn's hand, said something Bryn couldn't translate and left. He was off to start the enquiries and seemed very pleased about it. Mario turned to Bryn and started laughing – Bryn couldn't. He watched him cross the road – he did seem a really nice man.

Bryn tried to take his mind off his personal events and, in order to stop Mario continually taking the piss out of him, he turned their attention to the apartment across the road.

They walked slowly past the officer outside and went up to the top apartment. The door was already open and a middle-aged couple sat on the couch, the man cradling a very upset woman – the situation not helped for them by the fact that they were surrounded by *Carabinieri* officers. Bryn let Mario do the talking and it transpired that they had only rented the place three months before. Bryn got the feeling that they wouldn't be staying too much longer.

On their way back Bryn asked, 'Why do civilians carry on so much about death – they are so fucking squeamish about it – so what if someone died in your house. What are they going to do – haunt you?'

Mario looked at his friend. 'Perhaps the place might be haunted by those that have died violently,' he said as he pulled out into the afternoon traffic.

'That's rubbish.'

'How can you be so certain?'

'In my flat thirty years ago, the railway crossing guard killed his wife and cut her up and put her in bags all over the house then went outside, sat on the railway lines and waited for a train.'

'And you live in that place?'

'I do; and no ghosts.'

Bryn smiled; his case proved. Mario shuddered and quietly made the sign of the cross. The coldness of his British friend did worry him.

After making a quick stop back at the office, they sat in the same booth of the small cafe and ate a lovely meal. How he loved the food here in Italy! Bryn was so engrossed in conversation he didn't see Helena and Magda enter. They surprised him as Magda kissed him on the cheek.

'I am sorry about last night – you were asleep very well – I didn't want to wake you – and today I was in with my... *sovrintendente.*'

'Her supervisor,' Mario said, though he was now otherwise engaged.

Bryn stood up and took Magda by the hand and led her outside. 'You didn't tell me you were married – to a policeman too.'

'So – he is a pig. Our marriage has been over for some time.'

'Don't you think he would be upset if he found out about us? And besides, I have spent the whole day with him on this enquiry.'

'He wasn't at all *infastidito* – how you say, bothered.'

'You told him.' He saw people in the street turn and look – he hadn't realised just how loud he shouted, but Bryn was thinking of the firearm he carried.

'Michael wanted to know where I had been. He had been with his girlfriend. He was, how you say, *fresco.*' At last, an Italian word he knew.

'Cool – shit.' He almost choked as he blurted this out.

She couldn't get over just how upset he looked. There were plenty back at the office that wouldn't have cared at jot who her husband was as long as they could get between her legs. She kissed him, took his hand and with a smile led him back inside, sat him down and poured him a glass of wine. Slowly he relaxed for after all – this was Italy and he was now experiencing *la dolce vita*.

CHAPTER TWENTY-THREE

25th December 1974 01.30 hrs

Suddenly, light and sound erupted in his head. He opened his eyes but everything was blurred. He was very frightened. He closed his eyes again and tried to relax but it didn't stop the loud drumming that seemed to come from somewhere very deep inside his brain. He could hear people muttering but their voices seemed distant – it was as if he was hearing them through water. He opened his eyes again – this time very slowly. A dark shadow loomed over him. He was very afraid. He heard a woman's voice say, 'Hurry – tell the doctor Giovanni Salvati is awake.'

Over the next couple of weeks, the extent of his injuries became apparent to Giuseppe as he tried to move what he could of his wrecked body as he lay in that hospital bed. When he had first looked at himself in the mirror he started to cry as he saw what he knew to be his ruggedly handsome features ruined by a long, angry scar that ran along the whole length of his forehead. He had lost several teeth and his jaw was out of line. The headaches he got were excruciating with doses of morphine being the only relief. The most worrying thing, however, was the fact that his legs wouldn't work. The doctor said that he was sure he would, in due course, regain at least some mobility in them but Giuseppe was unsure if he would ever be able to walk again.

All in all, he was a mess. Perhaps this is God's punishment on me – not taking my life straightaway, but making me live the rest of it as a cripple. As he thought this, he again turned his face into the pillow and began to cry.

During the short periods of lesser pain, he tried to piece together his last movements. He now knew he was in the Instituto Ortopedico Gaetano Pini, a large hospital in the centre of Milan but how he ended up here he had to be told. The attending doctor told him that he was very lucky to have survived the accident, and that he had been in a coma for over eighteen months. He knew his name wasn't Giovanni Salvati, but Giuseppe Salvino, but something had told him not to correct them. He genuinely couldn't remember much about his past so it wasn't difficult to tell the authorities that he was a drifter.

By the following June he had undergone several more operations to fix his shattered body. He was now able to stand, unfortunately not without the aid of a frame, but it was a start. Walking any distance was still a way off. He had been fitted with some dentures and his jaw had been straightened so speaking and eating had become much easier. Also, his past too was returning – perhaps it was just a bad dream. Surely, he hadn't killed all those people all over Italy? He also remembered he had a family and he had received money from somewhere but for the life of him he couldn't remember who, or where. His memory was so fragmented and that frustrated him greatly.

By the following Christmas he was able to walk; not very far but enough to know he was getting better so he started to think about moving on. More of his memories were returning to him bit by bit too. He often looked at the bank deposit slip, from which the authorities had obtained his name. It was a lot of money. If only he could remember his family. It was strange that he could remember so many vile deeds he had done over the years but not that.

Against all advice Giuseppe discharged himself from hospital the following June. He could now walk okay as long as he used a stick. If what he knew of himself was true – he had been in this one place far too long. He hailed a passing taxi and made a beeline for Pazza Dela Scala in the city centre, and entered the Banka Commerciale Italiana. To his surprise, and without too much fuss – for they remembered the accident that occurred right outside – he collected his money from the account, and made his way straight to the railway station. He purchased a ticket for the first train out. It took him to Turin.

Two hours later he stepped out of Porta Nuova railway station and into Corso Vittorio Emanuele II – it struck him he had been in another place with the same name but he couldn't remember where – he still couldn't remember a lot these days except for the very bad things, they seemed to be with him always. He didn't want to be out in the sun too long for it hurt his eyes and brought on a migraine. He found a small, quiet hotel not too far from the railway station. The trip had exhausted him so he was asleep within minutes – the morphine he had stolen from the Milan hospital's medical room helped but the amount he had wouldn't last long so one of his first priorities was to find a new supply.

He sat in his hotel room night after night trying to figure out a plan of action. He found it difficult to concentrate for more than a few minutes at a time. Then it came to him. He pondered the same question over and over, who could get him morphine, and where could he meet such people?

Then it came to him. The answer was simple. He started watching the hospitals and noticed that nurses from Ospedale Gradenigo congregated at a small cafe on a Friday night. He spent three weeks every Friday at the cafe and eventually found someone that fitted the bill. He struck up a conversation with her once she had accepted a drink from him.

Her name was Dorotea Asaro. She was a fifty-three--year-old spinster, who, Giuseppe later discovered, had been a nurse for over thirty years. She was flattered by the attention for – as Giuseppe thought to himself, she was no oil painting –here was a wealthy man, who professed to have been wounded during the war and had recent surgery, taking such an interest in her. He asked if he could meet her sometime the following week and she readily agreed – the sooner the better, she thought. They met the following night, and the subsequent three nights. Giuseppe was always the gentlemen; kissing her on the cheeks as he dropped her off at her home. He thought that the slow tactic was best.

It was two weeks before he got her into bed – she told him she was worried for it had been a long time since she 'had been with a man'. He was very attentive and gentle – and she was easily hooked. It was easier than he thought – she jumped at the chance to help him get the morphine for after all she didn't want to lose him. So twice a week she would take a couple of vials from the hospital, ensuring that it was never the same store too regularly. She was delighted how grateful he was and how he showed that gratitude in the bedroom.

She begged him to move in with her but he always refused – he kept his small apartment on the outskirts of the town. He never wanted to make her another one of his victims – he realised that he needed her as much as she needed him, but for very different reasons.

The arrangement was working well – he would visit her regularly, stay the odd night, give her what she wanted then take her out for the odd meal and she ensured he had a regular supply of morphine. It was the ideal situation.

Then he was hit by the bombshell:

'I have been caught – they were watching me.' She was in tears when he entered the apartment. 'I will be fired tomorrow and I am sure the police will be there too.'

He didn't know what to say – he would have to find another source, and quickly. He felt no pity for her – just annoyance at her stupidity at getting caught and at the inconvenience it would cause him.

'Don't you care?'

He really didn't so long as he was kept out of it, but he could tell from her look that he wouldn't be.

'Well, perhaps the authorities would like to know all about Giuseppe Salvino? Yes, you talk in your sleep when you take the drug. It was laughable. You told me everything and I thought it was a joke, some kind of hallucination.' She said this to provoke a reaction – she hadn't believed what he had said. Then she saw his face change and she now knew that what she had heard was the truth – he had killed women all over Italy.

Then without another word and despite his infirmity he was on her like a flash – she didn't even have time to scream. He held her down, his hand over her mouth, his fingers pinching her nose. She tried to fight it; he pinned her arms down with his knees. She became desperate to get air into her body but, despite his age and injuries, he was too strong for her – she quickly passed into unconsciousness and once again he kept his hands there much longer than he needed and she was dead long before he got up.

He sat on the couch – this one had really taken it out of him. There would be no hiding the body behind a false wall now – he just needed to get out as soon as possible. He looked around the room to ensure he had left nothing incriminating belonging to him. He checked the rest of the apartment – nothing. He sat in the lounge with the body. He riffled through her purse and took what money he found. He remained in the flat, watching television and waited until well after midnight, when all possibility of meeting any of the neighbours had gone, and then he slipped quietly out of the small apartment, out of the building and walked slowly home.

He packed quickly and wondered where to go. In the bathroom he caught himself in the mirror. The three years he had spent in hospital and the four years here in Turin had turned him into an old man. He was pleased that he had slowly begun to remember things about his family and was surprised to learn that he had a son, Leonardo, who, his brother had informed him, had gone back to live in Britain, where he had lived for some time – he didn't remember that.

The money from his brother in Bologna had started again so he lived well. It was clear to Giuseppe that the nightmares he was having were in fact true.

Friday 4 July 1986 19.15 hrs

The two detectives were very tired as they got out of the police car outside the Salvino villa. There were several reasons for their condition – this protracted enquiry, the flight from Turin and the night of sex they had experienced in Turin with Magda and Helena. It was fantastic. Magda had come to his hotel and stayed all night but he was knackered now. Mario rang the bell. It was clear that they were purposefully being kept waiting which only increased their already foul disposition, especially Bryn's, for he had a short fuse at the best of times but when he was tired... Neither officer was in the mood to be messed about this time for they wanted that last diary and they wanted it now.

The door was eventually opened by the elderly lady herself. She moved aside without a word and they entered.

'We want that diary – and if necessary, I will remain here while Officer Fabrizzi obtains a search warrant and we will tear this place apart. Your brother has murdered many people and certainly Guido knew all about it and continued to pay him a monthly allowance right up until he died and for all we know you carried on paying, thus becoming an accomplice.'

The old lady smiled a sad smile, 'The book is gone – destroyed and I can tell you now that my brother Giuseppe is dead so my dear detectives – your troubles are over.'

'Dead? When? Where?' Bryn was losing his temper so he looked at Mario to take over. Neither officer wanted to believe he was dead. And besides, why hadn't she told them this before?

'He died in Bari in 1981.' She opened her purse and handed Bryn a photograph of a gravestone. Bryn handed it to Mario without looking at it. He realised now that searching this place would be a waste of time – the diary was gone but he also knew that in some strange way it was very important to them so they wouldn't have destroyed it.

Any compassion Bryn had felt for these people was now a thing of the past. He stood up and faced the formidable old lady and said, 'We will get the grave exhumed.' The old lady looked at Mario.

'*Riesumato,*' he said.

The old lady looked back in horror at Bryn, and made the sign of the cross. Bryn turned towards the door and walked out. Mario felt uncomfortable leaving the old lady, for she was now sitting in that high-backed chair, crying uncontrollably, but he followed Bryn to the car and they drove off without a word.

Once again Mario marvelled at the way his friend could suddenly be without a shred of compassion, his heart turning to stone – he really would hate to cross this man for there really was no telling how he would react.

Mario dropped Bryn off at the hotel and went home. Bryn went into the lobby and called Heather. He now felt very bad about his sexual wanderings and it didn't help that she was a little distant as it had been several days since he had called. He updated her on the investigation and told her that they were back in Bologna and at the end of the line in their search for Salvino. He told her that he might be coming home sooner than expected – depending what was found in that cemetery in southern Italy.

'If you need any help with the remains, I know a great pathologist who is willing to work cheap,' she said, trying to lighten the mood between them.

'I wish I could swing it too – but I will be home soon.' She could tell he was depressed. She had mixed feelings about the pills she knew he was taking.

They said their goodbyes and Bryn went to his room and tried to sleep but he knew that, with the inability to catch his prey and the guilt he felt about Heather, it was a forlorn hope.

It was still dark when the phone rang – it was Mario from his home: 'They have checked and Giuseppe Salvino was buried in that cemetery on the 10th March 1980. The *carabinieri* office down there is sending us the death certificate and burial notification. It looks like the end of the line, my friend.'

'Yes, it does.' Bryn put the phone down, opened his suitcase, popped a handful of pills, and tried again to find some sleep.

Both men were in the office when the photostatted copies arrived. They had both looked better – the black bags under their eyes were proof of their exhaustion. They were summoned upstairs and ushered into a large office. A man with a lot of gold braid, in very stilted English, congratulated them both on a job well done but he told them sternly that there would be no exhumation – and the file was closed. He went on to say that Bryn was booked on a flight to Manchester at ten tomorrow morning.

As they left the station he heard Mario mutter, '*Mason maledetti*.'

That day and night Bryn and Mario got very drunk – it wasn't a celebration binge, but one of commiseration – for they had failed to catch their man and all they had were bodies; lots of unavenged bodies.

A very hung-over Mario waved a very poorly Bryn off at the

gate. He walked down the gangway, pulling his suitcase, and holding the box containing copies of all the paperwork, except of course, the diaries. He would need all that for his report to conclude the Jennifer and Lucia Salvino murder case – he was ready for home now.

CHAPTER TWENTY-FOUR

Friday 7 March 1980 20.20 hrs

While he sat on the Turin railway station platform, Giuseppe formulated a plan. He knew he had to disappear – for good this time – he knew his luck couldn't hold out forever and besides he was getting old, his strength was fading, his body was fragile and his brain certainly wasn't as sharp and active as it once was.

He boarded the train – he was looking for somewhere far from Turin and settled on the town of Bari in the south. He took everything from his apartment and now settled into his seat for the long journey of almost the entire length of his country. He had plenty of time to work on the plan in detail.

Sunday 6 July 1986 15.35 hrs

Bryn woke and felt Heather's body next to his. She had picked him up from the airport and brought him home. They had made love a couple of times and she felt he was a little less intense with her. She dismissed the thought and they slept until late.

Although he was on a day off, Bryn got up and walked the couple of miles to the station. It was quiet even for a Sunday. Penny nodded as if he hadn't been away and he wearily climbed the stairs and went into the deserted office. He looked at his desk – the in-tray was overflowing with unattended work and his desk was strewn with telephone messages. He sat down – trying to decide where to begin. He started with the easiest. Most of the telephone messages were from Laura which he discarded by throwing them into the empty waste paper basket below his desk. That now left just a couple of work-related ones, which he put in date order. He didn't have the heart to look at the case files piled up in his in-tray so he went downstairs and put the kettle on. Then he heard Noonan's voice in the control room – he followed him upstairs.

'Well, well, the traveller returns. We were running a pool on how many bodies you would have by the end – how many was it?'

'I can't remember,' he said. But he knew full well.

He sat there for a while giving Noonan a quick synopsis of the time in Italy then thought, Why the hell am I here? He called Heather and she picked him up, took him for something to eat and then they went home and returned to bed where he took his work frustrations out on her and she loved it – the intensity was back.

Later that evening Bryn awoke and he was alone in the darkness. He got up and went into the front room and to his surprise he saw that all the paperwork he had brought from Italy was strewn all over the floor with Heather in the centre.

'God, you and your Italian friend are messy workers – you would have to shape up if you were on my staff,' she laughed and he did too. He went into the kitchen, on the pretext of brewing some tea, but secretly he popped several anti-depressants into his mouth and swallowed hard. He was sure she knew about the pills but he wasn't comfortable taking them in front of any body, especially her. He returned to the lounge and handed a cup of coffee to Heather, for his trip had made him addicted to the stuff. He sat next to her on the floor and looked at the pile of murder scene photographs – the women decayed; some with their throats slashed, some simply died through being unable to breathe, the skeleton of Mr Armstrong with its ribs broken where the knife had penetrated – but all with one thing in common – all killed by the same man, a man that Bryn had been unable to arrest. And that choked him.

He looked at the bottom of the box and picked up a picture he hadn't seen before. It was a close-up snap of Giuseppe and his son on a beach somewhere – he couldn't be sure, but it looked like somewhere in Britain. It must have been taken just before he disappeared back to Italy– they looked so happy – perhaps the picture was taken by Jenny herself. The boy had certainly inherited his father's distinctive dark eyes.

He sat there, sipping his hot coffee which was not a patch on the Italian drink, and he hoped for Heather to come up with some brilliant piece of detective work that he and Mario had missed – but she didn't and besides, the autopsy reports were in Italian. So they finished their drinks and went back to bed.

It was around three that Bryn woke suddenly – something had hit him but what? He lay in the darkness, his heart beating furiously as if he had just woken from a nightmare. Then it came to him – it was something he had seen in that box. He got up and didn't even get dressed. He rushed into the lounge and he sat on the couch, stark naked and stared at the photographs that still littered the expensive carpet. Yes, there it was. He felt physically sick he was so excited. He rushed back into the bedroom and hurriedly got dressed.

'What's the matter?' she asked, her eyes trying to get accustomed to the bedroom light.

'Can I borrow your car? There is something I have to do.'

'What – now? But it's the middle of the night.'

'Yes – now. This can't wait H – I think I can crack this fucking case.'

'Okay – you know where the keys are – and put the light out.'

He put the Audi Quattro through its paces as he tore through the deserted Quayside streets. He stopped the car outside a small terraced house. He knocked loudly on the door and eventually a light came on in the upstairs bedroom but it was a while before the front door was opened.

Bryn looked at the man who opened the door – yes, he thought, he now knew was right.

'*Ciao Signor Leonardo* – I think we need to talk, don't you? Can I come in?'

Bryn didn't wait for an answer but brushed past the man and entered the house. Lenny just let him pass and followed him into the small lounge of his lodgings. He had mixed emotions about this – but, if the truth be told he had longed for this moment since he had returned to Wales and strangely enough, he was glad it was Bryn that had discovered the secret.

They sat in silence – Lenny staring at the picture of him and his father taken so long ago.

'It was taken in Newquay, Cornwall. It was the only holiday we ever had, the last time I ever remember being happy. What are you going to do?' he asked – not really caring, for his life so far had been a series of disappointments that one or two more wouldn't make any difference.

'Well, that very much depends on you.'

Bryn suspected, correctly as it turned out, that Lenny had been kept up to date on the happenings in Italy by the Salvino family. He also knew that no matter what he wouldn't turn the young lad in, but he couldn't let him know that – not yet anyway for he needed to maintain a power over him to get what he needed.

'I think you have something I need to see. Something your aunt sent you recently for safekeeping. Something she didn't want me to have.' He stared into the lad's eyes, those dark eyes he saw in the picture and he got that buzz that all detectives get when they know their hunch was right. He watched Lenny get up and leave the room, returning a couple of minutes later with a large, brown envelope. He handed it to Bryn. He could feel his heart pounding as he looked inside and saw the missing diary – he studied the envelope with the Italian stamp, and postmarked Bologna. He smiled.

'Here. You'd better have these too.' He handed Bryn Jenny's wedding ring, a crucifix, and a printout from the council. 'I stole this from the property cupboard – it was my mum's and Lucia's. I was wrong to take them. It was difficult to know how to feel. I took it the night I saw what he had done to Lucia. I'm really sorry, Bryn.'

Bryn handed it back, 'Don't know what you mean – I've never seen these before in my life.' He kept the printout though – it clearly stated who resided at the house from 1946–1952. Lenny started to cry. Bryn stood up and put his hand on his shoulder then he left him to it – now all he had to do was get back to Italy with the book – but without having to say to his bosses exactly how the hell he got it.

The drive back to Heather's was a lot more sedate. He let himself in with his key and found her sitting in the kitchen with a large Scotch in her hand. He smiled at her.

'You look like the cat that got the cream. Now are you going to tell me what the bloody hell is going on? I think you took 10,000 miles off my tyres when you roared away.'

'What are you doing tomorrow, Miss Home Office pathologist? Do you fancy coming back to Italy with me? Can I use your phone?'

He dialled the number, and the call was answered after a couple of rings. Bryn heard a very groggy '*Sì?*' come from the other end of the line.

'Mario – *Buongiorno mio Vecchio amico*. I have the last diary but please don't ask me how I got it until we meet. Hopefully I will be back in Italy as soon as I can – I think our man is in Naples.'

At ten that morning Bryn stood in front of Chief Superintendent Curry and again asked permission to go back to Italy.

'How did you get this?' He held the book as if he could read it.

Twat, thought Bryn but settled for, 'I got it anonymously in the mail while I was away.' He hoped that he wouldn't ask where it was posted.

'Okay, but you have until Friday. You are needed in court on Monday. We need to nail Tif. We don't want to look like we are playing favourites.' He said this as though he thought Bryn was thinking differently.

So, he had a week to get the bastard.

There was a flight at 10 p.m. It was a rush but he and Heather made it. Once on the plane and the ordeal of the take-off was behind them, Heather turned to Bryn and reminded him of the holiday they had spent in Florida, just before their affair had ended.

'Do you remember being stopped by the police for speeding?' she asked as she sipped her wine.

He certainly did – they were driving to *Key Largo*, as Bryn was a Humphrey Bogart fan and he had been told, correctly as it turned out, that the *African Queen*, the boat from the movie, was docked there. As he drove along Route One, the sun baking down, the shimmering sea on both sides of the road where he spotted the occasional dolphin breaking the surface of the water, his brain was in neutral – then he saw the lights behind him – it was like Blackpool illuminations. He was stopped by the highway patrol for travelling at 100 miles per hour, the limit being 60.

'But once again you played the 'I'm a British bobby card' – the sure-fire passport out of trouble.' They both laughed for Heather also knew 'the Venice story' too.

That really had been a fun two weeks, Bryn thought as he sipped his Coke and looked down on the lights of what surely must have been Paris. And his thoughts went back to his mother again, who had only died six months before.

Mario would be waiting for them when they landed in Bologna and he would arrange flights to Naples as soon as possible. They all knew time was now pressing on them if Bryn was to be there at the kill.

They met Mario. He seemed very happy to see Heather and Bryn felt slightly embarrassed knowing that he knew about the women he had had while in Italy. Mario winked – all was fine;

policemen don't shit on other policemen.

They sat in the cafe of the almost deserted airport, Mario rapidly leafing through the diary to confirm that Naples was their next and hopefully last port of call. He would read the whole thing later, when he would also get the story of where it came from. Their flight to Naples was called at 6 a.m. They boarded the plane and all three passengers were no trouble to the flight attendants as they slept the entire journey.

They were met by a *Carabinieri* officer who drove them to their hotel and after a shower all three met in Mario's room to have a reading of the diary. Coffee and Danish pastries were waiting on the table.

'The final payment was recorded on the 10th October 1983 to the post office on viale Colli Aminei here in Napoli,' Mario said as he sipped his coffee.

Bryn looked at the tourist city map he had picked up in the foyer. It took a while but he found the road and saw it was situated on the outskirts of the town.

Mario went on, 'The final mention of any contact was a telephone call from Naples on the 15th. The last entry was on the morning of the 17th – the day of his heart attack. He looked at his two guests. 'I think we could chalk this death down to his brother too. All that stress,' said Mario as he closed the book.

'I think he was as guilty as Giuseppe – he could have stopped him from killing those women years ago but chose not to – he got what he deserved.' The other two looked at Bryn but chose to say no more.

I love having Bryn as a friend but I would certainly hate to have him as an enemy, Mario thought once again as he looked at his friend.

It was Mario who broke the silence. 'Well?' he said, waving the diary.

Bryn told him the story but only after he had sworn Mario to secrecy: 'I don't want Lenny being dragged in – he has enough to cope with, and besides he is a good copper.'

'*Inferno di fottere.*' There was no need to translate. The two Brits just smiled. 'I think it is time for you to make a list, my friend – what do we know about our man?'

Bryn turned to a fresh page of his notebook and stared writing:

Always uses the initials 'GS'

Now 74 years old

Very callous

Has a large scar across forehead

Walks with the aid of a stick

Women find him attractive

Worked as a solicitor

Worked as a law clerk

Worked as a tour guide

Money from brother stopped in 1983

Made quite a bit of money from some (if not all) the deceased

Speaks English well

Good with a knife

Commando trained

Was in Bari before Naples (to be followed up later)

VERY DANGEROUS

'Well – where do we start?'

'Lunch. I am sure that Heather is hungry,' said Mario with a large grin.

CHAPTER TWENTY-FIVE

Sunday 8 March 1980 12.10 hrs

Giuseppe sat in a cafe just off the Corso Italia. Years ago, he had passed through this place a few times and to him Bari seemed very poor and run down, the people very southern and to his way of thinking, being from the north of the country, were backward – but then again, he wouldn't be here long for he had already seen what he needed – now all he had to do was set the bait.

The following day he returned to a Parco Due Giugno in the town centre and engaged an old vagrant in conversation who told Giuseppe that his name was Emmanuel Sampa and was originally from Trieste in the north. Giuseppe had seen this man several times the day before and knew him to be homeless and more than likely hungry. The old man jumped at the chance of something to eat. Sampa took the man who had made the offer to be some kind of rich do-gooder but he didn't mind if he had to listen to a little Jesus-bashing in his ear, or give him a blow job in a back alley if it secured him a hot meal and perhaps a couple of lire.

They ate in a small out-of-the-way cafe and then Giuseppe offered to take the man back to his hotel room so he could bathe. He also told Sampa he had some fresh clothes there too. Sampa couldn't resist and besides he had been used by several rich men in the past for a variety of purposes so what the hell.

It was a short walk to his hotel on viale Luigi Einaudi, not that anyone in the hotel would recognise him anyway – his hat was well over his face when he checked in. He told Sampa to wait as he had to ensure the coast was clear – it was and he sneaked the man into the lift and went into his room on the third floor.

He gave the man a glass of wine and went and ran the bath. When it was ready the old man went in and Giuseppe waited outside. He had already disabled the lock on the bathroom door. He heard the man splashing about. Giuseppe waited a couple of minutes then rushed in and quickly grabbed the man by his thin legs and lifted. Sampa struggled but he was not strong enough. He tried to cry out but his head went below the water and after a couple of minutes all movement stopped. Giuseppe let go of the legs and walked out, leaving the body submerged in the hot soapy water. He needed to catch his breath and take a little snort of coke – his new drug of choice, since he couldn't get morphine any more.

I am glad that this is my last – I am getting far too old for this, he thought to himself as he sat on the balcony to catch his breath and regain some strength which he would need over the next hour or two.

It took three more full baths to get the body clean but when it was, he refilled the bath, ensured the vagrant's head was under the water, then leaving behind his papers and clothing, he walked out of the hotel.

The body, later identified as Giuseppe Salvino by Guido in the Bari mortuary, was found by the maid the following morning, drowned.

Giuseppe left by train late that afternoon– deciding on Naples as his next and hopefully final destination. He had been there when he was a child with his nanny, who was originally from there. It was a place he had very fond memories of and where he had always felt safe, away from his domineering father.

The train seemed very slow and it took nearly three hours to reach Naples. He walked out onto Piazza Garibaldi and stopped at a café; in the toilet he used the last of his cocaine but he knew that obtaining more he would not be a problem – this was a seaport after all.

He picked out a nice hotel, and checked in under the name of Georg Stanis. He put his occupation as a lawyer and his home town as Trieste this time. He explained that his luggage was lost at the station but it should arrive tomorrow. The clerk was satisfied and seeing that the old man was infirm, he gave him the key to a room on the ground floor.

Giuseppe spent the next two days looking around for a furnished apartment and found one in the quiet suburbs. The landlady was pleased to have a refined older gentleman in the house. He told her he was a retired lawyer who, still being active despite his age and infirmity, was going to seek employment as a tour guide. She thought that was a lovely idea.

With the extra money he had asked Guido for he bought a small Fiat and travelled to Pompeii. He had decided to set himself up as a private tour guide there. He bought several books and maps of the Roman city and took them back to his home to study. He also took several conducted tours, always with a different guide, and took copious notes of what they said. Within two weeks he had amassed enough knowledge to be a successful guide. His first group were from America and, although he knew he could have told them anything and they would have believed him, he gave them an informative tour and picked up some hefty tips.

Giuseppe thoroughly enjoyed his new job, and for the first time in nearly thirty years he was settled and he never missed a day at the ruins. He also ensured that he had nothing whatsoever to do with any women.

Monday 7 July 1986 22.30 hrs

'Officers have checked all the solicitors in the town. Three have employees with the initials, two are women and one is a man in his thirties – so we can rule that out.'

All three pursuers were very tired so they broke early to reconvene early in the morning.

Bryn and Heather went straight to sleep – it was a first for them, not to have had sex.

They met at nine and after a not-too-filling continental breakfast they went out into the traffic madness that was Napoli. Bryn had seen crazy driving all over Italy by now, but nothing prepared him for the chaos here. Heather held on to him – so ill at ease was she. Mario took it all in his stride as only a true Italian could.

They sat and looked out over the sea and planned the day. Bryn could see his time running out and he was certain he would not be given the chance to come back again. One entry in Guido's diary had given them some new hope, for it had mentioned that Giuseppe 'had gained employment as a tour guide, putting his knowledge of history and architecture to good use'. They decided that they would start with the obvious places and work back. It was agreed that Mario was going to check out the tour guides of Herculaneum and Heather and Bryn went to Pompeii. Bryn was so excited for this was a place he had always longed to see and now the police were paying for the privilege. He smiled at the thought. They were dropped off away from the site just in case they were seen getting out of a marked police car. They paid their admission and mingled with the other tourists. Bryn's eyes kept straying to the magnificent sight of Vesuvius towering above them – the path the lava had taken in AD 79 still clearly visible in the long, leisurely, southern slope.

Their first port of call on the tour was a brothel. They marvelled at the pornographic paintings still on the walls.

'Trust you Lawton to bring me to a bloody brothel,' Heather said with a smile on her face. 'Is that how you see me – as a whore?' Bryn just smiled for he knew even a whore wouldn't have done the things she did with him, and the thought made his groin warm. They viewed the 2000-year-old pornographic painting, each with a number below. She turned to him and whispered, 'It would appear that you have had 3, 5, 6 and 11 in the last forty-eight hours. I wonder how much I should charge you?' He blushed and she enjoyed it.

Then they moved into the city proper and Bryn was like a schoolboy – he even kept forgetting why he was really here.

They were standing viewing a mosaic of an angry animal. The guidebook explained that the Latin written there translated as 'Beware of the Dog'.

It was Heather who spotted him.

She saw a tour group coming towards them – the guide, an elderly man with a walking stick. A wide-brimmed hat was pushed back on his head. As he passed, she looked at him and saw the deep, large scar running across his forehead – she nudged Bryn and said, 'I don't want to disturb you while you are enjoying yourself but you have just missed your man, officer.' Bryn turned sharply but all he saw were their backs. She smiled. 'Some bloody detective you are, Lawton.' She was as excited as him.

They ran after the group and caught up to them near the ruins of the central baths. It was there that Bryn got his first look at the man he had chased over thirty years and all over this country. The killer of at least eight people.

'I have to get Mario here – will you stay with him? But for fuck's sake keep your distance and for heaven's sake, do not bloody approach him.' She promised she would do as he asked. He kissed her and she felt his excitement, as if an electric current had passed through her.

He ran off back to the waiting *Carabinieri* officer and he radioed to his counterparts in the ruins of Herculaneum and ten agonising minutes later he heard Mario's voice on the radio:

'Shall we meet for lunch here – Heather's buying.' He used the code that they had arranged that morning for they wanted no glory-hunting lawman getting in the way of them arresting this man.

'I will be right there.'

Bryn met Mario at the gate – he showed his identification and strolled in with Bryn in tow. Now was the difficult part – they had to find Heather and by doing so, locate Giuseppe Salvino.

It took a while but to both officers' relief they saw Heather near the Forum. She saw them too and started waving. They moved quickly to her, but couldn't see their prey. She said, 'Don't worry – he's over there, sitting on the steps behind that column eating his lunch.' Bryn saw him or at least his legs. He could feel his heart racing. He looked at his colleague and knew he was experiencing the same sensations. They told Heather to stay where she was, which, as Bryn and Mario could see, she had no intention whatsoever of doing. Bryn also knew he couldn't arrest him – for that honour fell to his Italian friend. They waited for the old man to stand and they approached him from behind and quickly grabbed both his hands, and Bryn was surprised how quickly Mario had him handcuffed. He didn't even know Mario carried them.

'Salvino di Giuseppe – *lei è in arresto per l'assassinio,*' he smiled and winked to Bryn. Their long search was over. Salvino didn't say a word. Bryn searched his pockets – he found a knife but it was just one for cutting fruit – but Bryn knew that this man would have had no compunction whatsoever in thrusting it into both officers if he saw it as a chance to escape.

They walked him out to the waiting car and Mario accompanied him back to Naples. There was nothing Bryn could do now so he and Heather continued their tour of the ruins – he tried to enjoy himself but his heart wasn't in it. In truth he envied his friend, now in the thick of it with a fantastic arrest under his belt.

'Let's go,' said Heather staring at him with a wry smile, 'you coppers always want to be where the action is and here the action took place nearly two thousand years ago.'

The *Carabinieri* officer whisked them back to Naples and Bryn ran into the office on via Salvitori Tommasi and was quickly taken to the interview area where Mario was talking to someone who, considering how much gold braid he had on his uniform and cap, must be someone very senior. He saw Bryn approach:

'*Brigadieri, Vi present L'ispettore Bryn Lawton, della polizia Gallese.*' The brigadier shook Bryn's hand enthusiastically and went on and on in Italian – Mario indicated to Bryn where and when he should smile and nod.

'We will interview him tomorrow – I don't know if we will get much out of him as he hasn't said a thing yet, not one single word since we arrested him.' Bryn liked the fact that his friend had used the word 'we' and not 'I'.

He declined to sit in on the interview for Bryn knew it would, of course, be conducted in Italian so he shook his head. It was sad but he had come to the end of the line. The death of Jennifer and Lucia Salvino thirty-four years ago were now just two of many. He knew the Italian murders would take precedence over his, and that pissed him off a little, but he couldn't say anything. He and Mario had caught their man and he should be proud of that, for that was what really mattered.

He walked back to the hotel and made love with Heather. He was gentle and relaxed – and she loved it. Tomorrow while Salvino was enduring his interview, he would take Heather a little further south along the Amalfi coast – Mario had said it was fantastic to see.

Positano was everything Mario had said and more, with the multi-coloured buildings cascading down the hill towards the sea. They ate a delicious meal in a cafe on the small beach and watched some artist paint the stunning views around the bay. Then they visited the breathtaking church of Santa Maria

Assunta. Both were reluctant to leave but as dusk closed in, they made their way back to the *Carabinieri* office on via Pastiniello, where their driver was waiting to take them back to their hotel.

There was a message from Mario waiting for him when they got back. Bryn called and Mario was there within half an hour.

'Do you know that file you picked up on that prostitute in Rome – Genevieve? He did it, and the man buried in Bari is an unknown homeless man he picked up there – he is also going to take us to the site of another murder outside Bologna tomorrow – we will be flying up there and you are both to come. By the way, you are to be the guests of honour at a dinner tonight so get dressed, my friends, for we want to show our gratitude for all your help.'

It was way past two in the morning when they arrived back from the dinner – Bryn was so drunk he could hardly walk so two burly officers took him to his room and laid him on the bed. The embarrassment Heather felt when he told the officers to 'put your foot down lads so I can shag this beautiful woman before I pass out,' was just starting to fade. He was however unconscious as soon as his head hit the pillow.

He wasn't feeling too well as he stood by the lake in Parco Regionale Storico di Monte Sole. But over the years he had become used to hangovers. He watched Giuseppe point out the spot where he had buried his young lover all those years before. The police doctor called Heather over out of some kind of professional courtesy and together they sifted through the undergrowth, finding small fragments of a body that the animals had left behind. She called Bryn and Mario over to show them a piece of bone.

'This is human and female. It is a piece of her pelvis and she was not very old – I think we have found Maria.'

They all glanced at Salvino who stood between two uniformed officers, smoking a cigarette – he didn't even flinch.

Bryn stared at that little piece if bone which was virtually all that remained of Maria Gambrelli aged twenty-two years, Salvino's secretary and lover, and suddenly his mind flew back to Fiona – they hadn't found too much of her either. He left the group and found a quiet, secluded place and threw up – now he felt a little bit better.

CHAPTER TWENTY-SIX

Wednesday 9 September 1987 04.15 hrs

Carlo Ricone, one of the night warders on duty in the prison, heard the noise of something falling just before 4 a.m. He was alone on the wing and, not wishing to enter a cell alone, he called his supervisor who was in the canteen – so it was well over ten minutes before Carlo opened the metal door to cell number 28.

'Oh *fotte*,' said the supervisor as they both peered into the cell.

'*Merde*,' whispered the warder as his mind went into overdrive to think of a way out of the heap of trouble that he would now be in.

Monday 7 September 1987 15.20 p.m.

Bryn had arrived in Bologna the night before, all prepared to give his evidence in the case against Giuseppe Salvino. He was met by the newly promoted Mario Fabrizzi. It had been over a year since the two men had met. They sat in a late-night cafe and caught up with each other's lives.

Mario told him that he and Helena was now a serious item, so much so that she had moved to Bologna and was working at the *carabinieri* office there, and they had married six months ago. He was proud of his promotion that he had received as a result of this case. Bryn thought about his return – he hadn't even received a 'well done' and besides which they had even refused to pay some of his expenses.

'How is Heather?' he asked, his mouth full of delicious pizza. He could tell by Bryn's reaction that the reply was not going to be good.

'It didn't work out – I haven't seen her for about six months.'

'So, is there anyone else taken her place?'

Bryn had had a string of one-night stands since the break-up but just replied, 'No – I've had enough of women for a while – I'm taking a break.'

'Then perhaps we can persuade Magda to pay us a visit while you are here – she is divorced now – she and Helena speak on the phone all the time.' He smiled and nudged Bryn's arm.

'Now that was something to think about,' he said and they both laughed.

Mario dropped him off at his hotel but even as late as it was, Bryn couldn't sleep. He got dressed and took a walk around the old city – it was beautiful at night. He walked into the Piazza Ravegnana and looked up at the Asinelli Tower looming high above him – his mind went back to when he and Heather had climbed it. He had been such a bastard to that lovely woman whose only fault was that she wanted to love and take care of him. He headed straight back to the hotel and after a handful of anti-depressants – enough pills, his friendly chemist had said, to stun a horse – he went back to bed but as usual sleep just wouldn't come.

The following morning, he and Mario sat in the magnificent

main court building on via Giuseppe Garibaldi in the centre of Bologna and awaited the start of the trial of Giuseppe Salvino for the murder of nine people here in Italy. The two British murders were to remain on file for the time being – Jenny and Lucia were not to receive justice – just the Italians and her mother and father for now and possibly forever but possibly Jenny wouldn't mind that too much.

Bryn had spent the morning with the *polizia giudiziaria*, the judiciary police, a branch of the police whose duty is to help a prosecutor during their investigations; the interpreter was one of the most stunningly beautiful women he had ever seen. She had the most amazing dark eyes and her perfume… it was all making it very difficult for the British policeman to concentrate, and when she crossed her legs, he completely lost his place in the proceedings. They wouldn't allow Mario in to translate as he was a material witness, which initially worried Bryn, but on seeing his replacement he couldn't have cared less. To Bryn's mind the preliminary interview was all over very quickly for such an extensive murder trial. He told them what he could and gave them his notebooks – they seemed impressed.

Now, as he sat with Mario he said, 'Have you seen…?' He didn't get any further with his question.

'Yes. Her name is Gisela Manutti – believe me, my friend, everyone has tried and everyone has failed – I think she is a nun, or something the devil sent to tempt us. She is *lei è fredda come il ghiaccio.*'

Bryn understood – 'cold as ice.' That was certainly a pity, he thought as he sipped a triple shot coffee – something he had missed back in Britain. They never seemed to get it right back home.

'So you tried?' he asked as he sat on the uncomfortable stone seat and waited – waiting for what, he had no idea.

'You have seen her – I think *il Papa* would try if he saw her.' Bryn smiled as he watched his friend cross himself for daring to mention the Pope in such derogatory terms.

Mario quickly changed the subject. 'The judges who are to hear the case are two of the few who actually like offices of law enforcement – we are far more likely to get a conviction with them than any of the others.'

'What about the jury? Don't they have a say in all this?'

Mario started to laugh: 'In Italy we do not have a jury – just a judge, or as in this case *due giudici,* who will decide.' Bryn didn't know if that was a good or a bad thing. Then again, having twelve idiots decide in British courts was a lottery anyway so...

He also noticed his friend would use more Italian without translating.

It was a long wait, but both officers were used to that – the courts never ran to time, no matter which country one was in. At 5 p.m. the prosecutor who Bryn had spoken to that morning came out of the most ornate doors. He approached Mario, who stood, as did Bryn.

'E'liberto di andare ritorni domani alle dieci.'.' With that he turned and walked briskly away, his robes flowing behind him.

'We are free, my friend,' Mario said, slapping Bryn on the shoulder 'until ten tomorrow morning. You will dine with us tonight. Helena will be so pleased to see you.'

Bryn just wanted to return to his hotel, take his pills, have a bath, and go to bed. The last thing he wanted was to see people playing happy families, but he couldn't say no to his friend who seemed so excited.

Mario lived in a small village over an hour's drive away called Crespellano. It was very picturesque. He parked his car outside a large house and Bryn followed him in. Helena rushed to greet them and to Bryn's surprise saw she was heavily pregnant. He smiled at them. 'That is my surprise. We would like to ask you if you would be our child's *padrino* – that is, how you say, godfather?'

Bryn was taken aback by the request, for he knew just how important that person was to the Italians.

'I would be honoured but do you think I am suitable? After all I am not Catholic.'

'Nobody is perfect, my friend,' Mario said with a smile.

'Don't you want someone more…?'

'What? *Normale?*' said Helena. 'No, we both want you,' she said with a smile and walked over and kissed him.

'Besides, Magda is going to be *madrina*,' Mario said as he turned to answer the phone.

'It is for you,' he said, handing the phone to Bryn.

'Lawton *di ufficiale* – this is the *ufficio di accusatore*.' Bryn knew enough Italian now to know who it was and also whose voice it was. But why was the prosecutor's office calling him?

'How can I help?' he said.

Within ten minutes Mario was driving him back into the city, back to the prosecutor's office. It was all very mysterious and also a little disappointing as the smell of the cooking food was fantastic and the promise of a chat with Magda on the telephone was in prospect – but once again duty got in the way of him enjoying himself.

They both entered the office and the prosecutor turned to Mario – '*La ringraziamo Ispettore Fabrizzi. La sua presenza non e'piu necessaria.*' he said and virtually closed the door in his face. Bryn knew when someone was being dismissed and that was one, leaving him alone with the old man; that was, until the gorgeous Gisela Manutti made her entrance.

The prosecutor sat behind his desk and signorina Manutti sat to one side, crossing those fantastic legs. If she noticed him looking, she gave no indication. She was, after all probably used to it. She took a notepad from the desk and read:

'Officer – the prisoner Salvino has heard you are here in Italia and would like the opportunity to speak to you in private. You cannot ask him any questions about the case but if you are willing to do it, we can arrange it now. We have promised that whatever he says will not be used in the coming trial – but it might lead us to make, how shall we say, other discoveries.'

Bryn was quite used to informal chats with prisoners – they usually wanted something in return like money or a reduced sentence for dropping an accomplice in the shit or recovering some property. Perhaps he has a body he wants to tell him about. Bryn then thought that throughout this entire enquiry he had never actually spoken to the man. So now here was his one and only chance.

'Sure, I would love to take the opportunity to speak privately to Mr Salvino.'

The gorgeous woman turned to her boss and in the most beautiful Italian said, '*L'Ispettore l'vorrebbe parlare in private con il Signor Salvino.*'

'*Benissimo, portatelo a vedere Salvino,*' said the old man and waved them away.

All Bryn could tell from the conversation was that the old prosecutor seemed very pleased that he had agreed. He wondered how the old man could work that closely with such a beautiful woman without having a permanent erection. Perhaps she is only allowed to work with the 'very' old men, he thought to himself as he stood up to leave the office. But a man would have to be dead not to react to seeing her every day.

'Please come with me, officer.' She stood up and Bryn followed her out. As his old friend Dave Knight would have said – 'her arse was like two ferrets fighting in a sack'.

Mario was sitting in the foyer, waiting for Bryn to return. She walked over to speak to him, he gave Bryn a quick look and Bryn just shrugged his shoulders, and Mario walked out. Bryn could tell he was far from pleased with this situation – whatever that situation was.

'Do not worry Officer Lawton – we will see you get safely back to your hotel,' she almost purred when she spoke.

Bryn was taken to a nearby restaurant and was surprised to see Salvino sitting in a booth in the corner, flanked by three burly officers. He walked to the table and the officers and his beautiful companion moved away.

'Giuseppe, let me introduce myself I am...'

Salvino held out his hand and Bryn took it – they both gave the Masonic third level handshake – Salvino seemed pleased. Bryn saw that he was handcuffed.

'I know you – you are Bryn Lawton, the officer from Quayside – the one who has chased me all over Italy.

'The one who has chased you all the way from Wales, to be

exact,' Bryn said with a smile. Salvino nodded.

'Can I please ask you some questions?' he said as Bryn took the seat opposite him.

'Sure, but what's in it for me?' He loved being a policeman. He knew he needed to control this meeting and not give too much away too soon.

'Okay – I will give you the two bodies you didn't find – if you will answer me.'

'Okay – ask away, but I can't promise I can give you the answers.'

'That is fair. Have you met Leonardo?'

'Now what I am going to tell you will further destroy his life if you tell anyone – so it is up to you.'

'You have my word, officer, that what you tell me will die with me.'

'Yes, I know him. He is a detective and my friend. He uses the name Lenny Sullivan. I am the only one who knows who he really is and at the moment I don't see the need to share what I know with anyone else. I work with him at Quayside. He is a good man but haunted by the past. He now also has Jenny's ring and the crucifix I think you put on Lucia – I gave them to him the other night.'

Salvino smiled, 'That was very kind of you.' Bryn saw his eyes mist over. He soon composed himself. 'How were they found?' he asked – his voice falsely strong.

Bryn related the story of the finding of Jenny and Lucia.

'I loved them both very much – she was leaving me and it all happened so fast – Lucia was an accident. She wouldn't stop crying – I did it by accident.' He started to cry. Bryn put his hand on his shoulder and he looked up. 'Can you give this letter to Leonardo?' he said through the tears, 'it might explain some things to him.' Bryn took the letter and put it in his pocket. He noticed Miss Manutti watched him do it.

'Now your turn,' Bryn said, pouring himself a glass of iced water that sat on the table before them. To his surprise the prisoner sipped on a glass of red wine.

'I spent some time in Venetia in the spring of 1970 or '71. I took a house on Calle Bernardo. I cannot remember the number but it is on the corner – not far from a little trattoria. I became involved with a woman I had to dispose of because she got pregnant. She is buried in the attic, behind a false wall. Her name was Maria Tomas. She was a hairdresser.'

'How did you kill her?'

'I slit her throat.'

It chilled Bryn by the matter-of-fact way he said it. 'And the other?'

'In Florence. She was a British tourist. I just couldn't get rid of her. I strangled her I think – I can't remember exactly. Her name was Hilary something. I left the body in the flat.'

Bryn quizzed him but he couldn't remember when or where this had happened – Bryn made his notes and put his notebook away.

'That is all the bodies, but I want you to do me one more favour.'

Bryn listened and when he had finished, he stood up, signifying to the guards that they had finished.

Salvino stood up and offered his hand to Bryn who took it. 'Give my love to Leonardo and don't worry – we won't see each other again.'

Bryn stood outside the restaurant. He needed some air. He

smelled the perfume before he saw her. They started to walk to the car.

'Where to, detective? The night is young and the city is beautiful at night,' she said as she started the engine. Without thinking he gave her the address of the hotel, for his mind was still thinking about Salvino and their conversation. He felt very disconcerted by Salvino's words. He didn't really take much notice when she went in the opposite direction. He said nothing during the short ride. She stopped the car outside a small restaurant. 'I am hungry – please let me buy you dinner,' she said. 'It is the least the prosecutor's office can do.' He realised he was starving.

He enjoyed her company and she laughed when he told her what he had been told about her.

'I do not sleep around and that makes me *apatico* – frigid – that is according to my work colleagues.'

He smiled. The rest of the evening passed quickly. She was great to talk to.

She stopped outside his hotel and to her surprise he leaned over, kissed her on the cheek and got out of the car without inviting her in. He felt good knowing she was watching him enter the lobby.

There was a message from Mario awaiting him – Bryn called him and arranged to meet at eight the following morning. He wanted to know what had happened but Bryn was tired and needed his pills. He said everything was alright and he would tell him everything in the morning. 'Don't worry, I will keep you in the loop, my friend.' They both laughed.

He had a bath and was in the process of drying himself when the phone started to ring.

'Do you not find me attractive, detective?'

'Very.' He was taken aback by the bluntness of the question.

'Then why did you leave me without word, with only a kiss my father would have given me?' He smiled for his plan had worked. They spoke for an hour and it was agreed that they would meet for lunch tomorrow in another secluded cafe she knew. He went to bed a very happy man.

Bryn sat in the dining room the following morning and waited for Mario for over an hour, but he never showed up, instead he saw Gisela. He was pleased to see her but a little confused. She sat down and he ordered her a coffee.

'*Salvino è morto – sì, è suicidato durante la notte*,' she spoke slowly, her voice full of emotion, but he understood.

'Suicide? How?' he asked, not that it mattered very much now. Salvino was dead.

'*Sì, è impiccato nella sua cella.*' Bryn shook his head to indicate he didn't understand. She made the gesture showing that he had hanged himself, much to the young waiter's amusement. She gave him a withering look and he disappeared back into the kitchen. 'Officer Fabrizzi is there with the body. He was a little busy and he asked if I could come and get you. I hope you don't mind.'

They drove back to the prosecutor's office in silence and Gisela disappeared without a word as Mario arrived.

'They found him in the middle of the night – he had used his tie. The imbeciles left him with his tie. *Merde*.'

Bryn took Mario over to a corner and told him all about last night's meeting with the now dead Salvino and the instruction he had whispered to him just before they parted.

'Do you still want to carry on?'

He didn't have to say anything – they both turned and headed for the car.

Once again, but this time as instructed by Giuseppe Salvino, they stood and knocked on the door of the Salvino villa. It was opened by a male servant who handed Bryn an envelope, then without a word, he closed the door. They returned to the car, both of them fully aware that they were being watched by that formidable matriarch.

They stopped on the side of the road and Bryn opened the envelope. He found a key and a slip of paper. On it was written

BANCA Di BOLOGNA, PIAZZA DELLA COSTITUZIONE BOX 127

Bryn felt the déjà vu. He shuddered. It was the Fiona thing all over again.

Neither man was sure whether they needed a warrant to search the box but as Bryn remarked, 'Salvino was dead so what the hell.'

The manager, a fussy little man, was most helpful and they took the box into a small cubicle. Bryn couldn't help remembering the time he did this with the box Fiona had left him and finding all that money hidden in it – a lot of which he still had in a box in a bank in Quayside.

Inside the safety deposit box, they found a ring with a large diamond and a small, purple velvet pouch, which Mario opened. He poured the contents into the palm of his hand. Both men looked in awe at the eight diamonds sparkling under the neon light of the small cubicle. Mario translated the note:

To whoever finds this:

I am dead and more than likely in hell for the things I have done.

I took this ring from a Jewish woman at Rab Concentration camp sometime in 1943 – just before she was deported to Auschwitz. Her name was Carlota Aschenazi. She came from a village called Colleferro in Lazio. She gave me it to save her child's life but I didn't – perhaps you could return it to her relatives (if any still exist) or if not, do some good with it.

I don't recall who I got the diamonds from. I do remember that they were all Jews but they will now be dead so again – do some good with them.

Signed Giuseppe Salvino
    October 1983

Was this the ring he tore from Jenny's finger before he boarded her up? he asked himself. He knew it was.

Back at the station, while Mario left to book the seats on the next flight to Venice, Bryn asked Gisela if she could check with directory enquiries for anyone by the name of Aschenazi who resided in the area around Colleferro. He couldn't help thinking about the irony of a Jewish family having the word 'Nazi' in their name.

She returned with a number – Fredo Aschenazi. He asked her to dial the number.

'*Pronto parlo con il Signor Aschenazi? Qui e' l'ufficio di polizia di Bologna, le parla Inglese?*'

'*Sì – un po.*'

She handed Bryn the phone. 'He speaks a little English,'

she said.

'Mr Aschenazi – I am a police detective from Britain – do you understand me?'

'*Sì* – sorry, yes.'

'Do you know of a lady called Carlotta Aschenazi who died in 1943 – I believe she was sent to a concentration camp at Rab and then to Auschwitz?'

'Sì. She was my *nonna* – my father's mother.'

'Do you know if she survived the war, Mr Aschenazi?'

'No – she died in Auschwitz, along with everyone on that transport, on the very same day she arrived.'

He told the man what he had in his possession and he heard him start to cry – Bryn told him he would have the ring returned to him as soon as possible. Mr Aschenazi was still thanking him as he put the phone down.

He turned and saw Gisela smiling at him. He smiled back and she saw that he had tears in his eyes. She kissed him on the cheek but the moment was lost as Mario came bursting in. Gisela left and Bryn, hiding his tears, told Mario about the ring. The diamonds were still in Mario's pocket and neither man mentioned them.

CHAPTER TWENTY-SEVEN

Tuesday 8 September 1987 08.10 hrs

The prosecutor received the telephone call from the governor of the prison, informing him that Giuseppe Salvino had taken his own life. He called the clerk of the court to inform the two judges, then he settled back to do some work, for crime in Bologna doesn't stop.

Gisela called Mario at home then went to collect Bryn from his hotel. It was a task she was very happy to perform.

The old, scarred body of Giuseppe Salvino was taken to the morgue, where the post mortem examination later that day revealed, to no one's real surprise, the cause of death to have been strangulation.

Tuesday 8 September 1987 14.40 hrs

Bryn and Mario caught the afternoon flight to Venice.

'I have contacted the *Carabinieri* – they are investigating a very old case of damage to a gondola a few years ago and they wish to interview you. They will be waiting with the handcuffs.' He started to laugh; Bryn just smiled. He wanted to tell him about the come-on from Gisela, but thought better of it, just in case he was seriously misreading the situation. He didn't want to look a fool in front of his friend, just in case she was playing a game with him.

They arrived at Venice's Marco Polo airport at a little after five and were taken directly to the *Carabinieri* office on Sestiere Castello, where they were introduced to the commander and together, they all went to Calle Bernardo and looked for the small trattoria. Venice was exactly as he remembered – beautifully picturesque. He thought back to something he had read recently – a gag quote from the humourist Robert Benchley to the editor of *The New Yorker* – 'Streets flooded – please advise.' He was shaken out of his reverie when the police car stopped suddenly.

There was only one small trattoria on the street, and it looked to have been there a long time so Bryn and Mario approached the large house on the corner. The local *carabinieri* let Mario take the lead. They remained in the cars. He knocked and the door was opened by a middle-aged woman. Mario explained their business and they were invited in.

Bryn and Mario were shown into the attic by someone who they took to be the son of the house. They thanked him and closed the door. They started tapping – Bryn had lost count how many times that had done this – then there it was again, that hollow sound of a false wall. Mario asked the boy, who had remained outside the door, if he could fetch a hammer. He ran down and within minutes he was back with two. Bryn hit the plasterboard and made a hole about a foot from the floor. He put his hand in and felt something carpet-like. He nodded to Mario who went down and called up the troops.

Ninety minutes later what was left of the body of Maria Tomas was being loaded into the hearse for its journey to the morgue.

Mario and Bryn walked to Piazza San Marco, where they sat in the sunshine and ordered a large pizza and a bottle of expensive wine – their search was finally over.

EPILOGUE

Friday 11 September 1987 11.35 hrs

Bryn and Mario kept a very respectful distance, while they observed the funeral and interment of Giuseppe Salvino in the family plot in the main Bologna cemetery. Bryn watched Gabriella the elder being supported by the younger. He knew the frailty she was showing was an act, but she played it very well. He also noted how it was a surprisingly well-attended affair considering who was being buried, but all the mourners were stony-faced. When Bryn saw the coffin lowered into the ground, he touched Mario on the shoulder. He had seen enough, so they walked slowly back to the car.

'I trust the bastard is in that box, and this isn't some elaborate Italian hoax just to get this annoying British policeman out of their hair.'

Mario just smiled but said nothing. Bryn wished he would confirm the death; after all he had seen the body in the prison mortuary – hadn't he?

'Come, my friend – let's get a glass of wine to celebrate,' he said and put his arm on Bryn's shoulder and led him to the car.

Friday 11 September 1987 19.30 hrs

So, for the third time it was Bryn's last night in Italy and he had been invited for that delayed meal at Mario's home. He had even suggested that Magda be invited but Bryn had declined, a bit too forcefully in Mario's opinion, but he thought he understood when Bryn surprised him by asking if he could bring someone.

You can imagine Mario's surprise when he walked in with 'the nun' – 'the devil's helper', Gisela Manutti. Mario was so dumbstruck that it was left to Helena to welcome them to their home. Throughout the evening he caught Mario looking at him in wonderment – he had to admit he didn't know how he had done it either – she was so beautiful and Bryn... well? That was another story.

The evening was a great success – the Italians around that table even refused to communicate with Bryn in English, forcing him to speak Italian, which he tried to do – very badly, causing the others to roar with laughter at some of his pronunciations.

The following afternoon Mario and Helena saw him off from the airport. They had promised to visit him back in Quayside once Helena had had the baby. He had mentioned the letter he was carrying for Leonardo and it was Mario who suggested that it wasn't worth anything and that the lad should have the last words from his father, without loads of prying eyes looking at it first. Bryn just wanted confirmation from his friend that he was doing the right thing. Neither man made any mention of the diamonds – Bryn believed Mario would do the right thing with them – but what that thing was he had no way of knowing.

He boarded the plane and took his seat next to Gisela - who secretly had boarded the flight and was coming to Wales for a two-week holiday – but at that moment in time neither was sure if she was ever coming back.

When they arrived at Bryn's new house – the house that he had only moved into two weeks before returning to Italy, he picked up the pile of mail inside the front door – one package interested him as it was postmarked Bologna. For some strange reason he did not want to open it in front of Gisela so he placed the letters on the coffee table and showed her around the house. He left her in the bedroom to unpack and he went downstairs to make her a cup of tea. He took the packet into the kitchen and while he waited for the kettle to boil, he tore it open. He took out the contents – a purple velvet bag. He looked inside but there was no letter. He slowly pulled open the drawstring and emptied the contents into the palm of his hand.

He stood there dumbstruck looking at his hand until he heard Gisela coming out of the bedroom and walking down the stairs. He put them back into the pouch and quickly put the envelope in a cutlery drawer.

He would have to think very carefully what the hell to do with four large diamonds.

He felt another trip to his safety deposit box coming on.

THE END

ALSO BY THIS AUTHOR

The Tiger Coat
A Bryn Lawton Mystery

Published by The Conrad Press (2022)
ISBN 978-1-914913-61-7
£9.99 Also available as an ebook

ACKNOWLEDGEMENTS

Although this is a work of fiction, I needed to rely on others to ensure certain things that are real – are in fact correct. I am therefore grateful to Mario Borrelli, for his assistance putting the correct words in all the Italian's mouths.

I would also like to thank my editor James Essinger and everyone at The Conrad Press, and Charlotte Mouncey for her editing skills and production of the cover. There is one job an author should never do on his own creation – that of proofreading and I wish to thank Gilly Brundle for undertaking that mission.